a

circle

of

chalk

a circle of chalk

Christina McClelland

LANIER
PRESS

LANIER PRESS *an Imprint of BookLogix*
Alpharetta, GA

ISBN: 978-1-61005-903-9 – Paperback
ISBN: 978-1-61005-941-1 – Hardcover
eISBN: 978-1-61005-942-8 – ePub
eISBN: 978-1-61005-943-5 – mobi

Printed in the United States of America   0 4 1 4 2 0

♾ This paper meets the requirements of ANSI/NISO Z39.48-1992 (Permanence of Paper)

Photography used in cover art by Katie Oblinger

For Walter,
with all my love.

*"I looked down . . . and what I saw was a
human blastocyst gazing up at me.
I thought 'we've done it.'"*

—Dr. Robert Edwards
winner of the 2010 Nobel Prize for his development of IVF in 1969

*"A mother's love for her child is like nothing else in the world.
It knows no law, no pity, it dares all things
and crushes down remorselessly all that stands in its path."*

—Agatha Christie

Contents

Author's Note   xi

PART I: The Broken and the Undoing   1

PART II: The Beginning of Everything, 1978–1985   19

PART III: The End of Everything   53

PART IV: Interlude   89

PART V: Eleven Years Later   111

PART VI: Snowflakes   239

PART VII: Remorse   259

Author's Note Continued   **267**
Acknowledgments   **269**

Author's Note

Since the birth of Louise Brown in 1978, over eight million births worldwide are attributed to conception via in vitro fertilization. That is eight million human beings that would not exist without the development of IVF. Pioneers in the field of IVF received public backlash and political assault in their pursuit to further science. Doctors Carl Wood, Alan Trounson, Alex Lopata, and the rest of the Australian team worked countless hours and many sleepless nights, along with Doctors Patrick Steptoe and Robert Edwards in the UK, and Sophia Kleegman in the US, making IVF the clinical success that it is today. The collective work of these clinicians as well as volunteerism by early patients who enrolled in experimental treatments changed the world in a way that is unlike any other industry in history. This book is a work of fiction based on the real lives of some of IVF's earliest innovators and recipients of treatment.

PART I

The Broken and the Undoing

one

Asheville, 2019

Ellie's phone rang three times before she answered it. It was her mother, or rather, it was Anderson Valley calling. Either way, it was not a phone call that she looked forward to. She checked the clock at the top of her phone's screen and guessed by the time, three o'clock on Wednesday, that it was her mother. It was a good thing that the rules were her mother had to call her on certain days of the week and not the other way around. If left up to Ellie, she may have accidentally on purpose forgotten to call, opting to punt the inevitable awkward and forced conversation for another week. But she couldn't *not* answer, that would be rude, and unkind, and a myriad of other things that she didn't want to be toward her own mother. But here she was, wanting to avoid her call and feeling like a terrible daughter for doing so.

Having that realization, however, made Ellie feel guilty—it was not that she didn't love her mother, she did, or at least she should—but as an adult in her midthirties, Ellie Mountain Harris (born Mary Ellis Mountain) had finally come to terms with the fact that it is hard to continue to love someone wholeheartedly when they in turn have only loved you halfheartedly. Her therapist called it "a person's capacity to love," and according to Dr. Hannah, that capacity was fixed, not adjustable.

"In other words," Dr. Hannah had said, "when it comes to the emotions of anyone other than one's own self, you get what you get, deal with it, and move on."

Throughout Ellie's life it had been abundantly clear where her mother's heart was divided—part of it was for her, and the other, larger part was for her ghost of a sister, Mia.

Jenna Ellis, Ellie's mother, had been at the Anderson Valley Recovery Center in Connecticut for almost a month by this point, and though her doctors told Ellie in the beginning that Jenna would need "an extended stay" for her treatment of depression following a failed suicide attempt, for Ellie, every day ticked by like a time bomb waiting to detonate. The seconds ticking down on the timer marched toward the day when Jenna would be released from treatment and would be sent home. At some point, Ellie dreaded, she would be better, whatever that might look like. And while Ellie had no idea what *better* would be, two things loomed over her. When Jenna *was* finally released from Anderson Valley, two things would have to happen: one, Ellie would have to find her sixty-two-year-old mother a new place to live—her previous residence still being under renovation following the fire—and two, far more terrifying, she would have to tell her mother the details of Mia's whereabouts.

"Oh honey," Jenna said on the other end of the line, five states away. "It's so good to hear your voice. Any news with you or Kevin? Have you made any travel plans for the holidays yet?"

"No, not yet," Ellie replied back. "Christmas really isn't my favorite time of year." *Why did I say that? She's just trying to make conversation with you.* Ellie tapped the phone against her forehead and closed her eyes, wondering how God could have dropped her into such a complicated life with little more than an inner tube to keep her afloat. Unbeknownst to Ellie, her mother wondered the same thing, and unfortunately for both mother and daughter, the turbulent course of their lives had been set into motion on a heavy track many years before, with little opportunity to change direction.

two

New York City, 1999

Jenna Ellis, formerly Mrs. Edward Clinton Mountain III and the mousey darling of the early '90s New York City society scene, stared down through the glass top to a large, cylindrical metal container. Hundreds of tiny, multicolored specimen tubes stared back at her as any remaining sanity that Jenna had clung to for the last year melted away like the clocks in a Dali painting. A coiling tightness wrapped itself around Jenna's heart, the aching telling her that she would never be able to forget the children that she lost that day. A much darker voice inside her heart told Jenna that she would never be able to forgive her ex-husband for his part in her loss.

Against her lawyer's advice, as soon as the divorce papers were signed and final that morning, Jenna went straight from the courthouse on Church Street, just a few blocks up from the World Trade Center, to the BabyGenix Fertility Clinic in Kips Bay. She needed access to the high-security cryogenic storage room inside BabyGenix's multilevel office, and she needed to see David, Carson, and Mia one last time before the disposition.

In her rush to leave the courthouse and get as far away from her ex-husband as possible, in the fastest way possible, it did not occur to Jenna in the cab ride from the courthouse to BabyGenix that she would need help gaining entrance to the room where her children were stored. It wasn't until she stepped off the elevator on the seventh floor that Jenna realized her rushing to get to BabyGenix might have been in vain. Her patient swipe card could get Jenna into the front door and up to the main In Vitro floor, as well as to the cryo-storage seventh floor, but no farther. Because the seventh floor was used mostly for storage, there was no nurses station, and no patient rooms, so for several seconds Jenna found herself all alone in the sterile and quiet hallway.

Miraculously, a male nurse that Jenna had never seen before turned a corner and began walking toward her, clearly on his way to a destination in the opposite direction of the storage room. When he saw Jenna standing alone in the hallway, he looked surprised — no one should be loitering alone on the seventh floor — and after an interaction that Jenna knew could be considered harassment, the young nurse reluctantly took out a security badge and swiped it across the door to the storage room and let Jenna in. She promised him that she would only need a minute, which did not seem to make him any less nervous, but Jenna put the nurse and his feelings aside as she walked straight to a container labeled EIGHT in the far corner of the room — right where it had been for the last nine years.

"Um, what's your name?" the nurse asked hesitantly in an accent that Jenna could not exactly place. It was European, but not British, French, or Italian — the languages that Jenna had the most exposure to. *Eastern European, perhaps?*

The young nurse scolded himself for only asking for the lady's identity *after* he had let her into the cryo room. What was the English word that his mind was searching for? Ah, yes—*shit*. His boss, Dr. Daugherty, had given strict instructions *never* to let any unauthorized visitors or patients into the container room without permission from the director of BabyGenix or Dr. Daugherty herself. He had broken an important rule already—he was sure that his job would be lost by the end of the day.

"Moun—I'm sorry," Jenna put a hand to her forehead to indicate she had made a mistake—which worried the nurse even more: *She does not even know her own name?*

"Ellis," she said at last. "My name is Jenna Ellis. I have been a patient of Dr. Daugherty's for a very long time. These are my embryos, here—" And she pointed at one of the large, cylindrical metal containers. With that, the nurse let out a deflated sigh, and Jenna turned from him and put both of her hands on the top of container eight.

"Hello, babies," she said, gazing into the container. "It's Mom here. Just coming to see my little darlings." Jenna pressed her palms into the top of the cold glass. She had always hoped that they— Carson, Mia, and David—could somehow sense when she visited them, that maybe they could even hear her. Dr. Daugherty had said herself that the science of IVF was only in its infancy and not to count any possibility, no matter how farfetched, out. Jenna had visited so many times in the last nine years, and she kept the black-and-white images that Dr. Daugherty had given her almost a decade ago in the back of her jewelry box. She breathed in, slowly through her nose and slowly out through her mouth. This was much harder than she had imagined—and she had imagined the worst.

The nurse that had illegally let her into the cryochamber coughed, but Jenna did not take her eyes off the tiny vials—three in particular—HN3-8A, B, and C, snugly resting in the back, all contained within a cartridge labeled *Mountain*.

"I love you all so very much," she said at last, and paused, searching within herself for strength that was no longer there, "and I want you to know that no matter what happens, I—" Jenna broke into sobs before finishing her outward thought. The moisture from her tears, not to mention the liquid falling from her nose, caught in the back of her throat and she choked as she tried to breathe. Over her hacking cough, Jenna heard the nurse say something to her, and though she couldn't make out what he had said, she saw him out of the corner of her eye take a step in her direction. She swiftly put a hand up to suggest that he stop in his tracks.

"I'll be fine," she said shakily, keeping her right hand extended in his direction. "I just, I just need one more minute." To steady herself, Jenna put both hands back on the top of the container and let her tears fall. She watched each tear burst upon impact and spread out across the clear glass top. There was no use telling herself not to cry or to simply *stop crying*. She was well past any point of return. She had crossed the proverbial line—one marked in bright yellow, and one that she could not *uncross* even if she wanted to. This was her life now. This moment and the next few moments were really happening. What Jenna felt was worse than horrifying. She was living out her worst nightmare, and there was nothing that she could do to stop it.

A pager on the nurse's hip beeped and he looked down at the number. "I have to take this," he said and motioned to the phone bracketed to the wall beside the door. He spoke quickly and quietly into the receiver, and when he was finished, he told Jenna sheepishly that she needed to step outside the storage room and into the hallway. He was sure that today would be his last day on the job at BabyGenix as he motioned Jenna's attention toward the door.

Jenna looked in the direction of his gaze and could barely make out a shadowy figure through the small, vertical frame of frosted glass. *It couldn't be*, she thought to herself. She would have no way of knowing that the next few minutes would change her life, as well as Ellie's.

When Jenna stepped back into the storage room after talking with her ex-husband, Ed, Ed's lawyer, and the director of BabyGenix, everything felt surreal. She stood next to container eight, but this time she found it too difficult, too painful, to look down into the lid at the vials containing David, Carson, and Mia. She felt unadulterated sadness, but she also felt shame. The same nurse who had let her into the container room escorted Jenna in the second time, and after several minutes, he spoke up, making sure his English was both clear and loud enough for Jenna to hear and understand.

"Ms. Ellis, it is time. I'm so sorry, but I need for you to step away from the container—for safety reasons," the nurse said in his most professional intonation.

The nurse slowly walked close enough to Jenna to carefully put both hands onto her shoulders and began to pull her backward and away from container eight with gentle force. Jenna yelped but allowed herself to move back several steps, only to break away from the nurse's grasp, lunge forward, and cling tightly to container eight's top.

"*Please*," Jenna sobbed, "Please, I *just* want one more minute. Can't I have *one* more minute?" The sterile room was all glass and stainless steel, and as Jenna's eyes darted around for someone, something, to save her and to save her unborn children, all she found was the cold, unyielding purr of medical machinery at work.

"I am sorry, but no," the man said nervously. "The director made an exception even letting you be in here for the disposition.

Please, Ms. Ellis, stand back, and do not interfere with the extraction process." This time, when Jenna did not budge, he was getting ready to say, *I beg you, Mrs. Ellis*, when the lab door made a loud buzzing noise. Both he and Jenna looked up. *For God's sake, finally*, the nurse thought to himself as Jenna released her grip on the container's lid and allowed him to, again, gently guide her backward into the corner of the room closest to the door. The red light by the door blinked and the high-tech keypad buzzed once more just before the large metal door unlocked and swung open.

A short, stocky dark-haired woman with tiny streaks of gray in her short ponytail suddenly appeared, and without stopping, silently walked past Jenna and the nurse. Her white lab coat made a swishing noise under her armpits, and for a moment that was the only sound in the room. Once the woman made her way to container eight, she lifted the canister's lid. A loud whirring noise filled the room and a plume of frosty white crystals released violently into the air. Without looking back at Jenna or the nurse, the woman pulled two of the tiny vials from the canister with gloved hands, checked the vials against the clipboard that she was holding, and without hesitation, dropped the two vials unceremoniously into the red biohazard waste box affixed to the wall. Jenna knew from her own research that it only takes a few seconds for a frozen embryo to thaw and die when exposed to room temperature. The woman, with her back still to Jenna and the nurse, removed the latex medical gloves from her hands and tossed them into a trash can on the floor beneath the biohazard box.

"No!" Jenna cried out from the corner of the room, where the nurse still held her by her shoulders. "No! No! No!" she wailed. "I am SO sorry," she sobbed, "I am SO Sorry! Goodbye David! Goodbye Carson! I love you, Mia! I am so sorry . . ." Jenna's voice trailed off as her body crumbled inside her and she felt her knees give way. Dark-green spots in the far corners of her vision became larger until the darkness converged on itself and everything went black, plunging Jenna deeply and immediately into the most vivid dream that she had ever had in her life.

Her mind swam through a deep sea of her saddest memories—the last vacation that she and Ed took together with Ellie, and the last vacation that she took with her own father when she was just twelve years old. And then, in the background of her mind's eye, in the far corner of the dream, there she was. Standing in a pool of light, a fully formed little girl—one that looked more like Ellie than Jenna, but nonetheless, Jenna knew exactly who the child was. The child stood still, just out of Jenna's reach. Jenna called out to the girl and tried to move toward her, but no matter how hard she tried, she could not will her own legs to move. It was as if she were standing knee deep in hardened cement. Unable to move any closer to the girl, Jenna kept her arms outstretched, and called out for the child to hold on and to wait. But the little girl only stared blankly back at Jenna, expressionless as she was beautiful, breaking Jenna's heart all over again.

Jenna Ellis, who had been Mrs. Edward Mountain III just hours before, collapsed onto the floor of the high-security storage room on the seventh floor of the BabyGenix Fertility and Embryonic banking facility, and Gunnar Sharp, in only his second week on the job as a medical assistant, was tasked with waking her up. His boss, Dr. Christine Daugherty, turned around when she heard the thud that was Jenna's body hitting the floor. Thankfully, Gunnar had seen Ms. Ellis's eyes roll backward as her knees buckled and he caught her head in his hands just before it hit the concrete floor. Dr. Daugherty's brow wrinkled when she saw Jenna on the floor, and Gunnar noticed that his boss's expression was not one of empathy or fear, but rather one of curiosity.

"Get her some cold water to drink and put a wet cloth on her forehead," Dr. Daugherty said, leaving the room in a brisk walk. When she got to the door, she stopped and turned around. "And take Mrs. Mountain, Ms. Ellis I mean, into the women's restroom. She looks like she is going to get sick."

Gunnar, kneeling on the floor, held Ms. Ellis's head in his lap and looked up at his new boss. *Get sick?* "What kind of sick?" he asked out loud, and inwardly he wondered, *How can you tell?*

"Vomit," Dr. Daugherty said flatly. "She's as white as a ghost."

Dr. Daugherty thought about adding an additional comment about following orders, but when she saw the look of helplessness and terror on Gunnar's face, she softened and held her tongue. She did not need another assistant quitting so soon after being hired. She took a deep breath in and looked to the ceiling. A low hum could almost be heard as a chant traveled through the closed windows from the street below. The noise had become constant, like a static background symphony inside the BabyGenix lab. It was the protesters. The picketing had grown worse in recent months, and in quick succession, several assistants had quit citing an "unpleasant work environment."

The crowds were relentless. "Fake babies!" they yelled among other obscenities. Whether it was two or twenty, someone gathered daily at the BabyGenix entrance to shout and stomp, stopping intermittently only to chant alternating verses of scripture—which for Dr. Daugherty was the most maddening part of it all. How could a person protest in the name of religion while at the same time hurl such awful and repulsive name-calling at Dr. Daugherty and her patients? The duplicity of Americans would never make sense to the Aussie Dr. Daugherty.

Dr. Daugherty went over to the window and looked out. Today, several protesters held up American flags while others held signs that read "STOP Making Designer Babies" and "NO ONE Wants Robot Babies in the USA." Negative press by hyperbolic right-wing news outlets had only made things worse. The stories being run were more like scenes from a science-fiction movie than science, and Dr. Daugherty was pegged as Godzilla in all of them. Just the week before, an op-ed article titled "Modern Medicine Gone Too Far" directly targeted BabyGenix and an unnamed female doctor designated as Dr. D "for Death" for what the article called "overt and grossly misguided medical practices" by BabyGenix staff. Christine Daugherty had spent over twenty years in reproductive medical research, and she had to clean egg yolks off her car every other day just to make the drive home to Long Island at the end of a long workday.

It was nearly enough to make her quit, which would have made her partner, Karen, a happy woman. "They don't understand what you are trying to do in this country. I'm not sure why you continually put yourself in the line of fire. For what?" Karen's heavy Welsh accent added a subtle layer of condescension to everything that she said, no matter how well intended, and though she cared deeply for Christine, even she was at her wits' end hearing about Christine's troubles at work. It had taken months to fill Gunnar's position. "It's 1999, you know," Karen reminded Christine. "Maybe the world is just not going to come around to your way of seeing test-tube babies. You are one person trying to do the work of a whole army—I am not even sure who you are fighting for anymore." The criticism, from Karen of all people, cut deeply no matter how hard Christine tried to block it out.

Christine wiped beads of sweat off her own forehead with the back of her hand and walked away from the window, bending down next to Gunnar and her unconscious patient. She hoped that Gunnar appreciated this; concrete floors were not kind to her knees anymore.

Gunnar's voice wavered as he looked from Jenna to his boss. "Does she have anyone?" he asked.

Dr. Daugherty nodded. "Ms. Ellis has a nine-year-old daughter. Her name is Ellie."

Gunnar looked back at Jenna's face. "Was she, the daughter I mean, was she a test-tube baby?" he asked.

Again, Dr. Daugherty nodded in the affirmative. "She was." Christine paused and went on. "That is why this is all so hard for her. All patients respond differently to the emotional toll of IVF treatment. Some are able to emotionally detach from the process once their family goals are met, but others, like Ms. Ellis, have a harder time." Dr. Daugherty looked down at Jenna's unconscious face. "Once she saw that what's stored in there—" Christine pointed toward the large containers in the back of the room—"put under the right circumstances, has the ability to become a living, breathing, child—well, everything changed. All the DNA markers and lipid levels, suddenly it all holds more meaning than it did before the first test-tube baby was born."

Gunnar knew that he was inching his way into uncharted and possibly immediate dismissal territory, but he asked the question on his mind anyhow. "And you?" he asked. "What do you think?"

Dr. Daugherty put her hands in the pockets of her lab coat and smiled, not a broad, proud sort of smile, but rather a very humble, almost reverent smile. She shrugged her shoulders.

"For me, it's science. It will always be about the science." Gunnar nodded and wondered what to think about his boss's response. He also had doubts about his new job—should he be allowed to keep it at the end of the day? And he wondered if his duties as medical assistant would entail reviving fainting upper-class white women on a regular basis—because if so, he wasn't sure that he would stay at BabyGenix for long. "She'll be fine, Gunnar,"

Dr. Daugherty said more softly than before. "Just get her a cloth and make sure she makes it into a cab." With that, Christine Daugherty stood up, and under her breath on her way out of the storage room added, "I'm just glad that this whole shit show is over." She shook her head, not bothering to address the three men standing in the hallway outside, all with hands firmly planted in their pockets as she coldly brushed by. Gunnar lifted Jenna's head to help circulate the blood flow and repeated her name until her eyes opened into tiny slits. At least she was conscious again. Although he had thought it highly unlikely for a moment, because Jenna's body was so limp, Gunnar wondered if he was holding a dead woman in his arms. She could have had a heart attack for all he knew. Dr. Daugherty was a fertility specialist, not someone versed in cardiac care. What if she had been wrong about what happened to her patient? Jenna's mouth began to move slowly once her eyes opened, but Gunnar could not make out what she was saying, so he asked her to repeat it. Barely above a whisper, Jenna repeated the words—"I saw her"—and her face contorted in anguish as she turned her head into his chest.

"Who?" Gunnar asked. "Who did you see?" he asked, thinking that perhaps she meant the daughter that Dr. Daugherty had mentioned before leaving him all alone. *Ellie?* he thought. "*Who* did you see, Ms. Ellis?" he repeated.

This time he heard her clearly. She said, "I saw Mia."

PART II

The Beginning of Everything, 1978–1985

three

Melbourne, Queen Victoria Medical Center, 1978

D r. Carl Wood paced the length of his small office as he waited for his colleague to arrive. Melbourne was over ten thousand miles from London, but word traveled fast when it was important, and he had finally received the earth-shattering news that he had been anticipating, if not dreading. He stopped pacing for a moment to look out the window and his eye caught on a pregnant woman crossing the street below. The woman wore a long, red-and-white-checked muumuu and was visibly uncomfortable; that was obvious from the look on her face, even from his fourth-floor window. A breeze blew strands of her blonde hair into her face. She was pretty, thirty years old perhaps? Maybe thirty-five?

The woman squinted in the bright sun and held one hand up to her forehead to block the light, and the other held the underside of her enlarged belly. She looked both ways before waddling across the side street closest to the hospital, then disappeared down the avenue among other Melburnians making their way hastily to work or school. Dr. Wood had no idea who the woman was, but he ached to help her. It had become his life's work and his life's purpose to ease women's pain during, before, and after pregnancy. His passion for his work was so profuse that he often felt isolated from his colleagues, who thought that he took his research *too far* and *too seriously* for a practicing obstetrician. "Just deliver the babies, Wood," one of them said years ago. "That's what they pay us to do, not to reinvent the wheel." This latest work in test-tube baby research had been the final nail in the coffin and definitively put him on an island with a handful of other researchers, separating him like a black sheep from the other doctors in the hospital.

"Did you get the news?" a voice asked behind him, and Dr. Wood turned to see his colleague, John Leeton, enter his office and take a seat in the black leather club chair opposite his desk. Leeton was tall and had a lanky build. Because of this, he often sat with his forearms resting on the top of his long legs—he sat this way in Wood's office, and he tapped his index fingers against one another nervously.

"I did," he replied. "We knew it was coming, but it still stings a bit that it couldn't have been us tolling the bells about the world's first IVF birth," Dr. Wood said, sighing. "Now Louise Brown's name, along with Pat Steptoe and Bob Edwards, will be forever etched into history." He tapped his black fountain pen on his desk, deep in thought. "Why wouldn't Edwards have mentioned the pregnancy at the Duphar lecture?" Wood asked aloud to no one in particular. "What have they discovered that we have yet to uncover? And why the secrecy? It doesn't make any sense. It doesn't serve a purpose if only one clinic in the world can help infertile women. The whole *point* is for in vitro fertilization to have proven clinical applications—globally."

"It's a giant leap, yes, but there is still much more that we can do," Leeton replied, breaking his colleague's monologue. Wood looked up, nodded, and looked back down at his desk, his fountain pen *tap, tap, tapping* continuously. Dr. Leeton wondered if he should excuse himself or sit in silence and wait out Wood's current thought process. He decided to stay put.

"Have you seen Trounson this morning?" Wood asked.

"The animal guy?" Leeton replied, a look of confusion crossing his brow.

Wood quickly corrected him, "Former 'animal guy'—he's on our team now and he may be the best shot we have at catching up to Edwards." Leeton confirmed he had seen Alan Trounson that morning in the lab, just before he heard Louise Brown's birth announcement on public radio. "Can you send him here to see me?" Wood asked, though he didn't look up from the notebook on his desk where he was furiously scribbling unintelligible notes.

"Sure," Leeton said, standing up and tapping the arm of his chair for good measure. "Right you are, I'll send him in." And he excused himself from Wood's office with an uneasy feeling in the pit of his stomach.

He found Alan Trounson in the team's tiny embryology lab an hour later. Trounson shared the pint-sized lab with Alex Lopata, who had been a part of the original Egg Project, which began in 1970, along with Leeton and Wood. The three men were the core of the test-tube baby effort in Australia. When Trounson joined the team, a small room that previously served the building as a maintenance closet had been retrofitted with microscopes and other basic tools, allowing the two scientists to view embryos in their earliest stages. But the setup was not ideal. The "lab" could fit a maximum of two people at a time inside—which was a bit tight for two men with vastly different methods of research.

Trounson was young for the veteran scientific team that had recently taken the new name of Test Tube Baby Team (TTBT) instead of Egg Project the year before. Then, in 1977, when Carl Wood had been awarded a Ford Foundation grant for contraception research, which included provisions for IVF research as well, the funding allowed for Trounson to join the team full time. The grant was a huge boon for the team, and most notably it allowed for Wood to pay Trounson a salary, thus wooing him away from specialized sheep embryology research at Cambridge to return home to Australia. But while the Ford grant was a major stepping-stone in Wood's dream of making IVF a clinical success, neither the Ford Foundation nor Monash University (the institution associated with the research team) wanted to be acknowledged if an IVF birth occurred. It was a sleight-of-hand trick that all research teams had to play into during the early days of infertility research and clinical trials.

Thankfully, Monash and a few institutions scattered around the world allowed fertility teams like Wood's to operate IVF studies under their roof. However, in the event of failure or some disastrous clinical outcome—say the birth of an IVF child with severe physical abnormality—only the clinicians would be held responsible, and thus institutions preferred to stay at arm's length when it came to IVF and other early infertility treatment research.

By the time Trounson sat down in Wood's office later that afternoon, Wood had devised a plan for the TTBT that would get Australia back in the IVF race and catch up to, if not surpass, Steptoe and Edwards in the UK.

"We need to get Steptoe here in Melbourne—a face-to-face meeting to see what he knows," Wood said to Trounson, who agreed, but had reservations about what information the Brit would share about the Brown birth, considering how mute both Steptoe and Edwards had been with their own British colleagues.

"Do you think he'll actually talk?" Trounson asked. "You were there with me in London last year, and neither Steptoe nor Edwards made mention of the success that they had achieved thus far—it couldn't have been more than fifteen weeks before the birth. I think they are just not keen on sharing information and don't see the value in it the way that you and I do."

"True," Wood conceded, "but we have to try. I put Ian Johnston on it already. He will buy two first-class tickets for Steptoe and his wife, Sheena, and we'll roll out the full royal treatment. Perhaps when he sees how close we are to achieving the same success that he and Bob had at Oldham, he will loosen up a little and give some insight into what made their pregnancy a success." Wood rubbed his chin and continued to think. "And I want you to get more involved—more hands on, so to speak—and I plan to as well. It will be round-the-clock work, but we are *this* close." Wood held his thumb and forefinger close together. "We just have to find the key to punch it through."

Trounson smiled. "I have been wanting to try my controlled hormonal stimulation technique—it is there that I found the most success in obtaining viable eggs from ewes at Jerilderie—"

"How confident are you that it will work?" Wood interrupted wearily.

Trounson looked puzzled. "Which part? Getting Pat to talk or using my hormone technique?" Trounson stood up from his chair, bent over at the waist, then lifted his torso back up, holding his hands close to his chest, his wrists flopped forward. "It is not a popular comparison, but if you take an ewe and bring her upright to two hooves, like so, you have the same basic female organs as in humans. I've done it hundreds of times in sheep with good results. It will work, Carl, of that I have no doubt. As for Pat

Steptoe, I don't know him well enough to guess what he will be like away from his colleagues in England, but we may not need him. I think we will have success with or without his help."

"All right, then." Wood rubbed his temples. "Get going right away. I want a live IVF birth in Australia by the end of next year." Trounson nodded his head and left Wood alone with his notes.

four

Los Angeles, 1978

A light breeze blew through the car window by Deputy Mark Newcomb as he sat in his squad car at the corner of Eagle Rock Boulevard and West Avenue 40 when his dash dispatch radio crackled to life. It had been a quiet day as far as dispatch had been concerned, which suited the deputy fine. He was not one of those cops who joined the force looking for adventure. He just liked the steady paycheck, and besides, it kept his father off his back about keeping a respectable job. Newcomb checked the time—he only had two more hours on his shift, at which point, he planned to go home, put his feet up, and enjoy a cold beer in front of his TV.

"Officers in the area of Glassell Park and Adams Hill," the voice on dispatch commanded, "respond to the scene of a shooting at 3539 Sunbeam Drive. Victim is a ten-year-old female inside the home. REPEAT, all officers in the vicinity of Glassell and Adams respond immediately to 3539 Sunbeam Drive."

Deputy Newcomb sat up in his seat and took the radio controller in his hand, pressing the side button to reply to dispatch. "This is deputy Newcomb, squad car 8751, responding to the call at Sunbeam Drive. Cross Street Sunbeam and Scandia, OVER."

The radio crackled once more and then went silent. Deputy Newcomb put the key in the ignition and took one more sip of his afternoon coffee before putting his police cruiser in reverse, switching on his active lights and siren.

He was the first to respond to the address and he noticed right away that the front door had been left open. It was a clear, sunny day in March, so it could have been open for a reason; lots of people in California moved to the state for exactly that reason— to be able to leave their doors and windows open and invite the sun and fresh air in—but Deputy Newcomb guessed that the reason for its position was not so benign as to let in fresh air. He opened the car door and stepped out. His boot crunched on something, so he looked down. A woman's compact mirror was shattered under his foot. He swore out loud and shook his leg before kicking the side of his tire to get rid of any residual glass. *What a day*, he thought, *what a week*.

The upscale neighborhood was eerily quiet, and when Newcomb looked in both directions of the well-groomed residential street for any signs of foul play, he found none. There were no skid marks on the driveway or road to indicate a quick getaway, nor was there anyone out jogging or walking a dog that he could get a statement from. In fact, aside from the now broken compact, the driveway was exceedingly clean, like it had been pressure-washed recently. In short, it did not look like your typical gunshot victim crime scene.

As a high-pitched scream came from inside the house, Deputy Newcomb put his hand on the gun at his hip and quickly ascended the stairs at the entrance two at a time. It sounded like a woman's scream, and it came from an upstairs room.

"LAPD!" the deputy yelled, and he carefully walked up interior stairs in the direction of the continued screaming. The high-pitched howl could have easily been confused for an animal in extreme distress, but Newcomb had heard it all, and knew when a sound was definitively human—however inhuman it may sound. He repeated his verbal arrival call as he followed the sound down the hall to the last bedroom on the right side of the home. With his gun thrust squarely in front of him, he entered the room and found a man crouched on the floor next to a bed, his face blank and expressionless, his hands clutching the telephone receiver. A woman, the source of the inhuman cries, lay sprawled across the bed next to where the victim, a young girl, lay motionless. *Stay cool*, Newcomb said to himself, and for added measure, *Stay very, very cool.*

There was a lot of blood on the bed, and a splatter of human tissue had reached the side wall closest to the victim. A single fatal gunshot wound—at close range, judging by the blood on the wall—to the forehead was evident, and it was fresh, maybe within the last hour or so. The pungent smell of death did not yet suffocate the room, but it would soon enough. *Stay cool.*

Newcomb quickly did a scan of the room. After several years on the force, his eyes were accustomed to the rhythm and cadence of a crime scene. He worked to locate any visual oddity before walking around the room and surveying the scene for something that might tell him who or what could be responsible. It was as he walked around to the footboard of the bed that he saw the revolver on the bed, half obscured by the woman's body.

"Ma'am," he said calmly, putting one hand out toward the

woman. "Ma'am, I am going to need for you to step back from the victim."

The woman was very attractive, and Newcomb guessed her to be in her thirties. When he spoke, her head jerked upward and she looked up at Deputy Newcomb as if she just noticed that he entered the room. Her hair and eyes were dark in that sultry South American way, and she wore a long, floral silk dress that was probably extremely flattering when it was not soaked down the front with dark blood. The woman's eyes were crazed, and Newcomb's heart began to beat faster. She did not trust him, and he could feel it. The room went completely silent as the South American beauty, stained in blood, stared with hatred at Deputy Newcomb. The smell of iron filled Deputy Newcomb's nostrils; decomp had begun. He took one slow step toward the bed.

"No!" the woman screamed. She turned her head back to the victim and resumed her cry, repeating the single word over and over, "No! No! No!" in a deep-throated howl. She was angry, but not violent, Newcomb decided. Still, he needed to proceed with caution.

"Listen to me carefully, ma'am," Newcomb continued. "I need for you to step away from the victim and the firearm, and slowly stand beside the bed with your hands in the air." The woman's eyes followed Newcomb's, and when they landed on the gun, soaked in blood in between the girl and herself, a look of genuine surprise crossed her face. She jolted backward away from the gun and clumsily slid from the bed to the floor, crawling over to where the man sat crouched with his hands covering his face. Newcomb watched them both. The man appeared to be older than the woman—was he her father or her husband? And though neither looked dangerous, because Newcomb was not sure who these people were or what their connection to the deceased was, in addition to the fact that backup officers had not yet arrived on the scene, he felt that he needed to secure the scene and keep everyone calm. Police training 101 made it impossible for Newcomb to ignore that, despite one being a woman, he was in a small upstairs room with three people, and only one of them was in uniform. It had been just over a decade since the infamous LA Watts riots, and though Newcomb had only been a young kid in August of 1965, the awful images from newspapers and TV, highlighting the violence that left thirty-four people dead, were never far from his mind when he was on duty.

"Sir," Newcomb spoke slowly and with an air of authority, "I need for you two to stand up slowly and put your hands in the air." The man hesitated but finally stood. Both the man and woman were South American, and while the woman put her hands carefully in the air, the man stared at Deputy Newcomb defiantly.

"This is our daughter—" the man began, gesturing his right arm in the direction of the bed.

"PUT YOUR HANDS IN THE AIR, SIR!" Newcomb commanded, but instead of the man putting his hands up, he put them out, reaching into the air toward the young white deputy.

"*Please*," the man said. "Please—we are good people. My name is Mario Rios, and this is my wife, Elsa." The man looked toward the woman, who was still holding both arms in the air. She nodded, not knowing what else to do. The man continued, "This is our daughter, Claudia." The man's voice cracked. "Someone has killed her! I am the one who called 911. Please, you need to help us!" Mario made the mistake of taking one step toward Newcomb.

"GET ON THE GROUND, SIR! AND PUT YOUR HANDS BEHIND YOUR BACK!" Newcomb barked, instantly flipping the scene from calm to volatile. He would have sworn that the tiny bedroom warmed up ten degrees in seconds. Sweat began to bead on Newcomb's neck, trapped between his rigid uniform collar and his skin. "GET. ON. THE. GROUND," he ordered one last time.

Mario lowered his hands and then he slid slowly to the floor, lying on his belly with his hands outstretched resting on the floor. Elsa stifled a cry and then let out a howl even louder than before. Deputy Newcomb could barely think straight because the screaming was so loud, and so, so inhuman.

"Quiet!" Newcomb yelled at Elsa. "F-ing foreigners," he said under his breath. Where in the hell were the other officers? Newcomb took a knee on the carpeted floor and yanked the handcuffs from his belt loop before slapping them across Mario's hands. Elsa put her hands to her mouth to stifle her own cries.

"Ma'am," he said, looking up at Elsa, "I am going to need you to get on the floor as well." Shaking and blanched white with shock, Elsa slowly lowered herself to the ground just as her husband had done, and Newcomb cuffed her tiny wrists. By the time he had read the Rioses their rights, a second cruiser appeared on the curb.

"Where did the gun come from?" Newcomb asked, nudging Mario with the toe of his boot. "Is this yours, sir?" Mario lifted his forehead from the carpet and nodded in affirmation.

"But—"

"Well, then it looks like we've got this wrapped up," Newcomb said contemptuously. "Either one of you shot her, or she shot herself. I'm good either way. I'll give you two a minute to decide what your story is going to be." Newcomb stepped over the bodies of Mario and Elsa on his way out of the room and down the stairs to meet the officers that finally arrived.

What Deputy Newcomb did not expect was the tongue lashing that he would receive from his superior officers. Mario Rios was not just another South American low-life immigrant, he was a millionaire who owned a quarter of the low-income housing in

Los Angeles County. Mario's personal contacts included several prominent city leaders and went up as high as the mayor's office. Deputy Newcomb had created a PR *nightmare scenario* for his squad, according to his next in command, and would take an indefinite leave of absence until desk duty could be found for him. As an act of reconciliation, the LAPD did not press charges against either Mario or Elsa, and in return, Mario would not leak the way that he and Elsa had been treated to the press. If he did, both he and the police force knew that it could spark an all-out riot.

Officially, within the confines of LAPD records, the death of ten-year-old Claudia Rios was deemed an *apparent accidental shooting* because the revolver used in her death belonged to Mario Rios. According to neighbors on Sunbeam Drive, a small, quiet suburban street just north of Los Angeles, both Mario and Elsa Rios maintained that they believed an intruder entered the house and killed Claudia on that deadly day in March.

Neighbor Peggy Dunham also maintained until her death that she believed the Rioses' claim that their precious daughter had been murdered and not accidentally shot. "That poor, poor child," Dunham expressed to an AP reporter for the *Los Angeles Times*. "The mother (Elsa) just adored her (Claudia) . . . she dressed her like a cupcake."

An investigation into the intruder theory was never taken seriously, and after 1983 it didn't matter. After 1983, the Rioses would be famous for quite another reason—one that would have a ripple effect on a global scale.

five

Princeton University, 1981

From her vantage point on the lawn, all Jenna Ellis could see was a mass of orange and black. Enormous banners bearing the illustrious orange P hung like leviathans from the stone facade of Nassau Hall, and streamers and balloons leftover from reunions, the weekend prior, mingled lazily with the variegated green ivy which covered every visible lamppost and doorway on campus. Jenna looked around and told herself to take it all in, remember this scene, remember how electric it felt to be standing amongst her classmates for the last time, each one full of so much promise and hope for the future, it could barely be contained in one courtyard. The energy was palpable, and it made Jenna both excited and a little nervous. What if she did not live up to all the expectations that people had for her—what about the ones that she had for herself? She took a deep breath in and told herself to relax. *Save that worry for another day*, she said to herself as she looked to the sky, closed her eyes, and let the sun warm her face.

If a person had never seen Princeton University at the end of May, deep in the wild heart of reunions and graduation, then they had not experienced true and complete adoration of which only Princetonians could possess for their alma mater. Jenna was no different from all the graduates that had come before—Princeton was a special place and could shape not only its graduates' next step in life, but all phases afterward. It was a golden key that unlocked many doors.

But in May 1981, Jenna's future was the least of her worries. It was uncharacteristically hot in New Jersey on graduation day, and while parents and other alums fanned themselves vigorously with programs, Jenna enjoyed the warmth and conviviality of her classmates—the class of '81. She barely paid attention to the commencement speech by Dr. Sissela Bok, daughter of two Nobel Prize winners and wife of Harvard President Derek Bok, and unfortunately did not remember a single thing that the scholarly woman said.

Some brave soul smuggled into the courtyard an enormous inflatable tiger and tossed it into the air at the end of the ceremony, causing Jenna along with twelve hundred giddy seniors to raise her hands high in the air to keep the animal aloft as they exited the lawn through FitzRandolph Gate and poured onto Nassau Street. After four years of living in a *work hard, play hard* mentality, Jenna could barely believe that she had donned a senior beer jacket and sung "Old Nassau" (*Hurrah! Hurrah! Hurrah! Three cheers for Old Nassau!*) one final time before heading to law school at NYU in the fall. It seemed like only yesterday she received her admission letter in the mail, making her mother scream with excitement and breathe a sigh of relief that her determined daughter's singular goal in high school had been achieved—despite

Jenna's senior advisor urging that she apply to other, "less impervious" schools. But then again, Jenna never had been one to take no for an answer once she set her mind to a task—and in this case she had decided as a sophomore at Westchester Preparatory School that she, Jenna Ellis from Asheville, North Carolina, would get into Princeton University.

And now here she was, standing at the corner of Nassau and Witherspoon Street, scanning the throngs of people for her mother, Janelle, who had made the ten-hour drive from Asheville to see her only child graduate from the esteemed Ivy League school.

"Mom!" Jenna shouted when she caught a glimpse of her mother's auburn hair. She waved overhead until Janelle saw her and began to make her way slowly through the multitudes of people exiting campus through the west gate, and over to where Jenna stood.

"Honey!" Janelle shouted as she came closer to Jenna. "I am SO proud of you, my dear," she said, holding firm to a tightened smile. Her emotions finally overtook her, and she allowed tears to fall merrily down her cheeks. She wiped them away with the pads of her fingers, smearing dark streaks of black mascara across the tops of her cheekbones and exposing a mass of tiny brown spots across her nose and face.

"Mooom," Jenna said, smiling, as she pulled her mother in for a hug. "You don't have to cry every time you see me, you know. I just left you, crying, an hour ago before the ceremony."

Janelle waved her daughter's protests away. "You just wait until you have a daughter," she said, now beginning to laugh at herself. "You'll see." She dabbed the corners of her eyelids with one of the wadded-up tissues from her bag. "It's not every day that you see your only child graduate from college. I just wish that your father could have been here to see it too."

Jenna had known that one of them would say it at some point during the graduation weekend, it was inevitable, but she held off being the one to bring him up thus far. It was too hard. Despite the years that passed since Rawson Ellis's death when Jenna was twelve, neither she nor her mother could talk about him without tearing up.

"He's here, Mom. I can feel him all around us." She rubbed her mother's back in soothing circular movements.

Jenna did what she always had done for her mother since her father's death; she played the role of solid grace, the one that held her fragile mother together, and kept Janelle from coming apart at the seams. It was a role that came easy to Jenna, and her stoicism had been noticed by more than a few of her professors. When other students panicked during classroom debates, Jenna remained calm, almost rigidly so, and so, when her academic advisor told her that this character trait would serve her well in law school, she took the advisor's advice, took the LSAT, and applied to NYU Law. She was one of many Princeton seniors that would be heading to New York City in the fall, each one eagerly following their own dreams, or at the very least, someone else's.

Janelle wiped her eyes again and stiffened her spine. "You are right," she said, rubbing Jenna's arm lovingly. "You are my rock, Jenna, and always so level-headed. He *is* here, and he's just as proud as I am. And, he would have never wanted to see the two of us standing on the street corner crying on such a happy day." Janelle laughed out loud at her own expense just as another parent walked past Jenna and Janelle, and gave an all-knowing wink to Janelle and a hearty congratulations to Jenna. The man could not know, of course, why Janelle was crying, but nonetheless, she felt a little embarrassed for being so emotional.

Janelle forced a smile, the same one that she used so often in the years since Rawson's death to put a stop to people feeling pity for her. If Jenna had been the rock after Rawson's death, Janelle had been the thrift store teddy bear, the one everyone felt sorry for, but no one knew how to help or put back together. The pity was something that had grown to irritate her beyond anything else. She decided many years ago that the best course of action in social settings when her husband's name came up was to smile, say she was doing just fine, and quickly change the subject. This tactic typically worked, and conversation would easily glide into who won the regional basketball tournament or whose child won the state meet in swimming. Around her daughter, however, Janelle was not as strong, and in the midst of significant life moments like graduation, she missed her husband terribly.

Losing a spouse to terminal illness at an early age like she had was hard for people to understand. It was not their fault, or for a lack of trying, but they simply could not understand the degree to which the world abruptly stopped turning. It was a loss of control that was irreparable, and a feeling of isolation so deep and so dark that Janelle would never wish it upon her worst enemy.

There was only one person, a colleague of Rawson's at the Eastern Carolina Medical Center, who said what so many others did not, and what, in retrospect, was the most poignant for Janelle's state of mind when Rawson was first diagnosed with malignant melanoma.

"No matter what happens," the colleague had said, "don't forget that *you* are alive, and Jenna is alive, and that is why you keep going." It seemed harsh at the time, but in the aftermath of her husband's death, it was those words that comforted Janelle the most and made her get out of bed in the mornings, despite wanting to hide away from the world in her dark and cozy bedroom.

She was thinking of the doctor friend and trying to remember his name when she realized that she had *drifted* again—the word

that Jenna used when Janelle suddenly got lost in old memories—
and she snapped herself back to the present. "Let's go get
something to eat!" she said enthusiastically. "What is the best
lunch around here?"

Jenna's eyes lit up. "Ooh, let's go to Barry's. It will be super
crowded today, but it is a nice day to stand in line." She linked
her mother's arm in hers and they crossed Nassau Street and
made their way down Witherspoon to join in the long line of
students and parents waiting for sandwiches and salads from the
best deli in town. Years later, Janelle would look back to this day
and remember with comfort that Jenna had been strong once, and
she hoped that her only child would someday find strength and
vibrance again.

six

New York City, 1981

A knock on his open door made Ed Mountain look up from the six-inch-thick computer printout that sat on his desk. He was one of the few employees of Mountain Chemical Engineering (MCE) that had one of the new IBM Personal Computers, making it monumentally easier to access internal MCE reports and files. The last seventy-two hours had been spent reviewing the quarterly financials for MCE ahead of tomorrow's board meeting, Ed's first, where he knew he would be grilled mercilessly for being the new guy on the block, and he still had a solid six more hours to go if he was going to get through the entire file before morning.

It had been Ed's idea to open the New York office, but it took two years for his father, grandfather, and uncles to see things his way and open one. Even then, his grandfather only allowed Ed to sign a five-year lease on the office space in the financial district. But Ed had let that go. When Goggin, the last remaining giant in the chemical manufacturing industry in the Northeast, fell to MCE in a merger engineered by Ed's uncle Don, the elder Mountains decided to give the younger Mountain what he wanted. Goggin had been based in Upstate New York and the plants that MCE saved in the merger continued to operate, so after the deal was done, a New York–based office for MCE made sense. The remainder of MCE's chemical plants were scattered across the Southeast and Texas, so it was decided that after making Ed cut his teeth in the home office in Birmingham, he could move up to "big boy" status and run his own part of the company from New York and oversee the former Goggin plants.

That was five years ago, and in that time, Ed had not only managed to buy out ten other smaller fertilizer brands and put them under the MCE umbrella, thus enlarging MCE's foothold to the Midwest and Northern California, he had increased production and profitability in the old Goggin plants in Upstate New York as well.

Because of this, his father pushed other board members to vote young Ed Mountain, just twenty-eight years old, onto the board of one of the most highly valued companies in the United States.

"What's up?" Ed asked flatly, not looking up from the green-and-white monster he had wrestled with for the past several days.

"Not too much. I just wanted to see if you wanted to go out for a drink. Can I twist your arm?" The person doing the asking was Dan O'Hara, and he had asked Ed to come out with him and some of his Yale buddies that lived in the city every Friday since he became an MCE employee, and every Friday, Ed said no.

"I'm too wrapped up in this report," he would say, or, "I would love to, man, but I just need a few more hours looking over this contract." It was never a good time, and time was something that Ed didn't feel like he had. His father and grandfather had made that clear on the day of his graduation from Ole Miss.

It had been like most university commencement ceremonies, the graduation march, handing out of the diplomas, and raging parties for several days following. It was during his fraternity's epic Take the House Down lawn party that Edward Mountain Jr. and Edward Mountain Sr. sat Ed down in a private room and told him that he hadn't made the cut and that he would not be working in the family business after all.

"What do you mean?" Ed slurred, drunk and high on the pills he had promised his mother he would stop taking. His four years in college had been one long and continuous debauched night for Ed, and he was more than a little sad to see it all ending. In fact, when the movie *Animal House* was released in 1978, Ed and his fraternity brothers swore that the movie had been based on their own legendary exploits.

His grandfather, Ed Mountain Sr., spoke slowly to make sure Ed would understand. "We are saying that we think that you should consider another profession, or industry, or whatever it is that you want to do. Be a writer, be a musician, hell, be a mailman for all we care. Your cousin, Greg, he's just finished at Harvard. He will fit in to the MCE culture—how shall we say it—*better* than you would have. No hard feelings though, son. It's just business."

Ed Sr.'s hand clapped down on the back of Ed's shoulder, and it felt to Ed like he had been struck by lightning. He could not have been more surprised. Ed Sr. then ran a hand through his per-fectly coifed silver hair and turned to his oldest son, Ed's father, to make a face that said, *See how it's done?* The old man was impec-cably dressed no matter the occasion or day of the week; Ed's grandmother made sure of that. Unlike Ed's father, Ed Sr. was the type of person that was so sure of himself, like nothing could stand in his way, and it was something that young Ed had always admired about his grandfather, but it was also one of many traits that made him afraid of his own grandfather. Ed Sr. would bulldoze a person over if that's what it took to get his way—in a Southern genteel way, of course. No need to make things messy, he would always say. It's just business, he would say. Ed was the third of the Mountain clan, and he had assumed that he would go into the family business after graduation. No one had ever said otherwise, until now. Ed looked from his father to his grandfather and suddenly had the sense that this was a conversation that they had planned well in advance of that evening. How long ago, he could not guess, but this was not spontaneous—it had been orchestrated behind his back. He could barely contain his rage and embarrassment.

"Does Mom know that we are having this conversation?" Ed asked, looking pointedly at his father, who shrank like a child in his father's shadow. Ed Jr. looked away and didn't answer. *You are such a coward and you always will be,* Ed thought to himself and looked away from his father.

"Fine. You don't want to answer, fine," Ed spat at both men. "What is it that you two assholes suppose that I should do, *for my profession,* that is?" He raised his hands to make air quotes and noticed that he saw four hands in front of his face instead of two.

"Whatever the hell you want, son! This is your *out,* just take it for once," his grandfather replied, acting exasperated. The Mountain family had always been this way, and Ed hated them for it. It was a hallmark, if such a hallmark exists, of the Mountain men. Dangle something of value in front of you, lead you to believe that you will have said item of value, tell you that if you "just work harder" that you may get said item, and then, at the last second, just as the gift is touching the skin of your palm, victory literally within reach, they reach down and snatch it away, telling you that you never really expected to get the gift. Surely not! How could a person be so idiotic? Sometimes, Ed thought it would be easier just to be his sister, Evelyn. At least they acted like she didn't exist and left her alone. She would end up inheriting almost as much as Ed when all was said and done, so a smarter person may ask themselves if putting himself in the line of fire repeatedly with his father and grandfather was worth it in the end. But Ed was tired of being put up against a wall by the bullies in the family. His uncles, more masculine versions of his father, had been lurking in the shadows for years waiting for the perfect opportunity to somehow screw him over, and put their sons, his cousins, ahead of Ed.

"Not this time." Ed looked straight into his grandfather's steely, cold blue eyes and counted to three in his head before he repeated himself to make sure the old bastard heard him. "NOT. THIS. TIME."

"Excuse me, young man?" Ed Sr. retorted, putting a hand to his ear as if to say that he had not heard correctly. He began snorting and shuffling his feet like a bull that had just been released from its pen. Then the old man squinted, and put both of his hands on the back of a chair as he leaned down and glared at Ed. He tapped the chair with his right hand, causing his large class ring (Old Miss, class of '29) to clank, and Ed Jr. physically moved to position himself behind his father. Ed once again felt pity for his father for being so weak.

"I am going to work for MCE," Ed said slowly and deliberately to both men. He was still drunk, of course, but his anger had temporarily sobered him up. "I will show up in the office on Monday morning, and I will take a desk, any desk that I want. I will prove to you that I am good enough to run your company, your precious baby that you have valued more than me for as long as I can remember. I will make my share of the quarterly commissions, and I will draw a paycheck equal to senior members of management. That is the deal—except . . . you know what, in this deal there is no negotiating. It is happening whether you like it or not." When Ed finished, he noticed that he had been pointing straight into his grandfather's chest, with his index finger only inches away from Ed Sr.'s Hermes tie. He must have stood up out of his chair at some point, but he didn't remember doing so and now he towered over his grandfather. Ed felt something he had never felt before, and certainly never in the presence of his father or grandfather—he felt powerful, and it felt good. He waited for one of the Mountains to speak.

Ed Sr. pressed his wrinkled, crusty mouth into a straight line across his face. He wiped his thumb across the corner of his mouth, smoothed down his tie, and looked back at his son and then to his grandson. He raised his hand and slowly moved Ed's still pointed finger away from his chest.

"I knew you had it in you, boy," Ed Sr. said in something between a whisper and a growl. "Glad to see that *some* of the men in this family still have balls." He did not need to look back at Ed Jr. for Ed to know what he meant. "I'll see you in the office on Monday—eight a.m. and not a minute late, do you hear me? Not one excuse for missing a day of work—ever—or you are *out*."

Ed nodded and exhaled all the breath that he hadn't realized he'd been holding in. Ed Sr. touched Ed's shoulder too briefly to call a pat, and too long for it to have been accidental, before shuffling out of the room with his son, Ed's father, trailing behind him like a puppy. This was the Mountain way. Nothing was ever easy, and nothing was ever straightforward. Even after joining the MCE team, his grandfather never missed an opportunity to remind Ed that he could be "put out on your ass in a minute" if he ever got lazy or was shown up by one of his cousins, who, as it turned out, all attended Harvard one after the other.

For this and so many reasons, Ed made it a personal goal to get onto the MCE board as soon as he could, ahead of Ed Sr.'s or his father's deaths, and ahead of them doing something irrational and stupid, like firing him just to prove a family point.

Dan O'Hara was from the Midwest and one of the young guys on the New York team. For reasons unknown, he liked Ed immediately, and had tried in vain to get the youngest Mountain out of the office and into the bars at the end of each work week. Dan was not the type of guy who needed more friends, he had more than enough, but something about watching Ed day in and day out in the office worried him. Ed seemed like a nice guy, a real guy's guy, and he worried that if Ed did not get out of the office soon, everyone in the New York office would witness Ed Mountain the Third have a public and embarrassing emotional breakdown. It happened all the time in the Wall Street firms, from what he heard from friends, anyway. Every happy hour with his buddies started with a new story about the guy who lost his shit and threatened to kill himself in the men's bathroom if his boss didn't take another look at his index report. Another story was about a guy who didn't show up for work one day, and several days later, his landlord busted down his door to find him passed out in a pile of dog shit. Breathing, but barely, because of all the pills he had taken "to calm down." His buddies howled in laughter as they recounted the stories to Dan, but Dan found the stories kind of depressing. He loved Manhattan for its contagious energy and electricity, so different from his small, quiet hometown, but he also watched Manhattan eat people alive. Ed didn't want to be that guy, Dan told himself, and Dan wanted to make sure it didn't happen.

"Come on, dude," Dan pleaded with Ed. "You cannot stay in this eight-foot-by-eight-foot cell all day and night. It's not healthy. It's kind of weird, actually. Aren't you like thirty? And . . . I shouldn't have to mention it, but you do realize what your last name is, right?"

Still, Ed did not look up. "I'm twenty-eight, you dick, and this office is a lot bigger than eight by eight—because of my name. Your spatial awareness is terrible. Where did you say you went to school again? Cornell?" Ed dragged a highlighter across the page in a straight line and turned another page over.

Dan smiled and he caught the faintest smile break across Ed's face too. "Aha! He jokes! He *is* an actual human being! Just one drink, seriously, dude. I'm not going to take no for an answer. My buddy, Cyrus, he knows this guy, whose cousin can get us in at The Jake tonight—The *Jake*, dude! Do you have *any* idea how many hot chicks will be there? It's like a free-for-all, crazy shit happening everywhere." Dan waved his arms in the air wildly.

"You aren't going to stop annoying me until I go with you, are you?" Ed asked. He was torn between being annoyed at Dan, and yet the old fraternity guy in him was glad to be asked to be a part of whatever the cool kids were doing. Truthfully, he didn't have many friends in New York. He had enough money to live in a place of his own, without roommates, and he worked such long hours that by the time his workday was over all he wanted was a glass, or bottle, of wine to himself and some peace and quiet. He had dozens of girls' numbers in his personal contact book, several that admitted to following him to New York from Ole Miss, so if he ever wanted female company, all it took was a phone call.

Ed pushed the giant stack of papers to the side of his desk and stood up. Dan already had Ed's jacket in his hand. "You are *not* going to regret this, my friend." Dan slapped Ed on the back as they walked down the hall to the elevators that would take them all fifty stories down to street level and out to a steamy July night in the city.

seven

London, 1985

J enna was exhausted, but she promised to call her mother that day and check in. Janelle worried about her only daughter living alone in New York City, and worried even more over the ridiculous hours that Jenna was expected work.

"The crazy hours are run of the mill for a huge firm like Schwartz," she told her mother reassuringly the last time they spoke—which was either three weeks ago or three months; Jenna was so tired that she wasn't sure which was right.

"It sounds like they are killing you," Janelle had countered, her worry seeping through the phone line and making Jenna regret letting her mom in on so many details of her life. "I'm just worried, that's all."

"I'll be fine, Mom, don't worry. I am a smart girl, remember?"

"The smartest," her mother had said before sighing and letting her off the phone.

Jenna turned her wrist over and looked at the time. It was one a.m. London time, so it would only be eight p.m. at home. But who was she kidding? She was too tired to have the long conversation that she knew her mother would want. Anything less would be disappointing to Janelle, and the entire phone call would be ruined and in vain. She took the postcard she had purchased earlier that day out of her work bag. She could post it from the Schwartz London office in the morning. It would have to do, at least until she got back to New York. And besides, she did have a little bit of exciting news to share with her mother.

Dear Mom,

I am in London (again) for work and I thought that you would like this postcard of Big Ben. I have not seen Princess Di yet, but if I do, I promise to get her autograph for you (ha ha). And though I still maintain that both William and Harry are WAY too young for me, I will ask Diana if she will entertain the idea of saving at least one of them for my betrothal (ha ha, again). But seriously, I hope that you are doing well, and I'm sorry that we have not been able to connect on the phone in weeks. My boss only sleeps for three hours a night and thinks that everyone else should too (not kidding). Anyway, I don't mean to complain, I am FINE. I was just thinking of you and wanted to let you know that I love you and that all is well here with me. Wish you were here—you would love London.

Love, Jenna

P.S. Oh! And some exciting news to share—I met a really nice guy last week while out with some friends from work— and guess what? He's Southern! His Alabama accent would rival yours—and Dad's. Hope that makes you happy and not

*sad. He's taking me to dinner next week when I get back to the
city. I'll keep you posted. X O X O*

The next week, Ed called Jenna as he had promised and asked
if he could pick her up at eight p.m. on Friday night—but their
dinner destination would be a surprise.

"Do you like surprises?" he asked Jenna over the phone. She
could hear the smile in his voice, and it made her feel like she had
butterflies in her stomach. Ed had a boyish charm that reminded
her of home in North Carolina, where people were honest,
genuine, and not as abrasive as the few local guys that she had
gone on dates with since moving to New York.

"I do like surprises, as a matter of fact." What Jenna wanted to
say was that she had only met Ed Mountain once in a bar in the wee
hours of the morning, but just based on that chance meeting, she
would follow him anywhere.

"Good," Ed replied. "I'll pick you up at eight." He was still
smiling.

"Perfect." Jenna tried to sound casual, but it was taking all of
her nerve. "See you then."

***

For their first date, Ed took Jenna to one of New York City's
bastions of haute French cuisine, and all throughout the extrava-
gant dinner, Jenna had to stop herself from pinching her own arm
just to be sure she wasn't dreaming. The candlelight, the music—
the entire night was magical in every way. Ed was incredibly
charming, not to mention good looking, and the food was fantastic. Best of all, Ed and Jenna both laughed more than either of
them had laughed in years. When Ed ordered a third bottle of

champagne at the end of the meal, the middle-aged couple sitting at the next table over scowled and swept out of the restaurant in a huff. The woman stood up and thrust her silk wrap over her shoulder in such a theatrical manner that it only made Ed laugh more.

"I want to see you again," Ed said at the end of their first official date. Jenna said that she would love that. Ed made good on his request and saw Jenna frequently over the following weeks. Six months later, when the lease on her rental (a tiny two-bedroom in Tribeca that she shared with three other girls) was up, Ed asked her to move in with him, and she accepted. Two months after that, at Christmas, he proposed. It was all so perfect. It all seemed so *easy. Surely that is a sign of a good thing,* Jenna thought to herself on her wedding day in 1987.

PART III

The End of Everything

eight

In 1993, *Vanity Fair* (VF) magazine ran a cover spread on the Mountains of Manhattan, which Ed's mother, Regina, cut out and framed and included photography by none other than celebrity photographer Lawrence Sweitzer. The photo chosen for the cover was a brightly colored close-up of Ed, Jenna, and their three-year-old daughter, Ellie, standing in the doorway of their century-old farmhouse just outside Asheville. All three wore relaxed, authentic smiles that came part and parcel with wearing couture, and Ed's arm rested casually around Jenna's shoulders as her long, multicolored designer skirt blew in the breeze behind Ellie, who was dressed in baby couture from head to toe. Dino Torres, the editor for *VF* at the time, said that the one word he would use to describe the Mountain family set in the backdrop of their North Carolina haven was *blissful*. Torres sent Jenna a forty-eight yellow rose bouquet with a copy of the magazine on the day that the copy hit the newsstand. A handwritten note was attached to the flowers that said the Mountains were "perhaps the most beautiful family" that had ever been featured on the cover of *VF*. *Much love, Dino.*

The caption on the front cover read: "For Three Months out of the Year the Mountains of Manhattan Trade in City Life for a Country Abode and Prove That One Really Can Have It All."

The farmhouse had been a total gut job. It was built in the early twentieth century and Ed had lighted on the property while he and Jenna were still newlyweds and were visiting her mother for the Thanksgiving holiday. Ed was excited as a kid on Christmas morning when he saw the for-sale sign at the front of the long gravel drive. He wanted to buy the property immediately, but after much thought, considering that Jenna still working full time, owning a second home, and much less one seven hundred miles from New York, seemed out of the question. Several years later, however, the property was still on the market, and without asking Jenna, Ed bought the dilapidated farmhouse and surrounding land for a steal. Ellie was three, and though Jenna had always planned to go back to work after Ellie's birth, once she held Ellie in her arms, she never wanted to let her go, thus her law career came to an abrupt but not a regrettable halt. At first, Jenna was furious with Ed for moving forward on the property without asking for her opinion, but the minute Ed showed her the new house plans for what the farmhouse and surrounding structures would become, Jenna fell in love with the project. There was the farmhouse, which would become the main dwelling, a barn that would be converted to a party barn (a term that Jenna had only just heard of), and several old smaller structures that would be converted to guest quarters for their friends and family from New York and Alabama to come visit. All in all, the property could host up to thirty people at a time. Photos that the previous owner sent to Ed showed two small ponds for fishing or small boats, and a stream that fed into the larger river at the back of the property. It was like a dream come true. A place that Jenna and Ellie could retreat to in the hot Manhattan summer months and Ed would fly down to visit as often as he could. What could be better?

Jenna was prepared to handle the decorating as well, but Ed informed her that he had already chosen a decorator to handle the entire project. Her name was Laurie Dewer of the New York City–based Dewar & Cowart design firm. Laurie was a petite blonde that had more energy than Jenna could ever imagine, and over the year and a half that it took to complete the project, Jenna and Laurie became close friends, spending many weekends at what they now officially called The Retreat, the name donned on the 130-acre estate in Buncombe County, North Carolina. They picked out fabric, watched Ellie catch frogs in the stream, and drank more wine than they should have, staying up late into the night, laughing about the ridiculousness of some of Manhattan's most interesting socialites.

Because Ed Mountain's pockets were deep and he had a propensity to lose interest in a project (of any kind) if it lasted too long, Jenna and Laurie worked fast to get the renovation and decorating done as quickly as possible. Three foundation companies, two building contractors, and four painters later, The Retreat was ready for move-in after a record-setting nineteen months.

As quickly as the work was done on the house and surrounding guest cottages, the same could be said of the ramp-up of Laurie and Ed's affair, which ran hot and heavy for the duration of the project. When Jenna and Ellie would fly down from the city to The Retreat to meet with Laurie, what Jenna didn't know was that Laurie would spend the night in Ed and Jenna's apartment before flying down to drink wine and laugh with Jenna the following day. Laurie met Ed at a client's home shortly before he purchased The Retreat, and they began sleeping together shortly after. Laurie thought that Jenna was a nice girl and fun to work with, but they certainly were not friends. It was a work relationship, and Laurie easily separated her time with Jenna and her nights with Ed without a single ounce of guilt. Ed came on to her; that wasn't her fault. He was already unhappy in his marriage to Jenna, and he hoped that The Retreat would give Ellie a place to go to get out of the hectic city. Laurie believed every bit and felt pity for Ed that he could be in such a loveless marriage. Much to Laurie's surprise, as soon as the final check had been mailed to Dewar & Cowart for the project, Ed stopped taking Laurie's calls and he instructed his secretary to "tell Ms. Dewar that Ed Mountain has no intention of speaking to her again." Laurie was devastated.

Six years later, *Vanity Fair* would run a second story on the Mountains. This time, there was no photoshoot with a famous photographer or quotes from the editor. The story was written by a young writer that had still been in college at the time when the first piece about the Mountains was run. Parker Espy grew up in Kentucky, graduated from Duke, and moved to New York after grad school at NYU. He despised people like Ed Mountain and when he wrote his damning piece, entitled "When Mountains Turn to Molehills," about the sharp fall from New York society that took place after the divorce, and all of the Mountain possessions had been very publicly divided, it had not been without a small amount of dark satisfaction. Espy went as far to say that the "Mountains treat everything in life according to its financial value—even their unborn children, who can be discarded by a lab by the snap of Ed Mountain's fingers."

The new editor, Marla Seegers, thought that the piece was a bit incendiary and should perhaps be edited down, but after looking at the magazine's lagging sales numbers in recent months, she decided to let it run just as Parker had written it. There would be pushback from readers and critics alike, she knew, but Seegers justified her decision with a gamble that readers would lap up the fall-from-grace angle of the piece. She wagered correctly, and the issue sold more copies than the past three editions had sold combined. Readers could not get enough of the gritty details of Jenna and Ed Mountain's contentious divorce that was so ugly it was labeled as "bloody" by many news outlets.

A freelance photographer caught Jenna taking lamps and rolled-up rugs out of her Seventy-Fifth Street building and loading them into a conspicuous-looking unmarked white van and sold them to a tabloid paper. This led to a contempt of court hearing for Jenna and a fine of over $300,000 to cover the items she removed from the Mountain penthouse during the divorce proceedings without Ed's agreement.

In response, Jenna leaked raunchy text messages that she had taken from Ed's cell phone between himself and his mistress du jour showing what a farce it was to think that Ed was the family man that he claimed to be.

It only got worse from there. Jenna and Ed slung mud at each other, like "two pigs in a pigpen," according to one editorial magazine that depicted both Jenna and Ed as pigs in a cartoon that poked fun at the fact that both Jenna, from North Carolina, and Ed, originally from Alabama, were both Southerners. "The city lights proved too much for this high-society couple bent on breaking into the New York social scene," ran one headline and, "Perhaps the Mountains should return to their Southern roots to finish their own Civil War," ran another.

Other papers were even less kind, and it was partly because of the press, and partly because of Jenna's mother, Janelle, who couldn't bear to see young Ellie caught in the middle. She suggested that Ellie come live with her and attend the same school that Jenna had attended, until the trial was over and the divorce was final. In a moment of brief solidarity, Jenna and Ed swiftly agreed and Janelle flew up to retrieve Ellie.

Those nights alone during the divorce in their large townhouse, Jenna's thoughts ran in a million different directions. One minute she wanted more than anything to beg Ed to come back home, to patch things up, and make their marriage work, but the next minute Jenna would think about all of Ed's affairs, his despondency toward both she and Ellie, and her resolve would be renewed that she was doing the right thing by divorcing him, no matter how hard it was to bear.

The hardest part of the whole ordeal was the night that she and Ed told Ellie that Ed would be moving out—immediately.

"We need to tell Ellie tonight," Ed said tersely. He was loosening his tie but had not bothered to take his shoes off at the door, which meant that he did not plan on staying in the townhouse for long. He and Jenna had just returned home from another failed therapy session, this time ending with Ed calling the whole endeavor of therapy "garbage" and accusing the therapist—one that had come highly recommended from an old college roommate of Jenna's—of being a fraud straight to his face.

"I don't think that is such a good idea," Jenna replied, defeated. She looked Ed straight in the face, searching for some amount of emotion. Anger, hate, jealousy, anything would be better than the absolute blankness that she got from him. She waited one more, long second. Nothing.

"That's ridiculous." Ed put his hands on his hips. "It's inevitable, Jenna. I've already set up an apartment for myself on

Seventy-First Street. Ellie's eight years old—she's going to figure it out. Better to tell her now and pull the rip cord."

"But—"

"But what? You heard the therapist." Ed put the word "therapist" in air quotes. "He said that the best way to handle Ellie was to show a united front—you need to get on board."

"But Ed, in two days it's *Christmas*. And she's not eight, she's nine—you know what, that doesn't even matter. How could today be the best day to tell her that her parents are separating and getting a divorce? She's just a kid. Christmas is supposed to be the most magical time of the year. We will ruin it forever for her by telling her right before Christmas Day. You are unbelievable!" Jenna threw her hands in the air and stared at Ed, begging with her eyes that he reconsider. When Ed stood still, and said nothing, Jenna opened her mouth to shout, and then decided not to. "You are unbelievable," she said softly.

Unfortunately, neither Jenna nor Ed heard Ellie creep down the stairs, but when Jenna finished, she saw Ellie standing just behind her father, her small stature perfectly framed by the doorway separating the entry hall from the family room. She must have been up in her loft, her secret hideout that she retreated to most days lately.

Ellie's eyes were wide and pleading. "Who's getting a divorce?" she asked, looking from Jenna to Ed and then back to Jenna. Jenna started to say *no one*, which would have been untrue, but Ed cut her off anyhow and answered for the both of them—a united front, as they say.

"We are," Ed said tenderly to Ellie. "Your mom and I have talked it over, and we *both* think it is best if I get my own place for a while, maybe forever, we're not sure at this point." He knelt down and gave Ellie a hug, but Ellie did not take her eyes off her mother, staring woundedly at Jenna over the back of Ed's shoulder.

"Both of you?" she asked skeptically. "Forever?" Ellie's voice was suddenly small and weak. At nine years old she seemed so grown up in many ways, but in this moment, she looked no older than the newborn that Jenna brought home from the hospital and rocked for endless hours, stroking her tiny face and hands. Jenna's heart was broken knowing that she and Ed had caused Ellie so much pain. Out of nowhere, Ellie wiggled out of Ed's arms and pushed him away angrily, "I hate you!" she yelled. "I hate you *both*!" And she stormed off, running back upstairs to her hideout without turning back.

"Well," Jenna said, looking pointedly at Ed, "I'd say that went about as I expected. Good job, Dad. She'll remember this Christmas forever."

Jenna knew it was an unnecessary comment, but she couldn't have stopped herself even if she tried. *Who does that to a kid on Christmas?* She walked past Ed and back to their bedroom at the end of the hall, closing the door behind her. A few seconds later she heard the front door open then close. She knew that she should go comfort Ellie, but all she could bring herself to do was curl up in her bathrobe and sit in her empty bathtub and cry.

Later that night, Jenna was in the kitchen watching pasta slowly boil on the stove, when Ellie finally emerged from hours in her hideout.

"Hey, you," Jenna said casually. "Want some dinner?" Ellie nodded. Her hazel eyes were bloodshot and puffy, as was her tiny rounded Mountain nose. Ellie slid into a kitchen barstool and put her head down on her crossed arms at the island. "I don't understand," she said, the sound muffled from her folded arms.

Jenna wanted to say, *I don't either*, but in this one instance she knew that Ed, or rather, Dr. Beasley, the therapist, was right—she did need to provide a solid, united front for Ellie. However terrible it felt to pretend that this was the life she was choosing, it was better than giving Ellie conflicting pieces of information making the whole situation worse, though Jenna could not imagine at this moment how it could possibly be worse than this.

"It's going to be okay," she said to Ellie, who shook her head from side to side without lifting it up.

"No, it's not," she said feebly. "Evelyn's parents got divorced last year and now she has a mean stepmother. I'll probably get a mean stepmother too."

What Jenna wanted to say, *I can't do this anymore. I thought I could, and I tried, but I just can't live like this for the rest of my life, so therefore, your life has to suffer, and for that I am so sorry.* What she said instead was, "Don't worry, sweetheart, I promise it's all going to be okay," and she walked around to where Ellie sat and put her arms around Ellie's small shoulders and squeezed her tightly in a hug.

Not that Jenna expected it, but Ed did not call or text later that night to check on Ellie, to see how she was doing, or to ask when he could spend some time with his daughter. Jenna wanted this to make her angrier so she could be so mad that envisioning a life without Ed in it seemed *better*, sensible, and the right thing to do, but all she felt that first night with Ed gone was a deep and intense sadness for all that was lost. She had stood by these last few years and let her own life and Ellie's well-being slip through her fingers, and there was nothing she could do to get it back now.

***

"All rise!" The courtroom was filled at capacity with journalists from local and national news outlets wanting the scoop on the final day of the Mountain divorce soap opera. Also in the room were what Ed called "the hangers-on," a group of over-makeuped, over-Botoxed, and underfed women in their midforties who sat in the benches behind Jenna. *Jenna is not even friends with these women,* Ed thought to himself, and ran his hands through his hair while letting out a loudly audible sigh. His eyes roamed the rest of the room; his parents and brother sat in benches on "his" side and a few of the board members from MCE sat in the back row looking bored. His girlfriend, Cassandra, insisted on being there to support him, though he wished that she'd stayed home. Her presence only added to the drama of the whole thing, and Cassandra thrived on drama. That was one drawback to dating a girl in her twenties. At the last court appearance, Cassandra made the news by slapping a reporter on the courthouse steps. The young guy, with his press badge prominently displayed, had innocently asked her if she was the Mountains' nanny.

He continued to scan the room, out of boredom if for no other reason, and his eyes rested on Jenna in the exact moment when she looked up. Her eyes were red, and she looked too thin. *She really doesn't look good,* Ed thought harshly. *She should get back to yoga. Maybe she will once this is all over, and we can go our separate ways, putting an end to this clown show.* At first, all the attention and media coverage of the divorce had been somewhat of an ego boost. Especially since one of the young, attractive news anchors at the local TV station had dubbed Ed the "handsome and formidable Mr. Mountain." He'd take it. He'd been called worse. But lately, as the trial endlessly lingered on, he had grown tired of the attention and just wanted it all to be over.

His eyes were still locked with Jenna's when she mouthed the words *I hate you* before looking away. Her attorney, Andrew, must have seen her do it, because he immediately put his arms around Jenna's shoulders and began to rub her back in gentle circles. Andrew was speaking calmly and slowly, and Ed watched Jenna nod every so often. *Bastard*, Ed thought.

"What's up, tiger?" Someone grabbed Ed by the shoulders and pretended to shake Ed in the same way that a trainer would prep a boxer for a match.

Ed turned to see his old fraternity buddy, Travis Duke, who wore a broad smile and an ostentatious pinstriped suit—over the top even for Manhattan, which harbored a special kind of jerk like Travis. Ed forced a smile, but he really wasn't in the mood for Travis today. He wasn't really in the mood to see anyone. He was exhausted, and for the first time during the trial, he felt all of his forty-four years.

"I'm just ready for it to be over, dude," he said to Travis, and he turned back around in his chair to face the judge's seat, empty before him, but that would soon hold the man that would make the decision that would change his and Jenna's lives forever.

Ed listened as Andrew gave a final plea that the judge consider the "respect due to embryos," as outlined in the famous Waller Report, the results of a committee formed by the Australian government in the 1980s to deal with embryos' rights and the benchmark upon which all United States law regarding embryos is based.

"My client, Jenna Mountain," Andrew paused for dramatic effect, "has a *right* to bear her own children. This could be her last—"

"Objection!" Ed's attorney blurted out. The man, named Jerry Bashier but called Guard Dog by his colleagues because of the overtly aggressive nature he brought to his divorce cases, did not look up from the legal pad in his lap. The judge nodded at Andrew and said, "Sustained," anyhow.

When it was Jerry's turn, he stood up slowly, and showed that he, too, had a flair for the dramatic, when he sighed heavily before beginning his final remarks.

"What we have here is not difficult, Your Honor. My client is not asking for much—just the right to decide that someone else," Jerry paused and looked back at Jenna, "is not at liberty to bring these embryos to term—his own genetic material, I might add— and to create children that he neither wants nor wants to see put through the hardship of living with a single parent. I think we can all agree that is a reasonable ask?"

Jenna wanted to jump out of her seat and strangle Jerry Bashier. Andrew put a hand over hers and whispered, "Stay calm." Jenna nodded, but she found it an impossible task.

Meanwhile, Jerry was still rambling on about *Roe v. Wade*, the *Davis v. Davis* case out of Tennessee, and other related cases, each one driving another nail into Jenna's case.

"It's just not prudent to allow any result other than destruction. I would even go so far as to call continuing the cryopreservation reckless and dangerous."

"Objection," from Andrew.

"Sustained," from the judge.

In the end, Jenna knew what the verdict was going to be before Andrew told her of the judge's decision to award all three frozen embryos, stored by Jenna and Ed jointly at BabyGenix, to Ed. What she did not expect was for Ed to elect to destroy all three embryos immediately.

"I have to get to BabyGenix," Jenna said to Andrew at the conclusion of the hearing. "I have to get there." Jenna's voice was sounding more panicked by the second, and Andrew was for once at a loss on how to calm his longtime friend and client. They had met in law school all those years ago, and at one time, Andrew had been head over heels for Jenna. He never told Jenna how he felt, and by the time he ran into her in New York several years after graduation, she was already engaged to Ed.

"Jenna," he said calmly, "I wouldn't do that. Just go home. I'll fend off reporters; you get home and get to your mother's house to see Ellie as soon as you can." Andrew scanned Jenna's face for a sign of deference, but he saw none.

Jenna kissed Andrew on the cheek. "I'll be fine. Thank you for everything. Really, I really appreciate it." And Jenna slipped out the side door to the courtroom.

***

Against her lawyer's advice, Jenna planned all along to go straight to BabyGenix at the conclusion of the trial. If she was truly honest with herself, she knew what the outcome would be. Of the few custody cases involving embryos up to that point, not one had been decided in the genetic mother's favor. All embryos in previous cases had been awarded to the genetic father and destroyed. But for all her preparedness, when the decision was read, Jenna's heart stopped. She willed herself to breathe to keep from fainting—something that, due to her chronic low blood pressure, was easy for her to do.

As soon as she could, she got out of the courthouse. Using a side door, she left the building alone and ran down the side stairs to street level just as Ed, Cassandra, and his lawyer were coming down the front steps. Jenna looked back only for a second before ducking into a taxi. Cassandra's arm was looped through Ed's and she pretended to cry. An inexperienced reporter yelled out, "Mrs. Mountain! Mrs. Mountain, can we get a statement from you?" to Cassandra, who blushed. Ed was clearly annoyed and stayed silent by putting his hand in the air and walking quickly, practically dragging Cassandra behind him, to the tinted-out town car waiting on the front curb.

Once inside her own car, Jenna gave the driver the address to BabyGenix and sat back against the seat and closed her eyes. She was glad she had gone ahead and legally changed her name back to Ellis, but a part of her was also sad that her marriage was now truly and officially over. How could this happen? How could she have let this happen? What could she have done differently?

Several blocks later, the driver stopped the car and turned around for his payment. Jenna paid her fare, took a deep breath, got out of the car, and walked into the lobby of the fertility clinic that had almost become a second home over the last decade. She took the elevator up seven stories, just as she had so many times before, to storage room B. She would need to find an administrator, or Dr. Daugherty, to open the high-security room for her, but to give herself a minute to compose herself, she sat down on a small bench in the hall opposite a door that had a large B on the placard along with words that read AUTHORIZED PERSONNEL ONLY.

In what felt like her only good luck of the year, a new young male nurse was walking down the hallway toward her with no one else in sight. After a little urging, the nurse let Jenna into the storage room, but only to call her back out a few minutes later. She could not have been more shocked to see Ed standing in front of her, no Cassandra in sight.

"What are you doing here?" Jenna asked. Seeing Ed suddenly gave Jenna a feeling of being on fire. After the fire came pure anger. She was beaten but not dead.

"Stop talking, Jenna." Ed put his hand out dramatically and used the same belittling tone that he always employed when they argued. It is said that some people have one speed; the same could be said for Ed Mountain's tone—he had one—and it was arrogant and condescending. And despite hearing it for the duration of their ten-year marriage, Jenna still allowed it to make her feel as

68

if she was the one being silly, or that she was the one being ridiculous. That tone—it reduced her to a childlike existence, and she hated the fact that she always backed down. She hated that she was a different person when she was around Ed, and not for the better, and she hated that it took her ten years to figure that out. She stared at the floor.

"This is part of your problem sweetie," Ed continued. "This whole time you have acted like what is behind those doors is *only* yours." He smiled and pointed accusatorily in her direction. "Well guess what—it's not. It was *ours*, and now it's *mine*."

"I hate you," Jenna said softly. The fire that had coiled itself around her body was beginning to break her body down, slowly turning her bones and tissue into dust.

"Yeah, you said that already, Jen. I got it the first time in court." At the sound of footsteps, both she and Ed looked up to see the director of the lab coming down the hallway toward them. The director slowed when he saw both Jenna and Ed standing outside of the storage room door, and a frown came over his face. At the same time, the elevator doors opened and Fredrick, Ed's attorney, stepped off the elevator and followed the lab director down the hall.

"Jenna, I know that you think I am some kind of evil monster," Ed said, "but if you would have only been reasonable over these last two years, then you would have seen that I am quite easy to work with if you are just willing to make a deal."

Jenna shook her head. "No, Ed," she said. "Nope. Not right now. I don't need one of your talks right now. You won, okay? You won. I hope that you are happy. Now you and Cassandra can do whatever you want. The only trace that our marriage ever existed will be in Ellie. But I'm sure Cassandra will think of something to do about that too."

"Dammit, Jenna, you won't even let me finish." Ed wiped his

forehead with his hand, and ran his hand backward through his hair in the same way that Ed Sr. did when he was nervous or frustrated. "You really are impossible, you know."

Jenna folded her arms across her chest and looked away from Ed. This is not how she wanted to spend the last moments with David, Mia, and Carson. She hadn't planned on Ed being there at all. Why would he be? What was his point? She wanted to be able to talk to her three unborn children before the cannister was turned off and her embryos were destroyed. She could barely say the word in her mind, but that is what she had hoped for—closure. A moment of peace that she could carry with her, to know that she told them that she loved them in the end.

"I wanted to tell you—" Ed started and then stopped, and Jenna looked up. Ed ran his hand through his hair again and Jenna noticed that he looked nervous. He never looked nervous.

"What, Ed?" She was tired of his mind games. It would be one thing that she would not miss about being married to him. Ed looked down the hall in the direction of Fredrick and then looked back to Jenna.

"Even though the court awarded me full custody of what's in storage—"

"You can't even say it, can you?" Jenna shrieked. "They are called *embryos*, Ed, and they turn into babies, into living, breathing children just like Ellie, unless you kill them. Stop acting like they are pieces of your investment portfolio."

"Okay, okay," he said. "Calm down. Embryos. I wanted to give you the option of keeping one—if you wanted—but there would be stipulations."

Jenna heard what he said but couldn't comprehend what it meant, or rather, she did not want to comprehend what he was saying. She put her face in her hands and secretly hoped that when she opened her eyes again, Ed would be gone, *poof,* disappeared like in one of Ellie's magic books.

"So . . . do you want to pick one?" he asked again. By this time Fredrick and Dr. Fielding were only steps away.

"You want me to pick one?" Jenna asked bewilderedly and more loudly than she had intended. "Who do you think I am? They aren't puppies, Ed! Why would you think that I would ever do that? Even consider it? So you can feel better about yourself and what you are about to do? You really are evil, Ed, evil of the worst kind." Jenna shook her head and felt herself unraveling on the inside. It was too much. She had been strong, or as strong as she could be during the divorce proceedings, strong when Ed got everything that his lawyer asked for, and strong enough to get herself to BabyGenix for the extraction, but she suddenly felt any remaining strength melt away.

"Okay, suit yourself," said Ed, putting his hands in the air and backing away one step. He turned away from Jenna and looked at Dr. Fielding, the director of BabyGenix, who had just walked up along with Fredrick. "I plan to have all three destroyed today," he said flatly, and then turned back to Jenna. "It wasn't an evil plan, Jenna, it was an olive branch, but if you don't want to take it, that's fine by me."

Dr. Fielding looked fatigued and Fredrick looked worried. Jenna wondered why Fredrick had shown up. Did he know about the deal that Ed was going to offer to her ahead of time? Or not? Ed was known to spring things on people, particularly in negotiations. It was a tactic that Jenna had seen or heard about him using prolifically throughout his career to get what he wanted. He would wait until the other party had played all their own cards, and then he would swoop in and offer an "olive branch" in which they had only seconds or minutes to decide to take or not, both

71

sides fully aware that Ed had left them with no way forward but his own. Now he had used it on her, and she hated him all the more for it, if that was even possible.

Dr. Fielding looked from Ed to Jenna, who was still sitting on the small bench outside of Storage Room 3. "Ahem, I am sorry to interrupt your discussion, but I was not made aware that either of you would be here for the extraction." The media attention that had swirled around BabyGenix for the last eighteen months was bad enough without the divorce of the century, making his patience for either Mountain thin.

"Of course, Doctor," Ed said in his smoothest businesslike manner. "We apologize for barging in. I just came to make sure that all, you know, goes according to plan, and then we can all go about our merry ways." Ed smiled and it made Jenna legitimately want to kill him. The thought raced through her mind that if a judge was looney enough to award three frozen embryos to a man that wanted to immediately destroy them, then she had a good chance of getting off scot free for murder, all rules being the same.

"Okay then," said Dr. Fielding slowly. "Well, let's get started. Both of you will have to stay outside the door, of course, but I will provide documentation to you both after the extraction that confirms the destruction of all stored material in your account, thus closing it upon you signing that is your wish. Oh, and we are just waiting for Dr. Daugherty to get here, of course. As your primary consulting physician at BabyGenix, she will need to be present for the extraction."

"Wait." Jenna looked at Ed. He stared back at her coldly. He *had* won, again.

"Yes, Jenna," he said nicely, casually tucking both arms behind his back.

"Your offer," she said, still only looking at Ed, "What are the 'stipulations'?"

Dr. Fielding and Fredrick looked on as the two Mountains faced off in one last showdown. Dr. Fielding, sensing that this most likely did not have anything to do with him, moved toward the storage room door, but Ed put out a hand to tell him to stop, not taking his eyes off Jenna.

"Here's the deal," he said. "You can pick *one*. I don't care which one, as long as it is *one*. That *one* will remain in storage for a time— I think all of us could use a little de-escalation to calm down and to begin thinking clearly again. After said time, the embryo is eligible for adoption. You would have just as much of a shot as anyone, Jenna, given you don't show your true colors in the interview, of course. That's the deal. Take it or leave it. You have thirty seconds."

Jenna had stood up when Dr. Fielding arrived, but now she sat back down. She tried to run through the ethical implications of what she was considering, but her mind was swimming and she felt like she was drowning. She was the smart girl, the one who liked to run through all her options, make an informed decision, and then run through all of them again, just to be sure. This wasn't enough time. She had Ellie, and she loved her, but all her adult life she had this feeling in the pit of her stomach that told her that she was meant to have more children, and that Ellie was not her one and only child.

"Ten seconds, Jen." Ed tapped his watch. Dr. Fielding looked horrified and Fredrick smiled. "Five, four, three, two—" Ed counted down.

"I'll take Mia," Jenna said, barely above a whisper.

"What?" Ed said obnoxiously. "I didn't hear you. You choose one, and that one is?"

"Mia," Jenna repeated through gritted teeth. "But I get to go in—*alone*—and say goodbye to Carson and David before the extraction."

"I had a feeling you would say that," Ed said. "Fred, hand me the contract please."

Jenna looked from Ed to Fredrick. The contract? It was already drawn up? How would he have known what she would decide? Was she that transparent, or was Ed that good at manipulation? Dr. Fielding started blubbering and his face grew red splotches. Sweat formed around his bushy white eyebrows and he fidgeted with his glasses, putting them on and taking them off repeatedly, wiping the glasses maniacally with a handkerchief.

"Mr. Mountain, I'm not sure that—" Dr. Fielding grasped for words but couldn't find exactly what he wanted to say. Was this legal? What was his part in the transaction, if any? He wished that the BabyGenix in-house counsel was here. They offered to send someone, but Dr. Fielding had said no need, that the process of extraction would take no more than fifteen seconds and would be lacking the fireworks of the courtroom. On this front, the lead PR director of damage control for BabyGenix had put out a fake news release stating that the extraction was scheduled for the following day at three p.m.— specifically to avoid a media circus around the building when the extraction would actually occur. The lab was closed the following day for maintenance repairs, with the entire building shut down, so it was something of a stroke of genius to have the press arrive on a day when there wouldn't even be an employee inside to decline commenting. But this, this was not part of the plan, and he was panicked. Meanwhile, Fredrick calmly rifled through his expensive cigar-colored briefcase and pulled out a short stack of papers.

"Mr. Mountain," he said, handing the paperwork over to Ed. Ed flipped through the first few pages and then handed the stack to Jenna.

"Sign away," he said, and he stood back and crossed his arms. Fredrick leaned over and handed Jenna a pen. She took it but could barely keep her hand from shaking enough to hold on to it.

The attorney in her told her to read the document. *Just read it,* she said silently to herself. But she could not get past the first paragraph because she could not get over the fact that Ed had predicted this moment down to every detail. The contract stated that while all three embryos were under the custody of Mr. Edward Clinton Mountain III, he chose to have two of the embryos destroyed immediately, being no later than five p.m. that day, and that one embryo, HN3-8B, would continue to be stored at BabyGenix until it was eligible for adoption, at which point, *any* approved adoptive parent or parents may be chosen by BabyGenix, not excluding Jenna Ellis Mountain, from any pool of applicants should she wish to apply. Why was Ed doing this? What was the catch? And then Jenna saw the catch. The date.

HN3-8 (B) WILL BE ELIGIBLE FOR ADOPTION NO SOONER THAN AFTER A PERIOD OF TWENTY YEARS FROM TODAY'S DATE 7-28-1999.

Jenna's heart sank. That was the catch. Twenty years. It was like telling a convicted criminal that he *only* had to serve a ten-year sentence when he was already seventy years old. It was a death sentence. By the time Mia would be eligible for adoption, Jenna would be sixty-two years old. The contract went on with pages of legal speak about how Ed and Fredrick had managed to prepay for twenty years of storage at BabyGenix (to the tune of $7,000) and gave BabyGenix full authority to choose a suitable adoptive family for HN3-8B once the twenty-year time limit expired. It was all there, laid out in black and white, as if Ed knew her every move before she made it.

Jenna looked up at Ed, who was subtly smiling, though she

could tell he was containing himself from breaking into all-out laughter over his coup. The pen fell out of her hand.

"What's it gonna be, Jen?" he said. "Dr. Fielding has a lot to do today, and the court order from earlier today states that all three will be destroyed no later than five p.m.—which is a half hour from now." He reached out, picked the pen up from the floor, and put the pen back down beside her on the bench.

It was at this point that Jenna's memory became fuzzy. The brain has a strange way of protecting itself. Her psychologist would later tell her that her "brain will purposefully and instinctively block out traumatic events, leaving only traces of the event in your memory bank. These traces can be smells, tastes, or often sounds." Jenna remembered getting to BabyGenix before seeing Ed, she remembered talking to all three embryos while snugly resting in their cartridge, and she remembered the nurse's pager sounding off, and him telling her that she needed to step outside. After that, all of her memory was one big, jumbled mess. Of all the sounds from that day, the one that stuck was the sound of Fredrick's pen hitting the marble floor when she dropped it. It was a simple sound that would haunt Jenna's dreams for years to come.

She did not remember signing the contract, but she must have. She also didn't remember Dr. Daugherty arriving, the woman who had first told her that she had six viable embryos, but she must have because she would later receive a note from Dr. Daugherty asking if she was all right. She would receive a copy of the contract in the mail from Fredrick two weeks later where she saw her own signature. She had to sign it, because Ed wanted proof that Jenna agreed to the "amendment to the settlement set forth by the state of New York and upon the goodwill of Edward C. Mountain III."

Jenna did not remember saying goodbye to her children, but she remembered the bathroom afterward, where she vomited until there was nothing left to expel. Apparently, she fainted in the storage room and a young male nurse helped her off the floor and onto her feet. He brought a wet towel for Jenna to hold across her forehead, and she recalled that he had a foreign accent that she couldn't place. Eastern European, maybe? She remembered taking the towel gratefully and faltering when she tried to stand up, so she slid back down to a seated position with her back against the cold bathroom wall. She was not sure how long she sat on the bathroom floor—it could have been minutes or even hours—but when she finally came out, Ed was gone, and so were Fredrick, Dr. Fielding, David, and Carson.

nine

Dr. Daugherty left the storage room and headed straight for her office. She needed to sit down, and she needed to smoke, but she promised Karen that she'd quit—twice. Her feet had been killing her all day, and if she had one more hot flash, she may have to throw herself out of an upper-story window. She leaned back in her desk chair and kicked her hospital clogs off one at a time. She had not thought about Elsa Rios in years. But seeing Jenna Mountain today reminded Dr. Daugherty of her former patient, when she worked as a clinical research assistant in Melbourne, Australia, in the Queen Victoria Medical Center. Dr. Carl Wood, an eccentric (and often called flamboyant) obstetrician, led a team of scientists and doctors jointly working under the project name the Test Tube Baby Team (TTBT). Christine joined the project in 1978, the same year that Louise

Brown, the first baby in the world to be conceived using IVF, was celebrated across the globe after her birth in England.

It was an electric time to be in reproductive medical research, and a contentious one. Without consistent government funding, the team could not afford to pay assistants like Christine, but this did not stop her from jumping at the chance to work with the virtuosos of fertility and embryology at the time. Big things were happening in Australia in the late 1970s, and Christine wanted to be a part of the medical revolution, paid or unpaid. The scientific director of the Test Tube Baby Team was Dr. Alan Trounson, and Christine had admired him greatly. When Christine joined the Queen Victoria program following medical school, Alan Trounson was only a few years older than she was, and they bonded almost immediately over both being young newcomers to the Test Tube Baby Team, and over their shared intense enthusiasm for the team's research and clinical goals. Dr. Trounson, Dr. Linda Mohr, and Dr. Wood ran the IVF program and Embryo Freezing Unit from the late '70s to early '80s until the hospital's closure in 1987 amid a firestorm of national and international scrutiny, and condemnation over the fallout following the death in 1983 of two of the clinic's high-profile clients.

Mario and Elsa Rios, the last non-Australians to be admitted to the Test Tube Baby program, never signed any paperwork detailing a directive on what to do in the special case of death, and their two frozen embryos—left in limbo in Australia for years while the court system in both the United States and Australia worked out details of their own—were in the meantime deemed *orphaned* by the media. It was not the best PR for any clinician working in test-tube baby research, in Australia or abroad.

Like Jenna, Elsa Rios was desperate to become a mother. She was tall and thin like Jenna, but had a striking beauty that announced her Argentinian birthplace without her having to tell you. Jenna was a pretty girl, but—Christine mused how to put it best—she was very *American*, being classically attractive but lacking any ethnic flare. Dr. Daugherty scolded herself for being so superficial, even within the privacy of her own mind, and returned her thoughts to the question that nagged at her. How old had Elsa Rios been when she and her husband, Mario, traveled to Melbourne for her first (and only) IVF transfer? *Ah-ha*, she said to herself at last once she remembered. Elsa had been thirty-seven years old. *So young*, thought Dr. Daugherty, *so young and so hopeful.*

Despite being in perfect health by all accounts, Elsa had been turned down by the few IVF clinics operating in the US at that time by reason of *advanced maternal age*, and that was how Elsa and Mario ended up in Australia seeking the help of the preeminent reproductive specialists in the world. It was 1981, and in vitro fertilization was still in its infancy, experiencing advances daily, but still experimental and poorly viewed in the callous court of public opinion, due mostly to fear and lack of education about what the IVF process was really for—to help infertile couples experience pregnancy and parenthood, and not, as some pundits put it, to create "bizarre genetically altered babies." Christine remembered those early days at QVMC well, and when protesters circled BabyGenix, shouting profanities and holding up their signs, she was taken back to Melbourne in her mind, and the backlash that the patients and scientists endured. Poor Annie Dixon, the world's third IVF mother, was spat at by protesters outside QVMC, and both Christine and Annie often used a side entrance to the hospital on days when crowds were especially raucous.

The Rioses arrived in Melbourne in April of 1981, just one year after the team at Queen Victoria celebrated the birth of Candice Reed—Australia's first baby born using IVF—and clinicians from all over the world were flocking down under to watch the procedure be done in person. Alan Trounson had already begun to experiment with a freezing process for embryos that would allow doctors to hold extra embryos harvested in one session for use in transfers at later dates. The new cryopreservation technology would not only dramatically decrease the overall cost of an IVF treatment, it would also negate the need for unnecessary invasive harvesting procedures each time implantation was attempted. It was a major breakthrough for the TTBT, and one that definitively placed Australia on the international scientific map. Throughout the '80s, scores of the best and brightest of the scientific medical community flocked to Melbourne for a chance to work with Drs. Wood, Trounson, Leeton, Lopata, and Johnston.

The new freezing process, using liquid nitrogen and stainless-steel storage canisters set at -321 degrees Fahrenheit, was showing signs of success by early 1981, just as Elsa and Mario prepared to leave Los Angeles for Melbourne. When the Rioses arrived in Australia, Mario was optimistic and chatted breezily with the scientists and doctors that would be caring for Elsa. The rigorous IVF treatment, especially in 1981, is not for the faint of heart. It is a grueling process that involves several phases of poking and prodding for both the male and female patients, all happening in careful sequence at just the right times.

In the first phase, doctors retrieved three eggs from Elsa's ovaries and fertilized them with donor sperm in a culture dish full of a carefully crafted medium of human fallopian tube fluid and other ingredients. Then, the team would have to watch and wait to see if the cells within the fertilized eggs would begin to divide and prove viable in the lab dish for at least three days. All three Rios embryos survived this phase of the process, and on the third day at the eight-cell stage, one embryo was implanted within Elsa's uterus, with the remaining two going to cold storage.

Mario, being fifty-four years old, and the parent to a grown son, had unfortunately undergone a vasectomy in recent years and was unable to provide the needed sperm for fertilization. The team was given strict instructions, with the threat of being discharged, that under no circumstance was anyone outside of the team to know that donor sperm had been used. Eight tiny cells grouped together in spherical shape made up a three-day-old embryo, visible only under a microscope. At first, the transfer appeared to have been successful, but Elsa lost the pregnancy after ten days. Distraught and depressed that the implantation failed, the Rioses left Melbourne and returned to Los Angeles, with plans to return at a later date and make another attempt with the two remaining embryos, frozen and safely stored at the Queen Victoria Medical Centre facility.

Unlike Jenna, Elsa Rios had experienced traditional pregnancy and childbirth prior to seeking Assisted Reproductive Technology (ART). Her ten-year-old daughter, Claudia, died in 1978 due to an accidental gunshot wound. It was an emotional blow that Elsa would never recover from, and when she and Mario sought the help of doctors in Melbourne, it was truly a last-ditch effort to have another child. Christine remembered watching Elsa cry tears of joy when Dr. Wood held her hands and told her that having a child was possible through new advancements in fertility and reproduction, and that he would do everything in his power to give her the gift of life that she so desperately wanted. If it were any other doctor, Christine would have questioned the confident and seductive air that Carl Wood possessed, employing it artfully to calm anxious patients like Elsa. But Carl Wood was not any other doctor; he was one that genuinely went into gynecology to make women's lives better and to give women like Elsa Rios and Jenna Ellis the one thing that eluded them—a child.

Elsa Rios would never have the chance to attempt a second embryo transfer. In April of 1983, almost two years to the day after leaving Melbourne, Mario and Elsa's small Cessna careened into an Andes mountainside just outside of Santiago, Chile. The couple was traveling back to Los Angeles from Argentina when their plane crashed, killing both Mario and Elsa upon impact. The Chilean newspaper *El Mercurio* reported that two bodies, those of Elsa and Mario, were recovered at the crash site and noted that four passports were found in the wreckage.

Two of the passports belonged to Elsa and Mario, and the other two each belonged to a male child indicated to be one month old. One passport was an American-generated ID bearing the name Joshua Nelson Rios. Officials confirmed that a US birth certificate had been obtained using a private clinic in February 1983, prior to the Rioses' trip to Argentina.

The second passport was in the name of Maximiliano Fanfani. Local officials and members of the small community close to the crash site confirmed what many believed. The two infant passports both belonged to one child — the baby boy that the Rios traveled to Argentina to adopt. The child's given name had been Maximiliano, the infant son to a poor Italian immigrant family, and the Rioses intended to bring him back to the US and raise him as their own, changing his name to Joshua — an act of desperation to heal the pain that still plagued Elsa after the failed IVF attempt in Australia and the death of Claudia.

Because Mario and Elsa had told so few people about their travel to Australia in 1981 for the IVF treatment, no one thought to notify the Melbourne clinic or Drs. Wood or Trounson of the Rioses' death.

It would take almost two years after the crash in Santiago for the Australian team to be notified of Elsa and Mario's deaths, and it was only then that the TTBT realized that they had no written directive for the Rioses' frozen embryos in the circumstance of death of the parents. Worldwide attention was focused on Australia and the Los Angeles County court system for the next five years. First, the rights of the Rioses' embryos had to be established. Were the two vials that were stored in Melbourne *human*? Or were they simply specimen, or perhaps tissue? If the embryos were deemed human, did the two unborn children have rights to the Rioses' hefty $8 million estate for which there was no will?

In 1983, a guardian was appointed by the Australian government to look after the Rioses' embryos and determine the best possible outcome to a very messy public relations nightmare. After years of debate in the California court system, the Los Angeles Superior Court ruled in 1985 that any children born from embryos in Australia would have no claim to all or part of the Rioses' large estate. To prevent future issues, they appointed Professor Louis Waller to form a committee and create a provisional set of laws related to unimplanted embryos. The report generated by the committee, known as the Waller Report, would remain the preeminent law regulating reproductive medicine and the rights of embryos for the next three decades both in Australia and other countries, including the United States and Great Britain.

As Dr. Daugherty thought of Elsa, Annie Dixon, and now of Jenna, she wondered if Karen wasn't right, and if she had, perhaps, chosen the wrong field entirely and should consider finding a new career—one without so much heartbreak.

***

Later that night, when she finally walked into the house she shared with Karen, all she wanted was a glass of wine and a slice of reheated pizza. She opened the kitchen cabinet to find it empty of plates of any size, so she reached down and opened the space-saver dishwasher. It was unclear if the contents of the washer were clean or dirty, despite her picking one of the plates up and smelling it.

"Karen?" she called out, not sure which of the townhouse's four small rooms she was in.

"Yes?" a voice called back in reply.

"Are the dishes in the dishwasher clean or dirty?" she said loudly, still unsure as to Karen's whereabouts.

"Yes, they are clean," the voice called out again, and Christine bristled.

"You are doing it again—"

"What?"

"Putting emphasis on the first and last word of your sentences, as if there is a silent but implied 'you idiot' at the end. 'Yes, they are clean—you idiot.'"

"Oh," Karen said, her face suddenly appearing from the laundry room door. "I'm sorry, sweetheart. You know it is just my accent—"

Christine let out a heavy breath. "I know it is. I'm sorry, honey. It's just been a long day and I'm in a bitchy mood." Christine wiped her face with her hand and pulled a plate, now determined clean, from the dishwasher rack. Karen put the clothes she was folding down and walked into the kitchen, putting her arms around Christine.

"Hey," she said softly, kissing Christine on the side of the neck. "I love you."

"I know you do," Christine said soothingly. "I love you too."

That night, once their bedroom lights had been turned off, Karen snuggled closely behind Christine and wrapped her arms around Christine's torso. In Christine's mind, Karen was too pretty for what she deserved, and with an almost fifteen-year age gap, they often bickered over trivial things. Karen all too quick in arguments to refer to Christine as *your generation*; however, despite this, all in all the two women complemented each other perfectly and beautifully. Christine was a doctor and researcher and was the pragmatic of the two. She paid all the bills, took out the trash, and made sure that their insurances were both (separately) renewed each year. Karen was an artist, a dreamer, and the emotional one whose loving care and support were the glue that held their relationship together. They had lived together for three years and had by now settled into a comfortable and reliable existence. It would be eleven more years before Governor Andrew Cuomo would sign the Marriage Equality Act, and while both women hoped for the best, history would tell them to not hold their breath when waiting for acceptance.

"Do you ever think about having a baby?" Karen asked softly into the back of Christine's hair. Christine was not prepared for the question and was taken aback.

"Well," she said, trying to choose her words carefully, "we've never really talked about it."

"We're talking about it now," Karen replied in a whisper. Christine took several seconds to speak, which she knew was making Karen feel self-conscious. It was one of those moments when you are glad that the lights are off, so your partner, your soulmate, doesn't see the hesitation in your eyes. Some things are best discussed in the dark, and after what Christine knew was too long a pause, she formed her words carefully.

"I would love to espouse the miraculous advances of reproductive medicine," Christine said finally, "but I think I am simply too old to become pregnant. There is a limit to what science can do— even at BabyGenix—" Karen's laugh startled Christine, and she turned her body around to face her partner.

"I wasn't talking about *you* being pregnant, silly," Karen said, "I was talking about *me*. What if *I* were to have a baby—for both of us?"

Though they were now facing each other, the room was dark, so Karen could not register Christine's reaction—that is, until Christine leaned forward and put her lips to Karen's, saying, "I love you so much, my dear. If you want a baby, then we will have a baby." And for the first time in a long time, Christine felt hopeful.

PART IV

Interlude

ten

Brevard, North Carolina, 2007

Janelle's breathing had become increasingly labored overnight. Her lungs began filling with fluid three days before, and although her doctors at Eastern Carolina Medical Center did their absolute best to drain the fluid and keep Janelle comfortable, she knew that the time was near when she would leave this earth, and she had come to a gentle peace with that certain possibility.

Jenna and Ellie had arrived on Sunday, and for each of the past four nights, one or both had slept curled up on the tiny, plasticky, convertible loveseat in Janelle's hospital room. Amidst the endless beeping, clicking, and interruptions from nurses, the three women spent their days talking and crying, sometimes laughing, and telling endless stories of Jenna's father, Rawson, and sharing funny memories of when Ellie was just a little girl.

Janelle could not believe that her only grandchild would be graduating from high school the following spring. "Where did the time go?" she asked her daughter and granddaughter on Wednesday afternoon. The night before had been one of the times when both Jenna and Ellie slept at the hospital overnight, taking turns to feed Janelle ice chips or tiny spoonfuls of chocolate pudding when she would allow them to. At one point in the middle of the night, Janelle woke and was glad to see that her only granddaughter and her only child were finally getting some sleep, as she knew that neither one of them wanted to show how exhausted they were. She pushed a button on the armrest of her hospital bed to raise the incline, so she could better see both of them. It must have only been an hour before Jenna and Ellie's sleep was interrupted by a night nurse checking Janelle's vital signs, but for Janelle, those minutes of watching her girls sleeping peacefully next to her seemed like the span of a lifetime.

She noticed Jenna's small scar on the right side of her left eyebrow; it was from when she ran into the back of the tailgate of Rawson's truck when she was no bigger than a toddler. The gash had called for ten stitches, but little Jenna had not cried during the drive to the hospital or when the doctor was threading a needle through her brow. She only cried at the end, when the ER nurse told her that she could go home.

"But I like this bed," Jenna had said, very matter-of-factly, as only a precocious four-year-old could. From the time that Jenna could talk, people remarked constantly that her vocabulary was well advanced compared to kids her age. "This bed has a TV," she had said excitedly, pointing to the large, square bulb TV mounted to the wall. "I would like to stay just a little longer," she said emphatically. The doctor and nurses chuckled and told Janelle and Rawson what a bright little girl they had. She was so bright and so happy then. They all were.

Janelle smiled at the memory and found tears falling from her eyes. Memory is both a cruel and benevolent ruler. Some of the best parts of your life fade away over time like dust in a sandstorm, leaving one to struggle to remember what exactly had made an experience so good, while other memories, mostly the painful ones, sear themselves onto the brain with such ferocity that they are immune to time's attempt to dull them.

And Ellie, sweet Ellie. Though Jenna and Ed's divorce had been tragically terrible, the year that Ellie lived with Janelle in Asheville while the divorce was being hashed out in New York was one of the best times of Janelle's life. Her granddaughter was so much like her mother, but she also had a personality and grit that was all her own. Ellie loved playing in the creek behind Janelle's house that year, and she found more lizards and tadpoles than one could count. That year was a time of respite for Ellie, a break from all that was New York, and Janelle had been grateful to offer such a gift to her granddaughter and daughter in a time of need.

It was no surprise that after the divorce was final, and Ellie had only been back in New York City for a semester, that she asked Jenna and Ed if she could transfer back to Westchester Prep as a boarding student. Her parents agreed for once, and every weekend for the remainder of Ellie's middle and high school years, Janelle drove over to pick Ellie up on Friday and dropped her back off on Sunday evenings, except for holidays, when Ellie flew home to New York to be with Jenna or Ed.

When Janelle decided to buy a modest ranch-style house in nearby Brevard last year, before her diagnosis, Ellie helped her grandmother move furniture and clothing in her beat-up Ford Explorer, and shocked Janelle by knowing how to take down old wallpaper left over from the previous owners, and reapplying a new, "updated" floral print in the master bedroom.

Those weekends spent together over so many years forged a deep bond between Ellie and Janelle, and Ellie would be lying if she didn't admit that in many ways, she felt closer to her grandmother than she did to Jenna. She confided in Janelle when she became a woman and passed her first cycle, and cried on her shoulder when Derek Allenby, Ellie's first love, broke her heart to pieces just after her seventeenth birthday. Ellie had never even mentioned Derek to Jenna or Ed, but Janelle knew even the tiniest details of the young love that had swept Ellie up and away for seven months of her life. Ellie could depend on Janelle in a way that she could not with her mother or her father.

And then there was Mia. If Janelle had any regrets, and she really had so few in life, it was that she would never meet her granddaughter Mia, and she would not live long enough to see Jenna whole again with both of the children she loved so much. Divorce changes people, and Jenna had been no exception to that rule. Janelle put her head back on the pillow. She was tired. Jenna and Ellie had gone to the hospital cafeteria on the bottom floor and wouldn't be back for little while. Janelle said a silent prayer to God for Jenna, Ellie, and Mia, and with an image of her beloved Rawson in her mind's eye, she closed her eyes and went to sleep for a final rest.

eleven

Long Island, 2007

C hristine had been on the phone for over an hour, and Karen
was beginning to worry that they would not only be late but
would miss their anniversary dinner altogether. She had gone to
special lengths, pulling in practically all her favors owed by
friends in high places to reserve a coveted table at Le Reminet in
Washington Square. It helped that it was the weekend before
Thanksgiving and many locals in the city swapped places with
tourists, leaving the city just as crowded as always, but also
leaving seats open at hidden gem restaurants like Le Reminet, but
still, if they did not get in the car soon, the restaurant would surely
give their table away to another customer.

Who could Christine be talking to for so long? Because the home
office door was closed, Karen couldn't even make out what kind
of conversation it was—work or personal—though smart money

said it was a blend of both. She loved her wife, but Christine's mind was never very far from her work, no matter where she was or what day of the week. Christine's work was a part of her, an appendage that was irrevocably fused to her mind, body, and soul, and it was something that Karen had learned to love and accept, for the sake of their marriage.

Things had gotten better, however, since the birth of their son, James. At four years old, James was a wild man, and though he suffered from asthma, it did not seem to slow him down one bit. He was good at using his inhaler when he needed it, and per his mothers' instructions, he obediently kept the small plastic device in his pocket at all times. James was a blessing that neither Karen nor Christine could imagine loving any more.

Once they decided that Karen was ready to be pregnant, Christine and Karen, like so many other BabyGenix patients, poured over lists of hundreds of sperm donors. Brown hair, blonde hair, Scandinavian decent, or would you prefer a sperm with fifteen percent African heritage? It was an intense process that took up most of their evenings for the better part of a month. Once they had both decided on a sperm donor, Christine gave Karen the secret news that she had been bursting to tell her for weeks.

"How would you feel about our child having both of our DNA?" she asked her over pizza one Thursday night. Christine smiled her Cheshire cat smile, as Karen called it, and Karen cocked her head to the side, confused.

"How would that work? I thought that an embryo was made up of the fusion of only two sets of DNA." Karen paused and realized that while they had spent hours choosing the perfect sperm donor for their child, they had not discussed which one of their DNA it would be combined with. Just because Karen would carry the child, it did not necessarily mean that her DNA was included at all. She had simply assumed that the child would have her own genetic material. This was a wrinkle that Karen had not thought of until this moment.

"It is very top secret," Christine began, putting her hand across the table, covering Karen's. "But we are working on a study at BG now that uses three sets of DNA in the fusion—three parents, so to speak—and we are looking for patient volunteers." Christine had been so excited about the scientific part of the new trial that, until she said the words out loud to Karen, she had not considered whether Karen would go for something so experimental, something potentially *dangerous* to their potential future child. Christine watched Karen's face carefully and found that she could not read her expression in the least.

"I think that is the most amazing thing I have ever heard," Karen said, getting up from the table and going around to Christine's chair to hug her tightly around the neck. "*We* are going to be mothers!" she shouted with glee.

Karen's pregnancy was routine and smooth in all the right ways. She was bloated and uncomfortable by week thirty, but Christine reminded her that all women feel that way when they are six months pregnant. James was delivered at Presbyterian Hospital at two a.m. in the morning on a beautiful, warm August night. Karen's parents, who purchased an old barn that had been converted to a farmhouse in Upstate New York, and since 2000, spent half the year there—the other half at their primary residence in Neath, South Wales—drove down in the middle of the night from Broome County to hold their first and only grandchild, and arrived in time to hold James in their arms only minutes after his birth.

***

The next few years mimicked any other of parents with a first child. There were late-night bottle feedings that Karen insisted she cover so Christine would not be too tired for work, and the occasional ear infection and stomach bug that would put all three of them in bed. Now at four years old, James was beginning to morph from toddlerhood to childhood, and doing it all with a broad grin on his face.

Beginning at six a.m. every morning, Karen and Christine would wake to the padding of feet quickly going down the stairs. Several minutes later, James could be heard coming back up the stairs and then settling outside his mothers' bedroom door, wrapped in his favorite blanket, until Karen and Christine woke and were ready to go downstairs for breakfast. The exception was Saturday and Sunday mornings, when James knew that he could open their bedroom door and climb into bed between his parents. The three of them would ease into those weekend mornings watching episodes of *Sesame Street* and *Yo Gabba Gabba* until Christine couldn't take any more and would offer to go to the kitchen and make pancakes.

"I am glad that one of us is young," she said to Karen after one three-episode marathon of *Yo Gabba Gabba*. "What are they even supposed to be? Aliens? I just don't get it."

Karen and James both laughed. "Mommy, they're not aliens, they're toys!" James squealed.

"One more episode?" Karen asked. "C'mon, Anne Heche is the guest on this one."

"You two knuckleheads can watch all you want," Christine bantered back. "I am going downstairs for much-needed coffee and pancakes."

"Yay!" James and Karen cheered in unison. "I love Momma's pancakes!" James added as Karen scooped him up out of the bed and all three of them headed down together.

They were good parents, Karen and Christine, and though Christine especially had been terrified about becoming a parent, once James was born, her heart belonged to her son, and she could barely imagine life without him or before him. Suddenly her work was slightly less important, and she left BabyGenix by five or six o'clock in order to be home for dinner, instead of staying until eight, nine, or much later like she done for so many years.

Karen looked at her watch. It was five minutes past seven—the reservation was for seven fifteen, and there was no way that it would take less than thirty minutes to get there. She waited one more minute and then started to knock on Christine's door when Christine opened the door herself and stepped out.

"I am so sorry, sweetie," Christine said hurriedly to Karen, kissing her on the cheek on her way to the closet to grab her puffy coat. Christine's hair was disheveled, but it usually was, and Karen noticed that Christine was wearing the new sweater that she had given her a few weeks ago on her birthday. "See?" Christine said smiling, noticing her wife noticing her gift in use. "I'm all ready!" She threw her hands in the air and waved them like a Broadway dancer during a showtune. "Let's go before we are too late."

The women went downstairs together; both gave James a quick kiss on the top of the head and made sure that the babysitter had the restaurant's information before stepping out into the frosty November night. Once they were in the car, Karen asked who Christine had been talking to for so long on the telephone. Karen was driving. Karen always drove when both she and Christine were going into the city, because Christine's erratic driving patterns made her nervous beyond words. At one point, Karen admitted that if she were going to be in the passenger seat of a car, she'd rather a rhesus monkey be behind the wheel over Christine.

"Oh," Christine said absentmindedly, "I am sorry, I was on the phone forever, wasn't I?"

"You were, but no worries," Karen said. "I just wondered who it was, that's all."

"It was my old boss, Alan Trounson." Christine caught the slightest glimpse of a flinch in Karen's neck.

"From Melbourne?" Karen asked curiously. She hadn't heard Christine talk about Dr. Trounson in years. She had once asked Christine what happened to all of the doctors and researchers that were on the Test Tube Baby Team when the program was shut down in the late '80s, but Christine had clammed up and said it was too upsetting to talk about, so Karen had dropped the subject.

"Yeah," Christine confirmed. "He's in California now, or at least he will be soon."

"Doing what?" Karen asked.

"Stem cell research. He's just been appointed the president of the California Institute for Regenerative Medicine—CIRM for short, like *sperm* without the p."

"I think I could have gotten that," Karen laughed, "but thank you, though, for never letting sperm get too far from conversation. You know how much I love talking about it." It was a light jab that Christine ignored. Karen was always telling her to *leave her work at the office*.

"Anyhow," Christine continued, "it's a huge appointment. He will be in charge of raising billions of dollars to fund research, not to mention having the authority to guide the direction of the projects in the program. It's quite amazing actually. Did you know that they are working on cures for everything from diabetes to Alzheimer's? He said that it is an incredible time to be in stem cell research, and he likened it to the exhilaration of working on the test-tube team all those years ago. I couldn't be more happy for him."

"Interesting." Karen could tell that the conversation had left Christine feeling excited, but also a little bit . . . what was the right adjective? Jealous? "I hope he is finding the road to success more smoothly paved than what you all went through, all the criticism I mean, when you were trying to get the Test Tube Baby Team up and running."

"Not at all," Christine said, sighing. "That is what we spent most of the time talking about. He said there are roadblocks at every turn. He believes in the future of stem cell research and its applications for treatment of all kinds of ailments and injuries, but he said he feels like he is often on an island when out on the funding trail."

"He's not one to shy away from controversial issues, is he?" Karen asked.

"No, quite the opposite," Christine laughed. "He described himself once as someone who sees an open window and jumps through it, before anyone can tell him not to. He is an amazing man. Parts of me miss working with him."

Karen stayed silent. She had a nagging hunch that she knew where the rest of the conversation was going. She did not want to move to California, and pull James out of his new school, and leave the townhouse, but she was worried that was what Christine was leading up to asking her to do.

"What else did he say?" she asked as coolly as possible. This time, Christine stayed silent.

"He offered me a job," Christine said finally. "There it is, he offered me one of the top research jobs in the lab. What do you think?"

"I think—"

"But first," Christine cut in, "I think you should really think about what an opportunity this could be for me, *for us*. He is looking for a cure for Alzheimer's, for God's sake, talk about important work. I think it could be exactly what I need to get me out of my professional funk." Christine knew that she sounded like a child begging for an ice cream cone, but she also knew that Karen would probably not go for it unless she begged. Karen loved New York, she loved James's new school, and she loved the community that she and Christine had finally found in their neighborhood that was years in the making. It was a big task to ask her to give all of that up.

Karen reached over and put her hand over Christine's. She squeezed it gently and said, "I know you do, sweetheart, and you know I do not ever want to hold you back from your dreams. But—you know that you are still doing important work, right? Thousands upon thousands of women have successfully had children because of you and your dedication to your field— including me, I might add."

"Yes, but—"

"No. Christine, please. Let me finish." Karen unexpectedly felt tears come to her eyes. She realized that in the five years since James's birth, six years if you counted implantation day, she had never told her wife how grateful she was to her for giving her the gift of motherhood. A single tear slid down Karen's face and she took her hand from Christine's to wipe it away. "Have I ever told you about my friend Fallon from when I was a kid?"

"No," Christine whispered quietly. Karen was rarely one to be forceful, so this must be something worth listening to.

"Fallon and I were best friends from kindergarten until the seventh grade."

"Why only until the seventh grade?" Christine asked, though she had a strong feeling she knew exactly what broke up the friendship. Being gay does that to friendships, especially the young ones. It's unfair and it's cruel, but it is the reality of being young and gay in a small town like Karen's.

Karen put out one finger and took a deep breath. "Be patient—
I'm getting there. Our favorite game in elementary school was a
game that we called 'baby.' We basically used our own dolls and
some of Fallon's sister's dolls and pretended that they were our
kids. We would bathe the dolls and feed them, and even walk them
around in the neighborhood using Fallon's mom's stroller, left over
from when her younger sister was a newborn. Being a mother was
the only thing that I wanted to be when I grew up. It was the only
thing that I could imagine myself doing and enjoying. Being a mom
was the most magical job on the planet to me. One day, in middle
school, Fallon was at my house and we were playing baby—I
realize that we were way too old to still be playing such an infantile
game, but we were, and we loved it. By this point, we had imagined
entire lives for our make-believe children—if they took ballet or
gymnastics, what school they went to. Fallon had even named her
husband—Johnny, she called him."

Now Christine was positive that she knew where the story was
going, and her heart began to break for twelve-year-old Karen
Rubin from Neath.

Karen continued, "It was something that I had been thinking
about for a while, you know, but just didn't know what to do
about it, or who to talk to. I had so many questions. I figured, who
better to tell than my very best friend, someone who knew me
better than anyone? Anyhow, I told Fallon that I didn't have a
husband, and when she asked why not, I said because—and I
really had to build up courage to say it—I said that because maybe
I had a wife."

"You seriously said that?" Christine was stunned and over-
whelmed with pride for young Karen. Karen nodded.

"I sure did. And do you know what Fallon said?"

"I can guess," Christine confessed.

"She said, and I quote," Karen put on her strongest Welsh accent yet, "she said, 'But there can't be two mummies. That's *not* how it works. If you have two mummies like Ms. Jane and Ms. Carmen (the only two lesbians that existed in our tri-county area), then that means that you *can't ever* be a mummy.'" Full tears were falling down Karen's cheeks and Christine leaned over with a tissue to wipe them away.

"I am so, so sorry, sweetheart," Christine said to Karen. "I wish that I could have been there to punch that kid in the face."

Karen laughed. "You would have had to have been fast. She never came over to play at my house after that ever again, and she never invited me to her house either. When my mum finally asked me what was wrong and why Fallon and I weren't friends anymore, I told her that I didn't know why—but deep down I was devastated. I had lost my best friend and my future all in one day, and all for simply being myself. I think it was probably that day that I decided I had to get out of Wales as quickly as I could and go somewhere where I could be accepted, if not understood and loved." Karen shook her head and smiled as if she were reliving that seventh-grade trauma all over again. "My point," she said, sucking in a big gulp of air and heavily blowing it out, "is that *you*, and your work in Melbourne, and here in New York, made it possible for me, *me*—gay, fringe, weirdo me—to become a mother. And I had given up on that dream until I met you. You have no idea what that means to me. It's a miracle what you do every day. Don't ever forget that."

Christine rubbed the back of Karen's neck and smiled. "This is why I love you," she said tenderly. "You are the strongest vulnerable woman that I know."

"That's my job," Karen replied, "and I'll do it for the rest of our lives." She squeezed Christine's hand once more as they pulled up to the curb at the valet stand for the restaurant.

Christine turned down Trounson's offer to woo her away from New York and work on stem cell research with him at CIRM. It was a tough phone call to make, but once it was decided that Christine was staying at BabyGenix, she felt a strange weight lift from her shoulders. She did not need to search for more importance or meaning in her job—it was there and had been there all along.

twelve

New York, 2008

J enna woke to the familiar and unsettling feeling of her heart pounding in her ears at a rate that felt like three hundred beats per minute. Her jaw ached from clenching, for how long she had no idea, and despite the thermostat reading fifty-eight degrees (she had forgotten to turn the heat on before bed again), sweat seeped through the front of her nightshirt from underneath and between her breasts. *Bam, bam, bam, bam, bam* went her heart as Jenna leaned over to turn the lamp on her bedside table on.

It was the dream again, the same dream that had haunted Jenna for the last nine years, and one that had become more frequent since her mother's passing in April the year before. Janelle had always called Jenna her rock, but these days Jenna felt no more sturdy than a wet cardboard box. Ellie was in college now, and while she appeared happy, she seemed to need Jenna or her father less and less every day. Jenna would get an occasional call on the weekends, and last summer Ellie spent six weeks living in Jenna's apartment while she completed an internship in the city. The two of them, Ellie and Jenna, had become distant over the last few years, and the gap had grown wider between them after Janelle's death, which Ellie took especially hard.

Jenna lay very still and tried to calm her breathing and her racing heartbeat. *One of these days*, she thought, *I am going to have a heart attack. This can't be normal*. Then again, taking the prescribed amount of valium that her doctor recommended at bedtime didn't seem normal either. The dream was always the same, with subtle differences in setting or time—Mia was in dire trouble and Jenna, in vain, tried to save her. Sometimes other people floated in and out of the dream—her mother, Ellie, Ellie's boyfriend Kevin, and even sometimes her ex-husband, Ed—but Mia was a constant; she was the link in every dream.

This time, the dream was centered on the pond behind Jenna's grandmother's house. Mutty, as Jenna and all of her cousins called her, had been dead for twenty years, but in her dreams, Mutty's voice was not fogged over as often happens in memories, but rather was clear as a bell, calling out, "Don't go too close to the water! Watch out for the water!" How many times had Jenna heard Mutty utter her urgent warnings about the pond, dozens if not hundreds of times?

"The pond," where Jenna and her younger cousins loved to play around its edges, was really no more than a large natural spring and could not have been more than thirty feet across at its widest point. But the water was very deep in the crystal-clear center, where tiny air bubbles constantly surfaced, disrupting the sooty floor of the spring. Underwater ferns flourished, and huge lily pads floated across the top, making the pond the perfect centerpiece of summertime games like throwing rocks or seeing who could stick their leg in the farthest without falling in. Even on the hottest July days, the water in the pond was frigid cold, because it had come down through the Appalachian Mountains (according to Mutty), and Jenna and her oldest cousin, Alexandra, would dare each other to jump in first, submerging themselves in the icy-cold water.

In the dream, Mia had been standing on the edge of the pond, near where Jenna and Alexandra would jump off from when diving in. She looked to be five or six years old, still with a baby face but not quite a baby anymore. Her face was innocent and, in the dream, like in all the others, she was blissfully unaware of Jenna's presence, caught up in her own game or song or craft.

Today, Mia was picking dandelions near the pond's edge when the dream began. She hummed a tune that Jenna knew but could not name, and walked carefully from one end of the pond to the other collecting flowers.

All was fine until Mia slipped on a muddy part of the bank while reaching out for a perfectly full flower just out of reach. She tumbled headfirst into the pond with a splash, her red coat disappearing underneath the glassy water's top. It was in this moment that Jenna realized that her feet were stuck in either cement or glue or some substance that would not allow her to move her legs forward toward Mia and the water. *Tick, tick, tick* went the seconds, coinciding with the *bam, bam, bam, bam* beginning in Jenna's chest.

Jenna screamed and fought with everything that she had, but her feet were stuck, and she could do nothing but watch as the ripples in the water cleared, and after only a few seconds there was no sign that a child just slipped beneath its surface. With every dream, Jenna woke exhausted and edgy, turning on her bedside lamp, getting up, and fixing a cup of tea, after which she sat in her recliner with one of the cats and waited for the sun to rise, so she could go back to sleep.

PART V

Eleven Years Later

thirteen

2019

Lucie Hernandez looked out of her bedroom window and saw the number-four bus pull away from the curb. "Mama!" she called out to her mother, who was folding clothes in the kitchen. "Llego tarde! I am going to be late! Otra vez." Lucie was bent over a wiggling toddler, and once she finished attaching the tabs to a diaper, she picked up the child, kissing her on the face and making her laugh.

"See, mi pequeñita?" she said, smiling to the drooling one-year-old. "All better, yes? Your auntie is going to be late for work—again." She bounced the girl on her hip and walked into the kitchen, where she put the petite girl into a high chair in the corner of the tiny room.

"I need to go, Mom! Carmen is all changed. I will see you tonight after your shift." Lucie picked up her jacket, keys, and a granola bar on her way out of the apartment. If she hurried, she could circle around to the back of her building, cross Tenth Street, and beat the number four to the stop at 170th Street. She could take the number-five train; it, too, would get her as far as East Eighty-Sixth Street (and for the same amount of time with light traffic), but she preferred the bus when she could catch it. Something about being underground on the subway always made Lucie feel uneasy. Estella clucked as Lucie opened the front door to the apartment. "Nah nah nah," she said, wagging a bony finger at Lucie. Her mother was not old, but Lucie had often thought lately that her mother looked much older than fifty. Lucie attributed this to the strains of hard living that her mother had endured and hoped that she could do something to help mitigate some of the financial burden that her mother had carried for the Hernandez family for so long since her father's death.

"Argh!" Lucie sighed, smiling but annoyed. "Aye yai yai, all right, all right, but I *have* to go." She hurriedly stepped back into the room to give her mother a hug and a kiss, before turning back to the door once more, this time stepping out quickly, closing the door behind her. Racing down the interior stairs to the front lobby of her building, Lucie begged karma to let the bus driver be running a second later today than usual. *Please go slow*, she said to herself all the way down several flights of metal stairs.

"Good morning, Ms. Chu!" Lucie yelled to her elderly neighbor, who sat on the front stoop of the apartment building near the door. Old Ms. Chu was blind and slightly deaf, but she raised her hand to Lucie and waved goodbye as Lucie walked with a clip to the street corner, her shoulder bag containing her lunch for the day and a water bottle bumping against her shoulder blades as she walked.

"Have a good day, my sweet Lucie," Ms. Chu called out. Lucie and Ms. Chu teased each other over the differences in their English dialects. Lucie loved Ms. Chu's staccato Chin-glish (as

Lucie called it). But today, she didn't hear her neighbor. She was in too much of a hurry, and already too far away to hear Ms. Chu's reply.

Unfortunately, it was not the first time Lucie had missed the bus at her own stop and had to track it down several blocks over. She built up a generous sweat on her brow and underarms by the time she reached the stop at 170th Street, and was happy to see other commuters still waiting at the curb, telling her that she had beaten the bus and would make it to her first house on the Upper East Side on time. She learned through trial and error that if she began her day behind, the entire day followed in that pattern no matter how fast she tried to make the time up at one client's apartment or another.

The number-four bus pulled to a squealing stop and a large black poof of exhaust let out from the back as the driver opened the sliding side door. Lucie waved the smoke away with her hand and found a standing spot with a hand strap in the middle of the bus. An elderly man dressed in a mechanic's suit sat in the handicap seat just beside her, and when Lucie reached up to grab the hand strap, the man kindly and silently motioned for her to take his seat. The man struggled to stand.

"Oh, no, please," Lucie said, "I couldn't take your seat. Thank you though." The man smiled and sat back down, moving over enough to make room for Lucie's shoulder bag. She couldn't help but take him up on the spot for her bag. It made her shoulders and back ache holding it for such a long ride. He looked wistfully out of the window and continued to smile as if he was thinking of some faraway place in his mind. Lucie wondered if the man was really on his way to work, or if, like so many others, the old man rode the bus system around the city like a tourist, having no other way to spend his days.

The ride would take another forty-five minutes one way before she got off at East Eighty-Fifth in Manhattan, close to her first job of the day, and one that would take her a good four hours from start to finish.

Cleaning apartments for rich people had not been Lucie's idea of what her life would be when she graduated from Lehman College the previous spring with a degree in biology. Her mother had adamantly protested against Lucie taking on any work at all while she was enrolled at Lehman, which was nice because as her mother put it, she could simply "focus on her studies." But it also meant that there was a large amount of pressure on Lucie, however self-imposed, to do well in school so that she could graduate and begin to make real money of her own. Lucie was the first person in the Hernandez family to graduate from college, and since immigrating to the US when Lucie was eight, all her mother and father talked about was the importance of education, going so far as to tell young Lucie and her older sister, Maria, that the sacrifices Estella and Alejandro made in leaving their native Guatemala and coming to the US was to give their daughters a chance at a better life. Maria graduated from high school and tried college, but boys were a distraction for her, and not completely at Maria's fault. Taller than Lucie, and with their grandmother's sultry eyes, Maria was always being followed by one boy or another. At eighteen, she enrolled in college, but found her then-boyfriend to be time-consuming enough, and by the second semester, Maria had dropped all but one class. She swore to her mother and to Lucie that one day she would go back to school—but then she became pregnant with Carmen. Estella knew then that her only hope of a college-educated daughter rested on Lucie.

Lucie excelled at school and graduated with honors from Lehman with a degree in biology and a minor in Latin American studies. She felt somewhat guilty taking advantage of low-hanging fruit for a minor curriculum, but Estella was proud that her youngest daughter was both excelling in an American university and keeping ties to her native heritage. Unfortunately, an undergraduate degree in science without a teaching certificate or graduate degree made it hard for Lucie to find a job. Her dream of working side by side in a lab with top researchers helping to make important scientific discoveries was just that, a dream, and after going on countless interviews over a six-month period, only to be told that she was "too young, too inexperienced, or just not the candidate that we are looking for," Lucie gave up hope of working in a lab. She took a job nannying for a young Manhattanite couple who had one son and were willing to pay her $25,000 a year plus benefits to work for them Monday through Friday eight a.m. to six p.m. and occasionally on the weekends.

At first, the nanny job seemed great. The couple, the Joneses, had even held out the carrot that if Lucie was still with the family a year from her start date, they would up her pay to $30,000 a year. This was almost more than her mother and sister made combined in one year. Estella's friend, June, told Lucie about the opening and suggested that she apply for the position. June was a nanny for a family that lived in the same building as the Joneses and said that they were looking for a full-time nanny for their two-year-old son, Jackson, to begin immediately. Apparently the last nanny (as had several before that) had abruptly quit, leaving Mrs. Jones in a tizzy and having to use up her precious vacation days from CNN searching for a replacement and taking care of her son herself, which, according to Mrs. Jones, was exhausting.

Lucie met with Annelle Jones on a Tuesday and was surprised when Annelle sprung from the white tufted sofa, squeezed Lucie in a tight hug, and offered the job to her on the spot and asked if she could begin work the following day. Lucie was flattered, and the apartment was certainly the nicest that she had ever seen in person, but the speed at which Mrs. Jones moved in hiring her made her uneasy. *Why would she meet me and hire me all within a ten-minute window if I will be the sole caretaker of her only son?* As if reading her mind, Annelle gave an answer to exactly that question.

"I *have* to get back to work," she said. "If I don't get back in there soon, some young hot twenty-something will have taken my spot. You understand English, right? I will have a key made for you today." Before Lucie could reply, Annelle was up and on her way to her bedroom, when she turned around and held her coffee mug daintily in both hands.

"You should know that we have cameras throughout the apartment, and my husband and I monitor them throughout the day," she said a little coldly. Annelle was now pouring herself a cup of hot herbal hibiscus tea, intently watching the steaming hot water pour over the tea bag in her china cup, not offering a cup to Lucie.

"My husband and I are both very busy people, but our son's safety is of upmost importance—as you would imagine it would be." She paused. "You look responsible. The Days' nanny, I can't remember her name, said that you come from a very good family."

Lucie nodded. There was something odd about this woman and the way that she could be warm and inviting one minute and stone cold the next. But she couldn't deny that the job offer was a good one. If her mother found out that she had been offered a $25,000-a-year job and turned it down, she would never hear the end of it.

"Yes," Lucie said, sitting up straight on the sofa and trying to look confident and mature beyond her years. "I completely understand, Mrs. Jones. I would be the same way if Jackson was my child. In fact, I will treat him as if he is my child, making sure his every need is met while you are at work." Lucie added in the last sentence on a whim and thought that it came out sounding very professional.

"But he's not your child," Annelle snapped, and then, as if using a calculating self-calming technique, she took a deep breath in through her slender nose, let it back out through her mouth, and smiled. "But of course, I know what you meant, Lucie. Thank you. You can go now. I will see you here tomorrow at eight a.m. sharp. Not a minute late, or I will be forced to cancel your contract effective immediately. I do not like to be late to work." Annelle had looked up when she spoke to Lucie, but when she finished speaking, she looked back down to her teacup. Jackson, the Joneses' son, had been asleep for the entirety of the interview. Wouldn't Mrs. Jones want Lucie to meet him before she began work the following day? When Annelle said that she could go, Lucie guessed not and stood to leave.

The kitchen was open to the living area, where the two women had been sitting together, and on the other side of the kitchen was the front door of the apartment. Lucie picked her bag up from the floor next to the coffee table and began walking to the door to leave.

In a moment of severe contradiction, when Lucie passed by the kitchen, Annelle stepped in front of her, blocking her from the door. Lucie stood still and was shocked when Mrs. Jones put her arms around her in a tight embrace, just as she had done when she offered Lucie the job five minutes before. "We are *so* glad to have you as part of our family, Lucie," she gushed as she twisted the long strand of pearls that hung from her neck.

Lucie stepped back, said thank you, and opened the door as quickly as she could without looking like she was an actress trying to escape in a horror movie. As it turned out, the interview with Mrs. Jones was the least strange of all of Lucie's interactions with Mr. or Mrs. Jones. When Annelle mentioned that they had cameras, she meant in every room. This by itself did not bother Lucie, it wasn't like she was doing anything incriminating, but

Lucie found within days that the constant mechanical sound of the camera's red eye moving back and forth whenever she moved from one end of the room to another was unsettling. Then there was the day that Mrs. Jones texted Lucie, saying in all caps, "CALL ME IMMEDIATELY." Jackson had just finished lunch, and Lucie had changed his diaper as instructed, regardless of whether he had soiled it. "A diaper should be changed every hour, regardless," Annelle had written on the notebook titled "A Day in the Life of Jackson Jones" that she left on the counter on Lucie's first day. It was at least fifty handwritten pages long and gave Lucie some hope that perhaps Mrs. Jones did after all care for the son that she couldn't wait to get away from every morning.

Lucie dialed Annelle's cell number and the call was picked up on the first ring. "What *is* that on Jackson's shirt?" she said excitedly. Her off-camera voice was shrill as is, but more so when she was nervous or upset. However, when the cameras were rolling, Annelle Jones turned into a hardened reporter with a voice almost as deep as her male colleagues.

"Um," Lucie staggered, "I'm not sure." Lucie picked Jackson up off the changing table and set him on his feet on the ground. He squealed and turned to run away as toddlers often do, and Lucie reached out to stop him. *"Don't* you *dare* touch him!" Annelle screamed into the phone. Lucie held the phone away from her ear and let Jackson go. She tried to get a look at Jackson's shirt to see what Mrs. Jones was referring to, but before she had the chance, Jackson said, "You can't catch me!" and took off running. He squealed louder than he had before as he ran down the long hallway separating the living spaces from the common areas and kitchen, but this time Lucie did not try to stop him.

"What is happening?" Annelle screeched. "What is that noise?" Lucie heard the tapping noise of a keyboard and before she could answer, she heard one of the camera lenses swivel and Annelle said, "Why is he running?! There is Absolutely *no* running inside! Our neighbors will complain! What do you think this is? A zoo?" By this point, Annelle was yelling so loudly and so vehemently that Lucie couldn't even remember what the initial text and subsequent call was about.

"Mrs. Jones?" Lucie asked. "Are you okay?" It seemed logical for Lucie to ask, since the woman was acting like a lunatic and presumably on a phone in her office where other coworkers could potentially hear her rant.

"I am fine!" Annelle spat into the receiver. "*You* need to be in better control of Jackson. He is acting like a wild animal. This is *not* the kind of behavior that is acceptable. All morning I have watched you let him boss you around like *he* is the one in charge. This is not good, Lucie, really not good at all. This is my *son* we are talking about, not some neighborhood kid that you are watching for free."

Lucie didn't have any idea how to respond. The morning had been completely innocuous. She arrived at eight a.m. on the dot, as she had for the past three weeks. Jackson asked for oatmeal for breakfast, so she made some for him. After breakfast they played fire trucks with the new set of building blocks that he received from his grandparents the week before, and then they sat in the library and read some of Jackson's favorite books—*Corduroy*, *Goodnight Moon*, and *Chicka Chicka Boom Boom*. Lunch was mac 'n' cheese and blueberries, and then she was in the middle of changing his one p.m. diaper when the text from Annelle appeared on her cell phone.

"Jones! On in five—" Lucie heard in the background of the other end of the line. "I've got to go," Annelle said tersely. "We will continue this discussion when I get home. Oh—and don't forget to vacuum in Clark's office at three, I noticed that you chose to skip the eleven a.m."

"Okay, will do," Lucie replied, trying to sound upbeat despite feeling completely irritated and offended. When Clark Jones arrived home that evening, he did what he always did upon arrival—he went straight to the wet bar separating the kitchen from his home office, made himself a strong gin and tonic with lemon, and closed himself in his office without a word to Lucie or Jackson. That was another of Annelle's requests. "Do not accost Clark when he gets home from the office, or let Jackson disturb him. His workload right now is extremely stressful, and he asks that Jackson and I wait to see him after he has some wind-down time alone in his *bureau à domicile*," she had said. Annelle had a habit of implementing French words in place of English whenever she could. However, when Lucie noticed this and asked Annelle if she would like for her to begin speaking Spanish around Jackson to introduce him to another language, Annelle made a sour face and said, "Ugh, no," quickly and without a trace of regret for her impertinence.

When Annelle arrived home on the day of the outburst, she swept into the apartment like one of those spinning tops that children play with on holidays. All makeup and hair and color from her scarf, she came in the door on a gust of wind and headed straight toward Lucie and Jackson, who were sitting on the carpeted floor of the living room playing a memory game with small square cards that had various Disney characters on them. Jackson loved the game and was good at it, Lucie thought, for only being two years old. He would turn his own cards over slowly and would stare at them intently before turning the unmatched pair back over. He had just made a match of two Donald Duck cards when the front door burst open, causing him to look up and see his mother throw herself into the room.

"Well," she said dramatically, "I hope that you two have had fun today." She was smiling, but something in her voice alerted Lucie that Annelle was still angry from the lunchtime call—although Lucie never could figure out what had made her mad in the first place. The trick was figuring out what it was before she pulled you into a long guessing game not dissimilar to Jackson's memory game that caused one party to ask if the problem was x, only to have Annelle say no it was something else, but not tell you what it was. It was a very frustrating game, and Lucie wondered if Annelle and Clark communicated this way often and how terrible it would be to live with them if so.

"We did," Lucie said, deciding not to engage in Annelle's game. "Hey!" Lucie said to Jackson, "Tell Mommy about how well you did in the game today! You had—"

Annelle cut Lucie off. "I'm not really interested in the game, Lucie," she said coldly. "What I am interested in is when you decided to give Jackson chocolate without asking my permission. Do you have any idea how bad sugar and caffeine are for young brains? I did a full report of it just a few months ago, I should know."

Lucie was caught off guard. "He hasn't had any chocolate," she said calmly.

"Oh really?" Annelle replied, and as she did, she bent down to where Jackson sat and pointed to his dirty T-shirt. "Then what is this?" she asked.

"The blueberries?" Lucie asked. "He had blueberries and mac 'n' cheese for lunch today. I'm sorry, I didn't realize that his shirt was so dirty with the juice."

Annelle looked like a deer in headlights. She was still crouched down next to Jackson, but she had taken her hand off of his shirt and put both of her hands on the floor, so she was in a strange position that looked like an animal that was about to pounce. With all her stage makeup still on, Lucie could see the papery lines that encircled Annelle's eyes. She wondered how old Annelle was and how old she had been when she had Jackson.

"Oh," she said after a brief pause, "I must have confused the blueberry stain on his shirt for something else. In my defense, on the camera it looked darker." Annelle stood up and walked toward the kitchen, where she poured herself a tall glass of wine. Lucie decided in that moment that she needed to quit, but was afraid for her safety in a bizarre way that made her not want to deliver the news to either Jones in person. She gave Jackson a hug and whispered in his ear, "Bye, buddy. I hope to see you around. You're a good boy, Jackson."

And that was how Lucie became a cleaning lady.

***

The number-four bus came to a stiff halt at the East Seventy-Fifth Street bus stop and Lucie nudged her way through the other passengers to get off. It was Monday, and on Mondays she had three cleanings in one day. It was a lot, but after the nannying debacle, Lucie preferred to work alone and found that she didn't mind cleaning other people's messes. It was therapeutic in a way, and because the client was almost never home, she could work at her own pace and be in her own mind for several hours and make money doing it. Of course, she would still rather be working in a lab doing real work with real scientists, but for now, if cleaning enabled her to let her mother work less hours at Brito Market, the Latin grocery around the corner from their building, then it was worth it.

She had a set of keys to all her clients' homes. It enabled them to not be home when she began or finished the job, and most had security cameras anyhow, so if Lucie was not trustworthy, they would know it and could fire her swiftly and change the locks. She put her key in the lock of 14B and was surprised when she heard music on the other side of the door.

She opened the door and was bringing her vacuum in when her client, Jenna Ellis, walked out of the back bedroom of the apartment.

"Hi, Lucie!" she said brightly. "How are you, dear?" Jenna was Lucie's favorite among her clients, and though Ms. Ellis was a bit eccentric and her cat-to-human ratio was severely skewed, she seemed to be a genuinely nice person. And anyhow, Lucie loved her cats. She could never believe that the building manager allowed a person to have as many cats as she had in one apartment, but here they were, and Ms. Ellis treated them each like human family members.

"Hi, Ms. Ellis," Lucie replied cheerfully. "I hope that you are well today."

Jacques, a white Persian, jumped onto the kitchen counter when he heard Lucie's voice, and he nuzzled his fluffy white head under Lucie's elbow. "You are not supposed to be up here," Lucie said playfully to the cat, and she picked him up and set him on the tile floor near the food bowl. Jacques looked up at Lucie momentarily, sniffed the food, and began to eat.

"Smart," Jenna said. "I will have to try that—a *distraction technique* is what they call it with toddlers . . . I think. I've been reading up on childhood behaviors lately." Jenna poured herself a fresh cup of coffee that smelled delicious, then took a second mug down from the cabinet.

"Coffee?" she asked, and Lucie smiled and obliged, thanking Jenna after taking the cup into her own hands. Lucie took a few blissful sips of the expensive tasting coffee, and then, not wanting Jenna to think she was taking advantage, thanked her for the coffee and got to work, starting with her bucket and scrub brush in the master bath.

125

fourteen

It was the media who coined the name Baby Mia in the press, but anyone close to Jenna knew that she had been calling the embryo by that name for more than twenty years—twenty-nine years, to be exact. She had named all three embryos on the fifth day of fertilization before they were placed in liquid nitrogen and cryogenically stored in 1990. She and Ed had been married for three years by that point, and Jenna had been thirty-three years old. Back in those days she had been young and hopeful and even a little entitled, if she was completely honest with herself. She felt that she *deserved* to be a mother. She deserved happiness and to have the perfect, harmonious family that came as a result of her hard work and good nature. It is not something that young girls are aware of, per se, the instinctual desire to reproduce—and sometimes, as in Jenna's case, that instinct is slow to arrive at all—

but when it does, there is nothing a woman wants more than to have a baby of her own. But Jenna envisioned more than that, promising herself that she would continue working after her children were born, vowing not to be one of those female attorneys who maintained a career only until the point at which they became the dreaded *stay-at-home mother*. She could do it all, she told herself, blissfully unaware the utopia that she was building in her mind was setting her up for an epic deluge of pain when that vision, that idea of what you think the rest of your life will look like, came crashing down, out of her control, and leaving only a blank void where her life, her future, used to be.

But Jenna did not yet know the pain of mourning a future that would not be. At thirty-three, she only worried for the baby that did not seem to grow so quickly or easily inside of her as they did for so many of her friends. She did not yet know that years of endometriosis had wreaked havoc on her fallopian tubes, filling the lifeline from the ovaries to her uterus with scar tissue, making it impossible for her to have a viable pregnancy on her own. After years of *trying*, she and Ed decided that they would try the new fertility option called IVF. Jenna knew from the start that she was more invested in finding a solution to their fertility issues than Ed was. By this point, having a baby was practically the only thing that Jenna thought about. She thought about babies while she was at work, she dreamed about babies in the night, and she even changed her diet to include more folic acid and began taking expensive prenatal vitamins, all so her body would be *ready* should she become pregnant.

"I don't know," Ed had said, "it seems kind of . . . weird. Like futuristic or something. Shouldn't we just wait this thing out? I mean, maybe it's just not our time."

Ed's mother, Regina, was less sympathetic, announcing to the entire Mountain family one Thanksgiving that Jenna had yet to become pregnant. "Sometimes God doesn't intend for certain women to bear children. It's a simple fact of faith. No need to take it personally, my dear," she said across the enormous lacquered dining room table, her deep-blue eyes boring a hole straight through Jenna's heart. As if the attack warranted an exclamation point, Regina added, "I'm sure God has some plan for you; the ladies in my prayer group will add you to our list. Surely if you became less self-absorbed with your *work*," she said the word work as if it were filthy, "you could hear God's call for you."

It wasn't so much her mother-in-law's lack of decorum that had surprised and enraged Jenna—it was that the woman could somehow use religion to explain away infertility, as if the right to have children was saved for *certain* people and not open to all. It had taken all of Jenna's nerve not to argue openly with the Mountain figurehead, so she did as Ed had instructed her: "Don't argue with my mother—you will never win."

The fertility specialist that Jenna and Ed were referred to was only slightly more hopeful. "IVF is your only option if you want to carry a child naturally in the womb. Waiting any longer to attempt pregnancy will only make it harder, as Jenna's body will not continue to create viable eggs at the same rate over the next few years." The doctor agreed with Ed that IVF could be a bit scary and the process futuristic, but he conceded, "Futuristic is your only option, and I assure you that the process is very safe. Science has made it possible for just about any woman who wants to have a child to have one. It is just short of miraculous."

The news had come as a half-answered prayer to Jenna, but Ed was still skeptical. The doctor continued, "With that said, cryopreservation—part of the IVF process—comes with its own emotional toll and risks. Not all embryos survive the thawing stage and there can be complications at implantation. Before going down this path, you should talk it over not once, but many times to ensure that this course of family planning is right for you." The doctor left Jenna and Ed with several pamphlets all showing bright-eyed babies on the covers and happy-looking families on the inside pages. Every baby looked perfect and beautiful, and the longer Jenna stared at the pictures, the more intoxicated with hope she became.

It was not easy, but in the end, Jenna won Ed over, promising him that he needn't come to any of her appointments that interfered with his work schedule, and that she would even pay the first installment of payments due to BabyGenix out of her own savings account that she kept separate from their joint banking account. Ed finally agreed, and in the fall of 1989, Jenna began her IVF journey, and was assigned to an OB-GYN at BabyGenix who would monitor her from pre-implantation to the birth of her baby. In the beginning, even the word *childbirth* Jenna said with glee when she was alone in the apartment, but IVF proved to be neither fun nor easy. Jenna was grateful in hindsight that she had not been aware ahead of the dozens of injections that she would have to give herself prior to several painful harvesting procedures. Months of enduring this plus the hormone pills, along with hoping and waiting, all culminated in seven viable embryos—three males and four females. Jenna guarded the printed images that BabyGenix sent her home with like an ancient treasure. Each embryo was labeled with letters A through G, and each image showed a single white circle containing eight grayish spherical cells—and all of it no bigger than a fraction of a typed period.

The sex of the tiny cellular beings had been determined with use of the most cutting-edge technology, explained to Jenna and Ed as genetic embryology. The process, still early in its developmental stages, was called Preimplantation Genetic Diagnosis, or PGD for short.

"You are lucky to be in New York, Mr. and Mrs. Mountain," Jenna's OB-GYN, a young female doctor named Christine Daugherty, had told them. Dr. Daugherty specialized in in vitro fertilization and had been recommended highly to Jenna and Ed through friends. "The genetic testing that we are able to do at BabyGenix is unlike what any other lab in the country can do."

"What exactly can you determine from these tests?" Ed asked, scanning the list of testing options and the corresponding price list.

"Much more than you could ever imagine," Dr. Daugherty had said. "Specifically, we can determine which embryos are the most viable and more likely to withstand the freezing, thawing, and implantation procedure. We can determine if chromosomal normalcy or if abnormalities exist, which would denote Down syndrome and other genetic disorders, and," at this she smiled and winked, "what most parents are interested in, we can determine the sex of the embryo with one hundred percent accuracy—before implantation."

"The sex of the embryo?" Ed chuckled. He looked around animatedly. "Did we somehow end up in China? Excuse me, Emperor Ming, why would anyone care so much about the sex?"

Dr. Daugherty was not amused. Jenna could not have been more embarrassed that her husband could be so callous about the birth order of their unborn children, and rude, in addition, to the woman that was trying to help them.

"Simply for family planning, Mr. Mountain," Dr. Daugherty replied, her smile gone. She did not look up from the clipboard in her hand. Deciding that she was finished with Ed, Dr. Daugherty turned her attention to Jenna and smiled. "Mrs. Mountain, we recommend that you choose at least two to three embryos for each implantation attempt. Science is good, but we are still a long way off from being able to guarantee you a viable baby without several embryos attempting to attach in one transfer."

"Whoa, whoa, whoa," Ed cut in. "What do you mean two to three? I didn't sign on for triplets or twins. No. Out of the question. We will implant *one* at a time."

Jenna was shocked. She and Ed had discussed how much she wanted a baby—how much *they* wanted a baby. If the doctor said that it took two to three to ensure one live baby, then that was what she would do. Twins would be a blessing, a two-for-one, so to speak, however unlikely.

"Ed, please." Jenna reached out and put a hand on Ed's forearm. "Please, I really want this first time to be a success—for both of us. Let's just listen to Dr. Daugherty. She's the expert, remember?" If the Jenna of the future could have spoken to the Jenna of 1999, then she would have told her that putting Ed Mountain in a corner and even suggesting that he was inferior to another person, another woman at that, was the last way to win him over to her side of the argument.

"Absolutely not," he said sternly. "One at a time."

Jenna sighed and looked to Dr. Daugherty, who looked miffed at Ed and sorry for Jenna. "Okay," Christine said smoothly. "Mrs. Mountain, I will do my best to make your implantation a success. Do you know which embryo you would like to select first?"

Before Ed could intervene again, Jenna jumped in to answer Dr. Daugherty quickly. "A female. Just choose the one that is most likely to succeed."

And that is how embryo D, or *Baby D*, as described on BabyGenix paperwork, was chosen for implantation first. Though currently empty, Jenna had put her hand to her stomach in that moment, imagining the soon-to-be little girl growing inside of her.

Her name would be Mary Ellis Mountain, Ellie for short. But after only five days, embryo D failed to attach to Jenna's uterine lining and was no longer viable. Jenna waited the requisite several months and tried again, with embryo E, only to have a similar result. Almost a year after the failure of embryo E, Jenna again went to BabyGenix for the transfer of embryo F, a male, and ten days later Jenna stared at an at-home pregnancy test with wonder. Two faint pink lines showed in the results box, and Jenna must have looked from the box to the stick a hundred times to make sure that two lines meant pregnant. She excitedly shared the news with Ed that evening over dinner, and she was disappointed at his non-plussed attitude toward her news. "Let's not get too excited, sweetie," he had said. "I think it is a little early to be calling yourself pregnant. It's just one test." When Ed left the apartment and went "back to the office" later that same night, Jenna cried herself to sleep hoping that Ed was wrong and realized that she cared more for the tiny being inside of her than about whatever indiscretion was keeping her husband out so late for the third time that week.

Unfortunately, Ed was right, and just three weeks after that joyous day of confirmation, Jenna's dreams of being a mother were once again dashed. It was bad enough to have your own body betray you in such a draconian fashion, but to endure the painful cramps and bleeding that did not subside for days afterward was salt on Jenna's wound.

It would take another six months for Jenna to be ready to try another transfer. On the day that Jenna went in for the transfer of embryo G, Jenna had stayed up all night the night before praying. "Please," she had asked God, "please let me become a mother. Please give strength to Baby G that she will be strong and that she will survive. Please." Regina's words ringing in her ears, Jenna hoped that the God that she prayed to was different from the one that her mother-in-law seemed to know so much about, and that Jenna's was more sympathetic to her deep desire.

After a harried first seven days of Medrol to suppress her body's natural immunity and counteract her body's inclination to reject the embryo, and twelve weeks of hormones, ten months after implantation day of Baby G, Ellie was born. She was a healthy eight-pound, ten-ounce bundle of joy that made Jenna happier than she ever could have imagined.

The pediatrician that visited Ellie in the hospital described her as a "picture of health" and an "absolute miracle" (alluding to Ellie's conception via IVF), and while holding Ellie in her arms, Jenna let her mind blissfully wander to her next child. With endorphins surging, Jenna put aside the failed pregnancies and allowed herself to name her remaining embryos. The others would be named David, Mia, and Carson, and would be thawed and implanted in that order. She couldn't wait for her children to forge the fierce sibling bond that she, as an only child, had heard about but never experienced.

fifteen

In the years following the divorce, Ed did what he thought was best for Ellie, but like many divorcees, he went about it all wrong. He threw expensive gifts at her on birthdays and at Christmas, and had a decorator create a new "Ellie Suite" in his new apartment, but none of it was personal, and Ellie (as most children can) saw right through her father's attempt at buying her love and affection.

One Christmas when Ellie was fifteen, she opened a pretty orange box from her father. Inside was a Hermes scarf and low heeled calf-hide boots that were a beautiful shade of caramel— and a size seven. The only problem was that Ellie inherited Jenna's oversized feet and wore a size nine and a half—which made her wonder if the gift was meant for some other woman—Cassandra, maybe, or someone else—and Ed's assistant had simply mixed up the boxes, or if her father just never bothered to find out what size shoe his daughter wore. Either way, Ellie said nothing about the gift, and later that night, she stuffed the pretty orange box with the brown satin ribbon in the back of her closet with all the items still inside, angry with both her father and her mother for ruining yet another Christmas.

That same year, Ed surprised Ellie in March with an all-expenses-paid trip to the Bahamas for Spring Break. Ellie could choose four of her best friends from school to take with her. Ed did not go; instead, he insisted that Ellie's friends bring their own mothers along as chaperones. Ellie was beside herself excited about the trip until she mentioned her mother in front of Ed, at which point he told her that there was no way he was paying for Jenna to go on a tropical getaway.

"But all the other moms are going—" Ellie had countered when Ed blew up at the mention of Jenna's name. "And you are not going—who is going to be there with *me*?" Ed acted put out by the whole conversation and told Ellie angrily that if she preferred not to go at all, that was her choice, and he was disappointed that she would be so rude about his thoughtful gift.

"If you want to take someone so badly, take Cassandra with you," Ed had said, only half in jest. "Cass loves the Bahamas—it's where we spent our honeymoon, you know."

"No thanks," Ellie muttered and went to her room without another word. She curled up under her covers and cried herself to sleep that night, vowing to never get married in the first place, or if she did, not marry someone like her father.

In the end, Ellie went on the lavish Spring Break trip with her friends Callie, Elisabeth, Mary Claire, and Bea, along with their mothers. It was *fine*, but not the trip that Ellie had envisioned. She lied and told her mother that Mary Claire's mom set up the whole trip, and while she *wished* that Jenna could join them, the bungalow that Mary Claire's mom rented only had room for ten and Mary Claire's older sister, Stephanie, wanted to tag along. Jenna might have believed Ellie, except that she took the story too far, adding some silly detail about how Stephanie hadn't been home from college in two years and it was *really* important that she go on the trip. Jenna let it go and hugged Ellie tight, telling her to relax and have a great trip.

The custody part of the divorce had been particularly messy. In the end, it was decided that Ellie would see her dad every other weekend per the court order, and live with Jenna full time. Despite this agreement, all too often Ed would text Jenna late in the day on Friday (because she knew that it was the most untrue), "Tell Ellie that I promise to make it up to her next time."

On these occasions, Ellie was half tempted to tell her father that if he was going to miss one of their weekends, he should tell his girlfriend Cassandra not to post pictures of their Bahamian getaways on Instagram, but she never did. She certainly never told Ed or Cassandra that her own Instagram name was Luckynumber9 and that Cassandra allowed Ellie to follow her posts without even bothering to see who Luckynumber9 really was. At first, it had been thrilling for Ellie, trolling her stepmother's Instagram feed. But after a while, when neither Cassandra nor her father seemed to care who followed them online, the game lost its fun and Ellie found herself nothing but hurt and angry. It was easier just to stay quiet, she decided.

And this was how the next few years rambled on—the three of them (Ed, Jenna, and Ellie) playing their parts, staying more, or less, calm; no yelling, no fighting, just living odd parallel lives of silent acquiescence. Ellie went off to college in Boston, and Jenna slipped farther and farther away from everyone.

After the divorce was final, Cassandra moved into Ed's penthouse apartment on West Seventy-Fifth Street. Jenna wasn't one to read society magazines, she found them ridiculous and shallow, but her friends told her about the constant pictures of Cassandra and Ed, donating a new wing to the library one week, and unveiling a new reptile house at the public zoo the next. "Good for her," was all Jenna would ever say in response, and for the most part, she felt no hard feelings for Cassandra. Yes, she had been the affair that had broken her marriage, but really, she was just the straw that broke the camel's back; there had been so many before Cassandra, and Jenna guessed that there would be many more after her as well.

***

But that was now years ago. Ellie finished college and toyed with the idea of staying in Boston after graduation. She got into a graduate studies program and spent the next two years working in a dive restaurant near her apartment and studying. She missed her mother, but she loved being out of New York, and having friends, and a life of her own for once, without someone mentioning her parents and the *messy* divorce. Despite this, she worried too much about Jenna and, in the end, moved back to the city after her graduate program ended and secured a position as a school counselor in a fancy private school for early learners (grades K through five). She was leading the safe, happy life that Jenna had hoped for her only child. Ellie married her college sweetheart, Kevin, and Jenna approved of her son-in-law wholeheartedly, seeing Kevin as the somewhat goofy but incredibly kind and loving complement to her serious daughter. Ellie and Kevin's dynamic appeared to be nothing like what Jenna had with Ed; they were kind and respectful to one another instead of jealous and competitive, and Jenna took this as a sign that her daughter's marriage may have a chance at defying national divorce averages and last. She hoped so, at least. Going through a divorce was something that she would shield Ellie from with all her might if possible.

After Ellie graduated from college, and even more so after the wedding, Jenna and Ed no longer had a reason to communicate regularly, or at all. It was a weight lifted off Jenna that Ellie could sense, and she felt comforted that her mother could now live her life completely free of her father.

But in 2017, all of that changed. One of the main ingredients in a chemical that MCE produced for its popular brand of weed killer was deemed a "lethal carcinogen likely to have caused death in thousands of people" by a New Jersey court, and a multimillion-dollar class-action lawsuit was launched against MCE and all officers of the board who had knowledge that the chemical known as "red nitrite 15" had been in use by MCE plants for half a century.

Ed's father, Ed Mountain Jr., resigned from the board amidst the allegations and lawsuit, and several of Ed's cousins left MCE under the cover of darkness, retreating to second homes in the Caribbean and Cape Cod to wait out the firestorm of media attention.

Ed and his grandfather were the only two Mountains left to answer to the lawsuit brought against MCE for over $300 million. Jenna kept up with the trial through Ellie and from tidbits that she could get from local news stations, but she knew her ex-husband and she knew that for Ed, watching his grandfather's company go down in flames right before everyone's eyes was killing him. And in the end, it did. Edward Clinton Mountain III died of a sudden heart attack on November 7, 2017. He was found in his office, on the floor behind his desk. He was sixty-one years old.

Ed's mother, Regina, called Jenna from Birmingham and broke the news in a syrupy upper-crust Alabama drawl. Just as Jenna was wondering why Regina Mountain would take the time to call her for any reason, much less to tell her about the death of her ex-husband, Regina revealed to Jenna that no one had yet spoken to Ellie, and it would be "oh so helpful, honey, if you could call her and let her know."

"Sure, Regina," Jenna had said. "I will call Ellie. No worries. I am so sorry for your loss. It's been a lot of years—" Regina cut Jenna off midsentence.

"Life goes on, sweetie. One of these days you'll realize that too," was all that Regina said before hanging up the phone.

sixteen

America is ruled not by ethics, but by law.

— Dr. Steen Willadsen, *New York Times*

"**M**om?" Ellie knocked on her mother's apartment door. "Mom? I'm coming in."

Ellie put her key into the lock of apartment 32B, her mother's home for the past fifteen years. After the trial, Jenna never truly recovered. She held herself together as best as she could for Ellie's sake, but when Ellie went to college in Boston, she knew that her mother became an all-out recluse. Jenna had begun painting during that same time, but as far as Ellie could tell, the paintings were the same every time—large, circular abstract paintings with spherical shapes in the center—eight to be exact—the same number of cells that a three-day-old embryo has before it is frozen, the same number of cells that Mia had. The canvases were large and filled up the tiny apartment. Some of the pieces were gray and white and others were painted in brightly colored primary colors like red or yellow. But every time, the subject, though appearing abstract, was the same, eight cells signifying a lifetime of hope.

In addition to the canvases, Jenna's apartment was littered with trash of all kinds. Ellie never discussed her mother's settlement in the divorce, but she knew that Ed had handed over a hefty amount to make Jenna quietly go away. What Ellie did know was that her mother had enough money to afford a housekeeper, which she needed desperately, but from the looks of Jenna's apartment, the woman had apparently not stepped foot in the apartment in weeks. Newspaper clippings, cat litter (both in the box and scattered around the living room floor because one of the cats, Pepper, preferred to kick the litter out of the box before peeing on it), and Chinese takeout containers covered every surface. On the corkboard in the kitchen, numerous pieces of scrap paper and newspaper articles were pinned one on top of another. One small piece of paper had Jenna's handwriting and said, "A person's a person no matter how small . . ." Ellie was not surprised by the quote. What did catch her eye and interest was the two-year-old article that was pinned directly next to the Dr. Seuss quote. The article was dated December 19, 2017. And though it was not current, Ellie did not remember seeing it there the last time she had been in her mother's apartment, so she stepped closer to the tacked paper and read the headline: "Twenty-Six-Year-Old Woman Has Baby with a Twenty-Four-Year-Old Frozen Embryo." The clipping was from the *Chicago Tribune* and touted the news that a Tennessee couple, Tina and Benjamin Gibson, adopted an embryo from the National Embryo Donation Center in Knoxville, Tennessee, and did not realize that the embryo that they chose from a list of over three hundred profiles had been frozen in time for over two decades.

Ellie didn't tell many people, even her closest friends, about Mia or her mother, or the fact that she may be getting a baby sister at the age of thirty-one. She figured most of her friends, however open-minded, would not understand. The article went on to say that the Gibsons turned to embryo adoption when they realized that Benjamin was sterile due to cystic fibrosis, and that embryo adoption was the only adoption path that allowed Tina to carry and deliver a baby of their own, even if the genetic makeup of baby Emma was different from both of her parents. Ellie found the article interesting and a little unsettling. Because despite the fact that she knew her sibling, Mia, would be put up for adoption when the time limit expired, she had not considered that anyone other than her mother would be interested in claiming an embryo to which they had no shared genetic material, and beyond that, one that had been frozen for so long.

"I didn't even know embryo adoption was a thing. That's *so* bizarre," Ellie's friend Rebecca said over lunch a few days later when Ellie told her about the twenty-four-year-old embryo from the article in her mother's kitchen. She wasn't sure why she brought it up, but if she was testing the waters on how the general public felt about frozen embryos, based on Rebecca's reaction, she got the answer that she was looking for. No one needed to know about Mia, ever.

Back in her mother's apartment, a cat jumped up onto the counter and began to eat out of one of the old rice boxes. Ellie picked up the cat and looked at it. She didn't recognize this one.

"Not another one," she said to herself out loud.

"Oh! You found Mr. Whiskers, I see," Jenna said, coming out from the bedroom. She was wearing the black sweatpants and top that she wore every day, except laundry day when she wore gray ones, and her hair was long and greasy looking. Ellie felt sympathy for her mother, but her sympathy was tinged with frustration. She had tried (hard) in the last few years to give Jenna advice on how to dress, how many cats were appropriate, and even how often one should bathe—suggestions that most grown children do not have to make to their parents. Each attempt had been fruitless, however, and ended with Jenna becoming defensive, and the visit would be ruined, so Ellie had begun to say less to her mother about anything, and Jenna looked more and more like the homeless people that slept outside Ellie's apartment building. It was better, Ellie had decided, to let her mother be who she wanted to be, but to check in on her often to make sure she was keeping herself alive. This time, though, Ellie couldn't keep her comments to herself.

"You know, Mom," she said, smiling, "I know that you are going for this whole eccentric thing," she waved her hand in a circular motion in her mother's direction, "but another cat? How many do you have? I'm worried that I am going to come over here one day and the damn cats will have attacked you and will be feasting on your dead body. And, didn't you hire a cleaning lady? When was the last time she was here?"

"Wow, aren't you a dark one," Jenna said, reaching down and picking up a gray tabby that had crawled out from under the sofa. "Numbers don't really mean much to me," she said coyly as she brushed her cheek against the cat's fur. "Oh, and yes, I do have a person that helps me clean—the term *cleaning lady* is very diminutive, in my opinion—and I gave her the week off. I think she was working through some personal issues last week when I saw her, so I told her that I would pay her two weeks in advance and she should take a little R&R."

"Okay . . . well, I guess that's nice of you, I hope that she gets better or whatever," Ellie said, stepping over two cats that lounged lazily in the middle of the entrance hallway. "But, going back to the cats, I'm pretty sure that three is the max for your building and there are at least ten in here—and those are just the ones I can see."

Jenna waved a hand playfully in her daughter's direction. "It's fine, sweetie. Nothing for you to worry about. Besides, if I get kicked out, then I just get to come live with you and Kevin."

Ellie laughed. "I know! That's what I'm worried about. But guess what—our building has a *no* pets policy, so Mr. Whiskers here, and his friends, would have to find someplace else to go."

"Stop," Jenna said, laughing too. "Kevin loves me; he would welcome me with open arms, even if you don't."

"Correct," Ellie said. "But his benevolence ends with one cat, I can assure you—the rest would be out on their ass, so to speak." Both women laughed, and it felt good for both of them to feel the old bond that they had once shared a long time ago. After the divorce, Jenna became distant and Ellie could not understand, so sadly they slowly grew apart. Ellie recently turned thirty, however, and she had decided that it was time to put her own frustration with her mother behind her and try to make amends with Jenna, whose birthday was fast approaching. She would be sixty-two.

But there was another reason that Ellie wanted to keep closer tabs on her mother these days. The date was almost here. The one that her mother had been waiting for over two decades to arrive. The date that sent Jenna into an emotional tailspin after the divorce and the date that she spent hundreds of hours of therapy in because she couldn't stop writing it in place of any other date. On checks, it was always July 28, 2019, no matter if it was January of 2007. On Ellie's school permission slips it was the same, every time: Jenna wrote 7-28-19, and Ellie would erase as much as she could and tell her teachers that her mom just made a mistake. That date, July 28, 2019, had been a wedge between mother and daughter for two decades, but it was also quite possibly the only thing that had kept Jenna from killing herself, and Ellie and Jenna both knew it.

After Ellie's father passed away suddenly of a heart attack, Jenna contacted an attorney to see if the contract with BabyGenix was now null and void. But, several thousands of dollars later (that Kevin and Ellie ended up paying because Jenna had been under the impression that the attorney would work pro bono for a good cause), the attorney determined that the death of Ed Mountain did not affect the contract because of the way it was written; the embryo was technically in possession of the cryogenic bank where it was frozen, not in custody of Ed Mountain. As long as the cryobank arm of BabyGenix remained open and operational, the contract stood, and embryo HN3-8B could not be put up for embryonic adoption until the twenty-year time limitation had expired.

seventeen

When the morning of July 28, 2019, finally arrived, Jenna found herself feeling a mix of emotions. She hadn't slept well in days, her stomach had been upset, and though her heart wanted to feel only happiness and excitement, something tiny and hidden deep inside warned her to be nervous. It was an unsettling feeling at best.

Until the night before, Jenna had not thought about the fact that she had not stepped foot in the BabyGenix facility since that awful day when she lost David and Carson twenty years before. She assumed that it was in the same location (over the years, she had checked periodically to make sure the lab had not moved or worse, closed). It was not unheard of for companies like BabyGenix to go out of business, in which case Ed would have been notified, not Jenna. But, according to the website, the lab was in the same location and had broadened its scope of fertility options substantially. Pictures of healthy babies held by smiling parents flashed across each page, and Jenna found her spirits lifting with each webpage that she opened.

She woke early on the twenty-eighth so she could be at BabyGenix as soon as it opened at nine a.m.. At seven a.m. she poured some refrigerated coffee over ice, read briefly through the day's *Wall Street Journal* (though her mind was anywhere but on Mia). At eight, she went to take a shower and realized that the water had been turned off in her apartment. She checked the sink faucet in the guest bathroom as well as in the kitchen, and sure enough, no water would flow forth from any of them. That's when she noticed a sheet of paper that must have been slipped under her door earlier that morning. She turned the paper over and read what she had already discovered, that due to a water main break in the adjoining building, water to her entire building would be shut off from seven a.m. until noon to repair the break. Scrawled across the bottom of the printed sheet, someone had written, "I am so sorry for the inconvenience!" Signed George.

"Well, that stinks," she said to Milo, her orange-and-white tabby, and newest addition to her brood of strays. She lifted her arm and made a sour face. "Actually, it's me that stinks. My apologies, Milo. Baby powder and dry shampoo will have to cut it today." She looked at the clock; it was 8:15. She would have to hurry if she was going to be there at nine. Kips Bay was not exactly close. "Okay," she said, speaking again to Milo, who looked up at her curiously, offering a faint meow in response, "let's go find something to wear."

Just then her phone rang, and Jenna looked at the screen. It was Ellie, and Jenna quickly swiped right to answer. "Hello, darling!" she said brightly.

"Hi, Mom!" Ellie echoed back. It sounded like she was in a wind tunnel.

"Where are you?" Jenna asked, holding the phone away from her ear when the whooshing became too loud.

"Out walking Ollie," Ellie huffed. "In the park. I'm near you actually and I just wanted you to know that I am thinking of you today."

"Thank you, sweetheart. You don't know how much I appreciate it, and how much I love you."

"I know you do," Ellie replied. There had been a time when Ellie finally had to share her feelings of resentment over Carson, David, and Mia with her mom. Her therapist had suggested it, and though Ellie knew that it was the right thing to do, it was also a very hard conversation to have with her mother. How can you ask someone to love you *more* than they love their other children? Can sibling rivalry exist without the existence of a sibling? Ellie knew that she was being nonsensical, but she had asked her mother for exactly that nonetheless.

To Ellie, her siblings were either ghosts of a dark and unspeakable past, or apparitions of an uncertain future. And though Ellie had tried her best to accept Mia's presence in her life, she couldn't help feeling that she had been cheated out of her mother's undivided love and attention for most of her life.

With that said, Ellie had to admit that in recent years, Jenna had tried to be more sensitive to her only living child's feelings and tried harder to hide the pain and scars brought about by her struggle with infertility.

"Are you sure you don't want me to go down there with you?" Ellie asked, still huffing, the sound of Ollie's collar jingling in the background.

"No, sweetheart, I can do it. Thank you for the offer, though. I will call you when I leave BabyGenix. There is nothing to worry about. I doubt that many people are busting down the door for a twenty-nine-year-old embryo."

"Okay, you are right. Nothing to worry about," Ellie said, though something in her gut told her different. Ever since she read the newspaper story about the couple in Tennessee that adopted a twenty-four-year-old embryo, she had a sinking feeling that her mother's plan for adopting Mia may not go as smoothly as she planned. What if there were other people, other couples, who would want to adopt Mia simply because she had been frozen so long—just to beat the record for the longest frozen embryo to be born? Ellie calmed herself and told herself that she was being silly. Her father had always said that her imagination ran away with her at times, and Ellie hoped that in this case, he was right.

By the time Jenna was dressed and finally out of the door it was nearing 8:45 a.m., and by the time her taxi ambled to the curb in front of BabyGenix it was 9:30 in the morning. Jenna got out of the cab and stood on the curb as the car pulled away. She looked up to a blue sky overhead, and took in the joy of the day, the importance of the day, the day that she had looked forward to for two decades.

The nondescript building where BabyGenix was housed looked the same from the outside as it had twenty years before. Plain and gray, only the sign on the street entrance door seemed to have changed. The BabyGenix logo was updated and featured bright-orange lettering and a heart layered over the text. Jenna pushed the call button outside the door and the call box buzzed. A staticky voice crackled through the receiver.

"What service are you here for today?" the voice asked.

Jenna leaned into the receiver and answered, "Embryo Adoption, please," and after a loud buzz the front door was unlocked, and Jenna stepped into the lower-level lobby.

If the outside of the building had remained unchanged, then the inside of the building was the complete opposite. Gleaming white marble floors led to a set of four elevators where there had previously only been one, and a security guard sat like a statue behind a large, clear glass desk, a high stark-white leather banquette just opposite him. There were several pieces of modern art hung on the walls, and some kind of strange-looking sculpture that, to the best Jenna could tell, was supposed to be in the shape of a uterus and baby stood tall in one corner. Jenna looked at the elevator marquee and noted how many more names were now listed than before. She had no idea who any of these providers were and was thankful to see Dr. Daugherty's name still listed under the fourth-floor listing. In all caps, EMBRYO ADOPTION INQUIRIES was listed as being on the sixth floor.

The elevator glided smoothly up six flights as light jazz music played, piped in through speakers expertly hidden in the all-mirror walls. This was not the BabyGenix that Jenna remembered. This was some swankier version of BabyGenix and Jenna began to wonder how many other things would be different about the clinic. When the elevator doors lightly dinged and opened to the interior lobby of the sixth floor, Jenna was shocked to see that the waiting area was even more luxurious than the street-level lobby. Textured white and pale-green leather club chairs lined the walls, and on each of the several Lucite side tables were brochures about an array of topics ranging from "How to Raise a Family If You Are Infertile" to "Gay Men Can Be Parents Too." Beyond the physical appearance of the waiting area, Jenna could not believe how crowded it was. There must have been thirty chairs divided into two spaces, and every seat was taken, with several couples standing in corners whispering to one another with looks of eager anticipation on their faces.

Once Jenna's eyes could focus on something other than how much the office had changed, she saw a youngish girl, probably in her midtwenties, sitting behind a desk, typing away on the computer in front of her, a clipboard sitting just in front of her keyboard. Jenna walked over to see what the clipboard said, and the girl looked up.

"Oh, hello there, how can I help you?" Her accent was Southern, and she smiled a wide toothy smile in Jenna's direction. Whenever Jenna heard a Southern accent in the city, it made her glad that after more than thirty years in Manhattan, she had finally almost lost hers. She remembered her first job interview after graduating from law school, and how the HR manager at one of the big firms had howled in laughter after Jenna introduced herself. After that, she vowed never to let her Southern background show, at least not when it mattered.

"I am here about embryo adoption," Jenna said, trying to speak softly. She peeked behind her to see if anyone could hear her, but not one of the people in the waiting area looked up from their smartphone.

"Perfect," replied the girl. She pushed her hot-pink tortoise-rimmed glasses up on her nose and handed Jenna a clipboard, different than the one sitting on the desk. "I just need for you to sign in here—" she pointed to the board on her desk—"and then fill out the paperwork here—" pointing to the clipboard now in Jenna's left hand. "Oh, and we will need a preliminary blood test. It is standard for all prospective parents. The bloodwork office is on the second floor—but you can do that on your way out if you would like."

"Oh," Jenna said, a little taken aback. What was all of this? The paperwork held to the clipboard in her hand must have been twenty pages thick. "I don't think I—" She was starting to read over the first page when the receptionist interrupted her thoughts.

"Every person that applies for an embryo must fill out the paperwork, ma'am. You are welcome to fill out the paperwork in the waiting area," and she pointed toward the crowded room. And then, to Jenna's shock, the girl added, "The good news is that BabyGenix does not require those silly home visits like other clinics. Once you are approved from your paperwork, you can begin the prep for your mock transfer. But, oh wait," the girl paused and looked at Jenna's face for a second longer than Jenna felt was comfortable, "are you the person adopting, or is this for a family member, like maybe a daughter or son? If so, they will need to fill out the paperwork in person."

Without thinking, Jenna's hand went to her long bangs and she tucked them behind her ear to cover the gray that had infiltrated her hairline in recent years. She was suddenly self-conscious of her age (sixty-two next month) and more than a little embarrassed by the girl's question.

Jenna nodded and said, "Of course," choosing not to answer the question positively or negatively, and turned to look for a place to privately look over what the girl had given her. The first several pages asked a million questions about her health history. Had she ever been diagnosed with cancer? No. Had she or any member of her family ever been diagnosed with cystic fibrosis? No—and on and on. Her pen paused and hovered over the section of the questionnaire labeled Mental Health. *Have you ever been diagnosed with depression?* She tapped the pen against the paper in thought. *How honest does one have to be on general health forms?* Jenna asked herself. Without much thought, she checked the box marked No and moved on.

The second section of the paperwork had to do with the financial obligations of the adopting parent. There were payment plan options, private financing options, and even a section for a request for financial aid in the event the adoptive parent could not cover the costs associated with the adoption. Included in the same section were required name and contact information for the attorney handling the adoption. Jenna had not even thought about needing an attorney, but it made sense to her. In most cases, the adoptive parents were surely worried about the parental rights of the donor parents, but in this case, Ed was dead, and Jenna was the genetic mother, so there was no issue there. She listed her own name and address under LEGAL COUNSEL and moved on to the third section, seemingly countless requests for Jenna's initials acknowledging the "imperfect science of assisted reproductive technology (ART) including and not limited to the process and procedures performed during in vitro fertilization (IVF)" and that BabyGenix would not be held responsible or liable for any transfers that did not result in pregnancy or full-term birth.

Finally, Jenna came to the last section of the paperwork, and she was stunned by what she saw. At the top of the page was the oval outline of a baby's face. The form asked that Jenna fill in her *ideal* genetic characteristics by drawing in facial features (large or small nose, green eyes or brown, full lips or thin) and to list her *ethnicity preference* on the provided template. *Is this really what IVF has become?* Jenna wondered. She just wanted her own baby back, not to order the *perfect* baby from a catalog.

The form continued with questions underneath the drawing. *What personality traits are you most drawn to? Is intelligence of the donor parents of interest to you? What about athletic ability of the donor parents? Please list here any activities that you enjoy, e.g. mountain biking, rock climbing, sailing, taking vacations abroad . . . This will help the BG team match you up with the ideal donor family and embryo so you and your child can enjoy similar activities in the future. And* finally, at the very bottom, as if an afterthought, a single empty box could be checked to pay for additional reprogenetics testing to rule out diseases and syndromes like cystic fibrosis and Down syndrome. Jenna did not make any marks on the final section and instead took her clipboard back up to the desk and the girl with the tortoise glasses.

"All finished?" the girl asked and reached out to take the clipboard from Jenna's hand.

"Not exactly," Jenna replied. "You see, I'm not here to choose an embryo. I already know which one I want." The girl looked confused. "Here," Jenna said quietly, and she pulled a small piece of paper from her purse. It was the original copy of Ed and Jenna's egg harvest from BabyGenix confirming the viability of her embryos A, B, and C and the cryogenic storage agreement. It was printed on the old-style computer paper used in the '90s, the kind with perforated edges on two sides. "See," she said, handing the paper to the girl and pointing in the center, "I want HN3-8B."

The girl looked at the paper and squinted. Then she said, "One minute," and got up with Jenna's printout in her hand and walked to the back of the receptionist's area and out of sight. Several minutes later, an older woman, but not one recognizable to Jenna from before, sat in the receptionist's chair and pecked away at the computer without addressing Jenna. The woman had short gray hair that was wild and curly and seemed to stick straight out from her head. She set a coffee mug down next to the keyboard that said "You can't make Man without WOman," and in any other situation, Jenna would have asked her what in the world that meant, or what sort of sentiment it was supposed to evoke. It was the same with odd bumper stickers; Jenna never understood the point of displaying them if the message was so obscure that no one understood what they meant.

"This is not how the adoption process works, ma'am, but for the record, that embryo is not even available," she said gruffly and stood up to walk back to her hidden office in the back of the room, obscure coffee mug in hand. The woman walked with a slight limp and set Jenna's printout down on a stack of papers just behind the receptionist's desk as she walked away.

"Wait!" Jenna said louder than she intended, and the woman turned around, half scowling as she did so. "What do you mean not available? That is *my* embryo. Maybe you typed the wrong letters in? Can you please check again? Please?"

The woman did not seem to be a person that was swayed by begging, and Jenna realized that must be how she sounded, but there must be some mistake. Where else would Mia be if not still snugly waiting in storage at BabyGenix? The gray-haired woman rolled her eyes but walked back over to the receptionist's computer, pulled her reading glasses dramatically down her nose, squinted at the screen, and then to the piece of paper again. She sighed loudly.

"That embryo is here, but it is not available for adoption. Mystery solved, case closed," she said unapologetically.

"No, that's not right." Jenna shook her head. "The date, please check the dates in your records. That embryo is available for adoption as of today, the twenty-eighth of July. Please, I have been waiting a long time—"

"Lady," the older woman said, "I don't know who you are—"

"Jenna Ellis," Jenna cut in.

"Okay, Jenna Ellis," the woman continued curtly, "you are correct. HN3-8B was available for adoption as of today. Despite what you may believe, I have all of the pertinent information right here in the computer. HN3-8B was released into the adoptive pool at 12:01 this morning. But it has already been assigned an adoptive parent. The application was filled out this morning—at 9:25 a.m., it appears. So, it is no longer available. You are more than welcome to choose from our many other available embryos—it's all there in the packet that you received at check-in." The gray-haired woman turned her back and walked away. Jenna's world began to spin. She clutched the top of the desk to keep herself steady. She felt hot and the act of breathing hurt in her chest. Each time she inhaled it felt like fire. A tightening that began in her throat coiled up her neck like a snake and continued its deadly traverse across her face.

"How is that possible?" she said quietly. "Another adoptive parent? You only opened at nine o'clock this morning, how could someone else have already put in an application?" Jenna was livid, shocked, and devastated all at once. And then suddenly she felt out of control.

"You *can't* give my baby to someone else!" she screamed at no one, holding her hair with both hands, and with that, every person previously engrossed in their smartphones looked up and stared at her, not with fear but with intrigue. Only in New York is a screaming lunatic interesting instead of scary.

The young receptionist stared blankly at Jenna. She was the only one that seemed slightly afraid. The gray-haired woman looked angry. No one told her what to do on her turf. Someone in the waiting area stifled a laugh and tried to pass it off as a cough.

"Ma'am," the gray-haired woman said, "I am going to ask you *one* time to respectfully leave this office immediately." She spoke clearly and slowly. "If you do not, then Hannah here," pointing to the receptionist, who was definitely now afraid, "is going to call security and the police."

And for the second time in her life, Jenna Ellis fainted at BabyGenix, her body falling hard to the floor with a thud, and this time, Gunnar Sharp was not there to break her fall.

eighteen

Cassandra Mountain squinted at the sun and pulled her oversized Chanel sunglasses down over her eyes. What a good day it was turning out to be. She had her usual 6:30 a.m. workout with her trainer, Luis, a mani-pedi at eight with SuSu, the best nail lady in Manhattan hands down, and then she went and bought a baby at nine. *I am the most productive that I've been in years,* she thought, and she silently applauded herself for her ingenuity and industriousness. Those were some of the characteristics that Ed always loved about her. He never said it, of course, but she knew what made a woman attractive: women that were tough as nails and went out and got what they wanted, unlike weak and shy women like Jenna who shrank away from any form of conflict—that was for losers. Cassandra thought back to the insufferable dinners that Ed insisted they have with Ellie, every two weeks, in the early days of their marriage. It was all Cassandra could do not to let her eyes roll right out of her head listening to that brat, Ellie, drone on and on about her mother and Mia. But now, the tables had turned, and Cassandra was grateful to her stepdaughter. If Ellie had not talked incessantly about July 28, Cassandra would have missed the date entirely. Cassandra smiled. Ellie had unknowingly handed over the key to a bright financial future. Sucking in a deep breath, she blew out a sigh of relief. It had all been worth it. Every last second. She looked down at her gold Patek Phillipe; she needed to get back up town. Next on her Monday to-do list was meeting her mother for lunch. Cassandra pulled her phone from her purse and began pecking away.

"Meet me at SA on Madison at noon—I have BIG news." Cassandra added a smiley face emoji, a double heart, and a tiny bottle of uncorked champagne before she clicked Send. Maybe she could sprint into Bergdorf's to pick up a little treat for herself and something for Mama on her way. Today was about celebrating, after all. She twisted the large ring that she still wore on her left hand. And to think that she had considered selling the four-carat Harry Winston diamond that Ed proposed to her with on the first Valentine's Day after his divorce was final—that was a close call. *No need to sell it now,* she thought. Her financial worries were over.

nineteen

J enna barely remembered being carried out of the BabyGenix adoption waiting area, down the elevator, and outside to the curb, but that was where she found herself when she regained full consciousness, propped against the building not too close to the front door, with her purse gently perched on her lap. She registered some pain in her right hip and gingerly felt a welt that was taking shape on her forehead. She must have hit something on her way down and wondered if what she had just experienced was real or if she was having a nightmare. She faintly remembered someone making mention of Bellevue while she was being carried out, and like a child, she pinched herself hard on the arm and said audibly, "Wake up, Jenna. Wake up."

A woman walking by on the sidewalk stepped around Jenna's outstretched legs and scowled. Jenna pulled her knees in close to her chest and put her head between her knees. *Breathe in, breathe out,* she told herself. When she lifted her head again she noticed that there were a lot of passersby—it was midmorning, after all—but not one of them stopped or even looked down to take notice of Jenna propped against the side of the building. This was one of the things that she did not enjoy about New York—everyone was a stranger. She put her head back down on her knees and closed her eyes so she wouldn't have to look at all the people not looking at her.

"There you are! I was wondering where they had stashed you." A voice broke Jenna's thought. She looked up and saw Dr. Daugherty standing over her.

"How—" Jenna tried to speak, but the words stuck in the back of her throat. She felt like she was in a trance, not sure of where she was or even who she was anymore.

"I heard all of the commotion from my office, but I wasn't really interested in what was going on until one of the nurses poked her head in and said that a woman had fainted in the lobby. You were the first person I thought of."

"Where—" Jenna tried to clear her throat and coughed. She rubbed the now fully fledged knot on her forehead. There was no Gunnar to catch her fall this time, no cool wet cloth, or someone to help her to the ladies' room where she could recover herself in private. She had been taken out of the building like a crazy person and discarded onto the New York City sidewalk. "Where's Mia?" she finally coughed out.

Dr. Daugherty sighed. "I don't know," she said. "But I'll look into it." She gazed down at Jenna, broken, disheveled, in shock, and a shadow of the woman that she met twenty-nine years before. That Jenna had been baby obsessed, yes, but she also had the youthful glow of a woman who was intelligent, optimistic, energetic, and resilient. All of that was gone now. Dr. Daugherty pulled a small, rectangular white box from her lab coat and smacked it hard into her left palm. Then, she opened the box and let a single cigarette fall from the pouch. She slid down the wall to sit next to Jenna with her legs outstretched—New Yorkers could walk around them—and sucked in strongly as she lit her cigarette, turning her head and blowing the first gasp of smoke away from Jenna's direction.

"Did I ever tell you about Elsa Rios?" she asked Jenna. Jenna shook her head no, but did not lift it from her knees.

"Well, she reminds me of you, or you remind me of her. I can't tell which," Christine continued. "She, too, wanted a baby more than anything." Dr. Daugherty paused to take a deep drag from her cigarette and then blew the smoke upward.

"She was thirty-seven years old when I met her. She and her husband, Mario, came all the way from Los Angeles to Melbourne—all in hopes that there was still a chance that she could conceive and have a baby of her own. No IVF clinic in the US would take her because of her age—can you believe that? Thirty-seven is in your prime by today's standards. Ridiculous." Christine looked at Jenna for a response, and when she finally got a gentle nod no, she continued her story, speaking calmly and methodically. "Anyhow, to make matters worse, Elsa's only daughter, Claudia, had died just a few years before. Gunshot wound to the forehead is what I heard, but to be honest I never asked Elsa about it. The girl was ten years old, poor child. LAPD said it was an accidental shooting, but Mario and Elsa never believed that. They believed that their only daughter had been brutally murdered in their own home one afternoon when Mario and Elsa were out of the house and Claudia was home alone. Mario found her lying on her bed, the gun beside her. That's why they came to see us in Melbourne, to have another child and replace the one that they lost." Dr. Daugherty paused her story and took another few slow drags from her cigarette. She waited for Jenna to speak next. She needed to get Jenna engaged in conversation, similar to the act of sobering up a drunk.

"Did she get pregnant?" Jenna finally asked. Her voice was small and weak, but Christine was glad to hear it. Christine thought about how to tell the rest of the story. How much to tell Jenna.

"No," she answered, picking a few stray pieces of lint from her black work pants, "she didn't, unfortunately. We retrieved three eggs and fertilized them. At the first transfer it appeared that Elsa had become pregnant, but she lost the embryo around ten days later. She never had the chance to transfer the other two. Elsa and Mario died two years later in a plane crash in South America. When our team in Melbourne heard the news, we were all devastated. Such a tragic ending to a tragic life." Christine took one last pull on her cigarette and then stubbed it out on the concrete sidewalk.

"Where's Mia?" Jenna asked again. A long pause filled the hot stagnant air of the city.

"I don't know," Christine said at last, "but as I said, I'll find out. Here—hold on for one minute."

Dr. Daugherty pulled her cell phone from her lab coat pocket and began scrolling through it. Jenna let her head fall back against the brick and she closed her eyes, still hoping that she was trapped in some kind of nightmarish dream. She heard the tearing of paper and opened her eyes. Dr. Daugherty had stood up and was holding out a small piece of paper that had been torn out of her prescription pad to her.

"Here, take this name and number. Her name is Susan Solaro. She is an attorney that specializes in reproductive law. Give her a call—today. I will see what I can find out about who filed the application for HN3-8B, but in the meantime, call Susan and then get some rest. You will need the energy if you are going to fight for your embryo."

"You remember the lab numbers for Mia?"

"Of course I do, Jenna, I could never forget it. I am not an emotional person, per se, but I know when something is important," Dr. Daugherty replied in her no-nonsense way. "Let's get you a cab." Just then, Dr. Daugherty's cell phone rang loudly in her pocket. She reached down and looked at the caller ID. "It's my son. I've got to take this," she said as she turned to walk back into the building. Just before answering, she turned back to Jenna. "Call Susan as soon as you get to your apartment." And then she answered her phone and disappeared into the lobby.

As Dr. Daugherty was going back in, someone else was rushing out. A middle-aged man with graying temples nearly ran into Christine as he came running out of the front door, where he abruptly stopped, and frantically looked down each side of the sidewalk until his eyes rested on Jenna. He ran toward where she still sat, her back propped up against the building.

"Ms. Ellis!" he cried, his accent still strong after nearly twenty years in New York. "What has happened to you?"

Jenna looked up at the man. He had aged, and not very well, over the last two decades, but there was no mistaking who he was. "Gunnar," she said in a croak, "it's so good to see you." She coughed again. "How did you know that I was here?"

"I heard someone say that a woman fainted in the adoption area and you were the first person that came to mind," he said matter-of-factly.

In her previous life, the old Jenna would have had a sarcastic quip for him as a comeback, but the Jenna of the present could barely bring any words to mind and thoughts that drifted to one name and one name only—Mia.

"Let's get you into a cab, Ms. Ellis. Do you need for me to help you home?"

"No," she said, "I can do it. But I can't get up."

Gunnar leaned down and put his strong hands underneath both of Jenna's arms and lifted her up to standing position. She swayed and he held firm to her while she steadied herself. He saw a yellow cab turn down Second Avenue and waved his arm to signal for it to stop.

"There you are," he said gently as he walked Jenna toward the curb, his arms still fully supporting her weight. He opened the door to the cab. "Upper East Side," he said and then, "She can give you the address." Gunnar poured Jenna Ellis into the cab, closed the door, and watched the taxi pull away from the curb. He had wanted to tell her why he was still at BabyGenix, why, despite wanting to, he could not leave during these last twenty years, but it had not seemed the right time. His wife—ex-wife (he was still getting used to the sound of it, though she left him five years before)—wanted Gunnar to find a job in a hospital, a "real medical hospital, not one for making monsters," she had said about BabyGenix. But Gunnar couldn't confess to her his reason for staying at BabyGenix. She wouldn't have understood. She had not been there the day that Jenna fainted (the first time) and had not seen all the life sucked out of a person the way that it had been sucked out of Jenna Ellis the day that two of her three frozen embryos were destroyed. The image of Jenna's transformation that day had stuck with him all these years, and that was why he stayed at BabyGenix—to watch over Mia, to make sure she was safe until the time limit was up and Jenna could come and retrieve her. It was a ridiculous notion, he knew; HN3-8B was not a person, it was merely a collection of eight cells containing genetic material that took up space less than that of a period on his phone.

But to Ms. Ellis, HN3-8B was not a medical specimen, she was a potential person, a *snowflake baby*, as frozen embryos were beginning to be called because of their frozen and unique nature. HN3-8B was Ms. Ellis's child, and he would do everything that he could to help her get Mia back.

Meanwhile, in the cab, Jenna's thoughts drifted. She muted the tiny TV screen on the back of the cab driver's seat to stop the noise, but she couldn't do anything about the flashing of the commercial changes. She felt sick. She put her face in her hands and an odd memory came back to her. As hard as she tried, she couldn't push it back down.

***

It was Christmas 1989, and as soon as Jenna had entered the corporate ballroom, she wanted to run right back out again immediately. The annual MCE Christmas party was the last place she wanted to be. Held in MCE's building on the seventeenth floor, the cavernous room had sweeping views over the East River and the Brooklyn Bridge, and although it was beautifully decorated as always, it never ceased to amaze Jenna that amongst all the glittering chandeliers, glasses of champagne, and artfully constructed hors d'oeuvres, she could not find a single normal person to talk to. Beyond that, it bothered her that a company as large as MCE could put so much emphasis on Christmas, with the party, the visit from Santa mid-December when employees were encouraged to pull their kids out of school, and the incredibly expensive decorating that, strangely enough, was put up by the Human Resources department.

"I would hate to be a Jewish employee of MCE, or heaven forbid, any other religion other than Christian," Jenna had remarked to Ed at last year's party. Ed had rolled his eyes and accused her of becoming more and more of a liberal with each passing day.

"Didn't you grow up in North Carolina?" he had asked with a frown.

"That has nothing to do with—" Jenna paused and decided that it wasn't worth the argument. "Never mind. You are right. I shouldn't have said anything." But Ed had already turned away from her, and she could tell that his mind was elsewhere. She wondered on *whom*.

Jenna was brought back to the present when Ed cupped her left elbow with his hand in preparation for the elevator to stop. "This should be fun," Jenna said, trying to sound upbeat.

"At least we finally cut the admin staff this year," Ed snorted when the elevator doors opened. "You couldn't pay me enough money to socialize with those degenerates for another year." He tugged at his bow tie and turned to Jenna, who noticed the elevator attendant flinch ever so slightly at Ed's remark, so she had smiled at him, hoping that the elderly man took her smile for its intention—an apology for her husband. "Is this thing straight or not?" Ed asked irritably. "I can never get these damned things straight."

"It's fine, sweetheart, you look great," Jenna replied soothingly as they walked down the long corridor toward loud music and the sound of a crowded room. "Just leave it alone and it will look fine."

"You know I don't trust your judgment, right?" Ed replied under his breath. Jenna reached up to pick a piece of lint from Ed's shoulder and he swatted her hand away childishly. "I don't need you to be my mother," he said gloomily just before smiling broadly and taking his hand away from Jenna's elbow. "Jack!" he bellowed to a red-faced man in his midthirties, "What's shakin', man?" he said, giving the man a playful punch in the arm.

"Not too much man, not too much," the man replied. A blonde

suddenly appeared at Jack's side and the several seconds that Ed stared at the woman up and down embarrassed Jenna for the second time in the past five minutes.

"This is Stephanie," Jack introduced, and the woman held out a slender hand toward Ed.

"Very nice to make your acquaintance, Mr. Mountain," she said in a heavy European accent. "I have heard much about you."

"Well," Ed said slowly, staring intensely at Jack's date, "the pleasure is all mine." He turned to Jack and spoke as if he wasn't standing right in front him. "I don't know where in the hell Jack Rogers finds all of the beautiful women." Jack blushed and pulled his date in for a tight squeeze, clearly proud of the prize date he had landed and the fact that he had impressed his boss.

"Stephanie's a model," he said arrogantly, though Jenna thought that the comment sounded like one a teenage boy would make. She looked down to keep from making a face. "Well, we are heading back to the bar, Ed, I'll catch you later," Jack said, and then as an afterthought, he turned his head around as he walked away. "Good to see you, Jenna. Keep an eye on your tiger tonight."

Jack and Stephanie walked away, and before Jenna could fully digest what Jack had said, another man hooked his arm around Ed's neck and pretended to choke him. A woman, even more perfect looking than Stephanie, stood just out of reach of Ed's mock flailing arms.

"*Where* have you been?! The party's half over already—did you find a better one to pregame at first? You did, you son of a bitch!" The man was clearly drunk and took his arm off Ed's neck only so he could grab a glass of champagne from the tray of a passing server. He offered one to Ed, who laughed and took two glasses from the tray, handing one to Jenna.

"Jenna, meet Dan O'Hara. Dan, this is my wife, Jenna." Jenna

169

put her hand out to shake hands with Dan, but he had already turned his attention back to Ed, so her hand hung loosely and embarrassingly in the empty space between them until she put it back by her side. Ed did not notice, and obviously Dan did not either, as he had already moved on in his conversation with Ed.

"When are we getting out of here, dude, it's super lame—no offence, of course, since this—" Dan waved his hand in the air dramatically—"is kind of your deal."

"None taken, my man," Ed laughed. "But we just got here, so I need to do the rounds before I can skip out. Oh," Ed put his finger to his head to show that he had suddenly remembered something, "Jenna, you need to talk with—" he pointed in the direction of the woman standing next to Dan and hesitated. This happened often when Ed didn't know a person's name. Usually out of respect or avoidance of awkwardness, the person would quickly say their name out loud. This woman just stared back at Ed. Jenna liked her immediately.

"Oh!" Dan smacked his forehead. "I'm such a jerk. Honey, this is Ed Mountain. Ed, this is my girlfriend Zara." As if a switch had been flipped, the woman smiled, extended her hand. Jenna watched the woman's eyes as they did a once-over of *the* Ed Mountain. When she spoke, she sounded as if Ed was a long-lost high school boyfriend. Unfortunately, by this point, Jenna was used to other women fawning over her husband in public.

"Ed Mountain," she said charmingly, "I am so glad to finally meet you. I'm glad to see that at least one of Dan's playmates is a sensible guy—and by that, I mean employed," she laughed, and the rest of the group laughed too. Then she turned to Jenna. "Hi sweetie, I'm Zara. It is a pleasure to meet you as well." Jenna took her outstretched hand in her own and noticed Zara's firm grip. There was no way Zara was older than Jenna, and if anything, she looked as if she was a few years younger. Who called another person *sweetie*? The condescending ones, that was who. Jenna wanted to hate her, but there was something interesting about Zara, something rebellious that was appealing—or maybe it was just that she was, by all physical measurements, generally appealing to look at.

"Yes, of course," Ed said, snapping his fingers high in the air. "Zara." Ed stared for an embarrassingly long time at his employee's girlfriend. "I assure you, it is not because you are forgettable." Zara smiled and touched Ed's upper arm lightly. When Ed finally snapped back to reality, he acted as if the whole awkward situation had never happened.

"Zara, this is my wife, Jenna. You guys should have a lot to talk about." He turned to Jenna and winked. "This is the girl I was telling you about—the IVF one." Jenna almost spit her champagne all over Ed's shirt in surprise. How could he be so embarrassing?

"Oh honey," Jenna said, trying to stay calm, a plastered smile across her face. "That is hardly talk for a cocktail party. I doubt that Zara even—"

"Nonsense!" Ed bellowed. Dan's arm was around Ed's neck. "She'd love to talk about it. Right, Danny boy?"

Dan drained the last few drops of his champagne and put his arm around Ed's shoulder. "Right! Ladies, we are headed to the bar—you stay here and chat, or whatever it is that women do at these lame events."

Jenna wanted to say, *No, don't leave me,* and she wanted to call Ed out on how rude his behavior was toward both Zara and herself. She hated it when he pawned her off on random people for her to talk to while he made his way around a room, but this time, despite her embarrassment, she wasn't altogether upset about being left alone with Zara.

With the men gone Jenna turned to Zara. "I am so sorry for—"

Zara waved a hand in the air as she gulped the last of her champagne and grabbed another from a passing tray. "Honey, don't be," she said to Jenna. "Seriously, not a worry. I'm not that sensitive anyway. So . . ." Zara said, taking a sip of her drink, "you are thinking about IVF?"

Instinctively Jenna looked around to see who may be listening to their conversation. After infertility was confirmed by her OB-GYN, Jenna felt waves of shame, fear, sadness, and frustration, but most of all alienation. Despite what her doctor had told her—that thousands if not millions of women are unable to conceive naturally every year—it did not stop the bleeding wound that Jenna felt every time another month passed without a baby.

"We are thinking about it," she said shyly. "I'm not sure if Ed will get on board or not. A lot to think about."

"True," Zara said, squinting her eyes as if she was concentrating hard on her words. "But just remember that Ed may never get on board. Sometimes the woman has to take matters into her own hands. You need something that is just yours, you know?"

"I guess," Jenna said slowly, unsure where Zara was going, "but I don't think of a baby as just mine. It would be both of ours—just like for you and Dan."

"You know Dan and I are not even married, right?" Zara said, looking around the room. When she saw Jenna's eyes go to the large ring on her left hand, she put her hand out in front to show it off. "He did finally buy me a ring, but I had to pick it out. I even paid for it, out of his account, but I did the back transfer. He was *too busy*, he's always *too busy*, but I'm sure that you know all about that." Jenna nodded. "Here's the thing," Zara continued slyly, "it's not a baby, it's just an *embryo*."

Zara may have been beautiful, but she had a devilish grin. "I wanted some insurance, that's all. None of us is getting any younger. I had my eggs frozen at thirty, and I had twenty embryos frozen at thirty-three. So, he can wait until I'm forty if he wants to get married, but at least I have some insurance that it will happen."

Jenna wanted to tell Zara that having frozen embryos did not ensure that Dan would propose, and more importantly she wished that she could tell her that an embryo was absolutely a baby—it was the tiniest, most beautiful beginning to a baby—but Zara didn't seem like the type of woman that enjoyed being contradicted. Jenna nodded instead.

"Where?" Jenna asked instead, taking a small sip of her own champagne, ready now for the conversation to be over but curious enough to get one or two more tidbits of information from Zara before letting her go.

"Where what?"

"Um, sorry," Jenna gulped down the rest of her glass, "where are the embryos? Is there a storage place or something? Can you visit them?" Zara laughed out loud, thinking that Jenna had made a joke. Several people standing nearby turned and looked in Jenna and Zara's direction. When Zara realized that Jenna hadn't been joking, she looked confused.

"You are a funny one, aren't you?" she said. "I just love meeting interesting people. It is one of the things I like best about New York. But, to answer your question, two different states— half are here in New York and half are in California. Dan wanted us to, how did he put it, 'diversify.' And no, I don't visit them— that would be really weird."

"But they're your—" Jenna started and then stopped. "I mean, Dan must be really excited that you will have children together at some point."

"Right," Zara said slowly. "Well, I've gotta run." She looked past Jenna and smiled at someone standing somewhere in the background. Or maybe, Jenna thought, she just acted like she was smiling at someone so she could get away from Jenna. Her eyes came back to Jenna.

"It was good talking to you, though, and if you ever have questions about the process, I'd be happy to talk. My guy here in New York is the absolute best. He's not cheap, but then if it was, everybody would be doing it—but I guess *for a Mountain* the cost doesn't matter anyway. How nice for you." Zara put her empty drink glass on a high-top table, smiled, and walked away, stopping to say hello to at least ten people while Jenna stood alone.

***

When Ellie did not hear from her mother all day, on Mia's release day, the small bundle of worry that had nagged at her that morning grew larger and larger. Finally, around six o'clock, she tried Jenna's home phone. No answer. Then, Ellie called Jenna's cell phone—twice—no answer there either. She was almost ready to get into a cab and drive over to Jenna's apartment when her cell phone rang and showed Jenna's name in the caller ID.

"Hi, Mom," she said nervously. "How was today?" Ellie held her breath. She could not say how, it sounded crazy, but before Jenna said a word, Ellie knew. There was only one reason why a jubilant Jenna would not have called Ellie once the adoption process for Mia was underway earlier that day.

"Hi, honey," Jenna said, slurring into the receiver. For as long as she could remember, Ellie had seen her mother drink alcohol on only a couple of occasions. But she sounded drunk, and it was only 6:15 in the evening.

"Mom?" Ellie said, more loudly than she intended. "Mom? Are you okay? Tell me what has happened."

Jenna seemed to be attempting to string words together, but because the sounds she was making were so slow and entangled, Ellie was only catching every third word that Jenna said.

"Ablam . . . annnd . . . Mia . . . shlepth . . . nootld . . . sommmone . . . else . . . "

"Mom!" Ellie shouted this time. "I am coming over. Stay right where you are. Don't move, okay?"

Jenna slurred an okay back to Ellie and Ellie hung up quickly and raced down the stairs to hail a cab. When she let herself into her mother's apartment, the entire place smelled like cabernet, vomit, and cat feces. Jenna was lying facedown on the sofa and one of the cats had jumped on top of her back and curled up for an evening nap.

"Shoo!" Ellie swatted the black-and-white feline and rolled her mother over onto her back. "Mom . . . Mom . . . Mom?" Finally, Jenna opened her eyes and smiled when she recognized Ellie's face.

"Hi, sweetheart . . ." she said slowly.

Ellie went to the kitchen and poured a tall glass of water to take back into the living room. She held the glass up to Jenna's lips and forced her to take a couple of small sips before she took the glass away from her mouth and set it on the glass coffee table.

"Tell me what happened," Ellie said again. Jenna wiped her face with her hand, and told Ellie about going to BabyGenix, how different it was, and how she hadn't recognized anyone that worked there until Dr. Daugherty and Gunnar found her outside on the street. She told her about the long application paperwork, and about how the burly nurse told her that Mia had already been assigned an adoptive parent.

Ellie was horrified. "Is there anything that we can do?" she asked, though the situation was so unreal that she could barely believe it was real, much less figure out how to fix it. Jenna told her about the contact that Dr. Daugherty gave her and that she already had an appointment to meet with her, but that she was not hopeful.

"It's over," Jenna said and slipped out of Ellie's grasp and lay back down on the sofa, her body curled into a compact little ball, and Ellie could not help but notice how much she looked like a fetus in the womb.

For the remainder of the evening, Ellie rubbed Jenna's back and held her hair back when she was sick, which was several times until there was nothing more for Jenna's stomach to expel. Ellie called Kevin and told him the news about Mia and asked if he would mind if she spent the night at her mother's, to watch out for her overnight. Kevin said of course, and in the morning, Jenna was incredibly hungover, but at least she was more lucid than she had been the night before.

twenty

Three days later, Jenna sat in the small waiting area for Solano, Burke, and Hampshire on the Lower East Side, only blocks away from BabyGenix. As directed by Dr. Daugherty, Jenna called Susan Solano's phone number as soon as she was back in her apartment on the day that she was physically removed from the fertility clinic. She had no idea who could have put in an application for Mia's adoption, and though she had called (several times) the BabyGenix adoption line, the receptionist would not release the *extremely sensitive* information to Jenna, and asked her to stop calling or BabyGenix would file harassment charges against her.

Her world had once again been turned upside down on its head, and Jenna had no idea how to turn it right side up. Jenna looked around the tiny reception area and hoped that Dr.

Daugherty was putting her in the right hands. For the divorce, Jenna had used an old law school buddy, Andrew, to represent her, but for this, for this she needed someone that she could place one hundred percent of her trust in. She needed someone really good.

"Ms. Ellis, I presume?" A strikingly beautiful late-middle-aged woman stuck her head out from an open doorway. The woman had a headset on and was listening intently to whoever it was that she was on the call with. She put one finger up to indicate *just one more minute* to Jenna, and Jenna nodded and half smiled.

A minute later, the woman was back in the reception area extending a hand to Jenna. "Susan Solano, very nice to meet you. Christine called and gave me a heads-up that you would be calling. I am so glad that you did—it sounds like we have our work cut out for us. Christine told me that you yourself are an attorney. That's great news. We are going to need all our firepower."

Jenna immediately liked Susan's energy, and she noted a hint of feistiness that was a good quality to have as a female attorney.

"Yes," Jenna replied, "I went ahead did a little digging of my own, into precedent cases, that is, but I can't find any case that is similar to what I am faced with."

"You are right," Susan said, motioning that Jenna follow her out of the reception area and down the hall to her private office. "There is not a precedent case for our purposes, but that's okay. We are going to set precedent. Come on back, let's get settled so I can go over some general questions that I have for you."

Jenna nodded and followed Susan back to her private office, which was even smaller than the reception area. The website described Solano, Burke, and Hampshire as a boutique firm, but this looked more like a mom-and-pop operation. Jenna took a seat in the undersized club chair opposite Susan's desk, and as Susan settled into her chair, Jenna glanced at the bookshelves lining the wall behind the desk. Rows and rows of books on IVF, fertility, reproductive law, surrogacy, and adoption filled the shelves. Susan followed Jenna's glance.

"You could say that reproductive law has become a passion of mine," Susan said, smiling.

"Dr. Daugherty said that you were the person to call. I appreciate her putting us in touch."

Susan noticed Jenna's shoulders relax slightly. "Jenna, you are absolutely in the right place. I have more experience than anyone in the city in this area of law. But you must know what you are in for. I would be remiss not to give you a lay of the land before we even begin down this road." Susan's face wore a serious expression that took Jenna a second to follow. She nodded. Susan took the cue to continue.

"You lost your embryo in your divorce, correct?" Susan's pen was poised and ready, hovering over the notepad on her desk. Jenna nodded, and Susan asked for the date of the divorce. When Jenna gave her a date of twenty years before, Susan raised an eyebrow.

"The embryo has been at BabyGenix for *twenty years*?" Susan asked incredulously.

Jenna shook her head, "No, ahem," and cleared her throat. "Twenty-nine years, to be exact. Mia, the embryo, was harvested and frozen at the same time as my daughter Ellie. After several failed implantations, Ellie appeared to be the strongest of the embryos that we had left. Thank goodness she pulled through. I was at my wits' end. Ellie was born in late 1990." Susan listened patiently and scribbled notes furiously on the notepad.

"So, the divorce was in '99, is that correct?"

179

"Yes, that's correct."

"I'm going to need to pull those records. Was Mia the only embryo in question during the divorce proceedings?" Susan squinted at something that she had written on the notepad, and then pulled out a pair of thick-framed black reading glasses.

"No, there were three. I had three viable embryos frozen at BabyGenix at the time of the divorce. Ed was awarded all three."

"What happened to the other two?" Susan waited for Jenna to answer.

"They were destroyed on the day the divorce was final." Jenna painfully recounted the ordeal at BabyGenix in which Ed first decided to have all three embryos discarded, and then, at the last minute, asked Jenna to choose one to save. She told Susan about the "catch" and how she never imagined that it would be something as outlandish as a twenty-year waiting period. And finally, she told Susan about collapsing in the storage room of BabyGenix, and that was the last time she saw Mia's tube. When Jenna was finished, she looked to Susan for a reaction.

"Well, your ex-husband sounds like a real charmer. Here's the thing—we could spend all day talking about how it is 2019 and we are still living in a man's world. We could talk about the Octomom and uterus transplants and all the other crazy advancements in reproductive medicine. But the reality is this: ninety-nine percent of custody disputes involving frozen embryos fall in the man's favor, and that's if the embryo or embryos in question are even deemed children. We have *Davis v. Davis* from 1989 to thank for that. Those Tennessee hillbillies had no idea the firestorm that they created by ruling in Junior Davis's favor. Anyhow, as I am sure you are aware, in most states, frozen embryos are considered property, and thus not protected by custody proceedings at all. It's not fair, and it may or may not be right, but this is the reality of the state of reproductive law in this country. That is what we are up against." Susan paused. She didn't want to scare Jenna away, but she needed for Jenna to fully understand the uphill battle that faced them.

"Mia is the only thing that has kept me going, Ms. Solano. I have to give it a shot. I understand that the chances of winning her back are low, but I could not live with myself if I didn't try."

Susan nodded. "I agree with you, and I am going to do my absolute best, Jenna, I can promise you that." Both women stood, shook hands, and Jenna let herself out of the office with the knowledge that Susan would call her the following day with a plan of action.

Once Jenna left, Susan sat at her desk writing nearly intelligible notes as fast as she could in her notepad. Question number one was to find out who had put in the adoption application for Mia. Question number two was to find out why, and what that person had to gain or lose by choosing that embryo of the thousands of available embryos stored at BabyGenix. Three, she needed a court order to suspend the application process on HN3-8B, Mia's BabyGenix ID number, to at least put the brakes on the process until she could build a case for Jenna and against BabyGenix. She knew from previous experiences that BabyGenix was a "no waiting period" adoption clinic, meaning, unlike other agencies that required background checks on the adoptive parents, several home visits by a social worker, a psychologist to assess the safety and environment of the home, and several rounds of paperwork between the donor parents and the adoptive parents, BabyGenix simply took payment for the embryo of the adoptive parents' choice, handled the legal paperwork that terminated the donor's rights, and scheduled the implantation right away—all performed within the walls of BabyGenix, and all done quickly.

Susan tapped her pen on her desk and began to brainstorm on her position for Jenna. The first call that she would make would be to her friend Christine Daugherty, and she hoped that Christine did not feel especially loyal to her employer of over thirty years.

***

The media loved Cassandra Mountain. She was an attractive woman in her early forties and cried every time she mentioned Ed's name, which was every interview, and spoke of his dying wish that she carry and raise his child as a living legacy. Cassandra had rehearsed at home, of course, and decided that the best *look* for her was to be seen each interview clutching a tissue in one hand and resting the other on her size 2 waistband.

"But Mia is not your genetic child?" each interviewer would inevitably ask.

But Cassandra was always ready. "Yes, sadly we discovered years ago that I am unable to have children of my own. Charlotte is her name, not Mia as presented in the press, and she is Ed's biological offspring—she is the only opportunity to make his dying wish and my dreams of becoming the mother of Ed's child come true." Pan camera right and cue more tears from Cassandra, smiling sweetly despite her camera-induced pain.

"So, you have named her Charlotte? Not Mia?" the interviewer would then ask.

"Yes," Cassandra would say emphatically, and at this point in the interview, she would look directly into the camera as if speaking only to Jenna. "Her name is Charlotte. No matter what anyone else says."

"So, you plan to conceive Charlotte using IVF?"

"Oh, no no no," Cassandra laughed lightly and then turned her serious face back on. "No, I plan to use a surrogate. You know, it is just very hard for a woman of my age to keep her figure, am I right?" She would wink at the television host, who would look uncomfortable.

"Charlotte will be given the highest-quality care from start to finish. There is nothing more important than my child, so we will be interviewing only the best in the search for a surrogate."

"We?" the interviewer would ask.

"My mother and I," Cassandra put her hand to her chest and feigned tearing up (again). "My mother has been my rock and my salvation throughout this horrible time. If not for her church prayer group thinking of me and little Charlotte every week, I don't know if I'd survive all of this." Cassandra put her hand to her face once more and counted to three before taking it away, pretending to wipe nonexistent tears from her cheeks.

"Oh," the interviewer put a hand lightly on Cassandra's knee, "I am so sorry, Mrs. Mountain. I—and the viewers, I assure you—wish you all the best in your search, and we know that baby Charlotte will bring a new light to your life."

"Thank you," Cassandra would say sweetly. "Ed Mountain, my husband of almost seventeen wonderful years, was a man of his word, and a man who wanted another child. I am just trying to fulfill that wish." Then Cassandra would stare into the camera lens once more and flash a perfectly poised smile that she would hold for exactly two seconds, knowing that the shot would result in good still photography prints for magazines and newspapers after the segment aired on television.

"This is garbage," Jenna said to the TV. "Ed didn't want any more children, you dimwit. Why would he have locked down the contract so tightly if he wanted *you* to have his child? Answer me that, Goldilocks. You are just as much of an idiot as I always thought you were."

"Mom," Ellie said warningly, "no need to get all worked up. This is just Cassandra's tactic, to get the media on her side. She doesn't have a leg to stand on."

"No, but she has George Allgood, and that's scary enough for me." Ellie agreed with her mother but didn't want to say so out loud. If anyone could get a decision in their favor, it was Allgood. The media loved him and, in turn, loved his clients. Cassandra was off to a good start.

***

By the time Susan and Jenna met again in Susan's office a week later, Susan had devised a strategy that would give Jenna the best chances of adopting Mia and annulling the previous application put in for her. There were only two big problems. In the time between when Susan saw Jenna last: she had found out from Dr. Daugherty the identity of the adoptive parent in Mia's case. She had planned to tell Jenna (or not, depending on Jenna's emotional state) in person, but the media beat her to the punch. Once the stop order was put in place against BabyGenix, Cassandra lashed out with such vehemence that one would think someone was trying to take *her* biological snowflake baby away—and that was exactly the point. Her legal team was good and extremely well connected and well versed in using the media to pull public support to their side.

Just days after the stop order, Cassandra appeared on the biggest morning talk show on cable television. Her tearful plea to viewers to keep her and Mia in their prayers sent TV ratings soaring.

"Why didn't you tell me that it was Cassandra who put in the adoption application?" Jenna asked furiously when she sat down in Susan's office for a second time.

"I planned to, Jenna, but I thought—" Susan began.

"Well, clearly you didn't think enough," Jenna cut in. Based on their only other meeting, Susan never would have guessed that such fire could come from sweet, demure, shy Jenna Ellis. Susan guessed that she was seeing a small slice of what had made Jenna a good lawyer before Ellie was born. It was dormant, but the passion and willingness to fight for her side was still there.

"Agreed," Susan said calmly. "But how or when you found out the identity of the other party is now inconsequential. Now it is time for us to get to work. We can fight this, Jenna, we can fight her, and get Mia back where she belongs, in your custody. Trust me on this." Susan hesitated and put both hands on her desk in a clasp which made Jenna nervous. "Jenna, we have another problem." When Jenna started to speak, Susan gently held a hand out to quiet her client. "Hold on," Susan said, "I'm getting to it." Susan took in another deep breath. "BabyGenix alerted my office this morning that Cassandra is not the only application put in for Mia's adoption."

"You mean besides mine?" Jenna asked slowly, confused about where this could possibly be heading.

"No," Susan replied, "aside from yours. In all, there are three applications for Mia's adoption." Susan paused to let the information sink in. "We don't know anything about who it is, and this time BabyGenix isn't taking any chances. They will not release the identity of the prospective couple, and unfortunately, they don't have to."

Jenna put her hands to her head. "But," she stammered, "But, how can they do that? What are you saying? That an *anonymous couple* can end up with custody of my child?"

"That's exactly what can happen." Susan had learned over the years to be as straight as possible with her clients from the start. "But Jenna," she said looking Jenna straight in the eye, "I am not going to let that happen. WE are going to fight, and YOU are going to fight—you need to trust me."

Jenna let out a big sigh and Susan saw her relax. Her facial muscles around her eyes and mouth softened, and her shoulders lowered away from her ears just enough to let Susan know that she was on the right track. Knowing your client intimately—what makes them tick, what motivates and what depresses them, and how you can use their emotional energy for the good of the case, is one of the keys to good lawyering. Rightfully so, Jenna was extremely emotional over losing Mia, and Susan planned to use that emotion to get court on their side. After that, she could worry about public support.

"What do you think we should do?" Jenna asked.

"For now, I think we should keep you out of the spotlight. Cassandra is hitting the public hard, and I want to wait it out for a bit longer to see if she gives us something that she can hang herself on."

Jenna nodded. "People like her usually do. They take an argument just one step too far."

"Exactly," Susan agreed. "So, that takes the media off our plate for the time being. I want to talk over strategy." Again, Jenna nodded, eager to hear how in the world Susan could turn the tide in their favor from such low odds. "I spoke to Christine Daugherty," Susan began. "She is the one who told me about Cassandra, not that it matters now. But she also gave me great insight into the Waller Report."

"What is the Waller Report?" Jenna asked. Something in the far reaches of her memory recognized the name, but not well enough to recall the specifics.

"Valid question," Susan said. "Louis Waller was a legal guru that was appointed by the Australian government in 1984 to lead a groundbreaking council tasked with creating legal framework concerning IVF and, specifically, embryo rights. Much of the legislation adopted by Australia, and later the US and much of Europe, was based on Waller's ideas and model."

"Interesting," Jenna chimed in, though she was not yet following how any legislation drafted in the '80s could help her case forty years later.

"You are wondering why this matters." Susan smiled a sly smile. Not much could get past her eagle eye. "It matters because the laws have not changed since then. What we use in this country for IVF and embryo rights is still basically the same framework that Waller gave us."

"Why?" Jenna asked, now confused again. "Most law, especially medical law, has to evolve over time to match the current scientific advancements. It has been twenty years since Mia was taken from me. Surely some of the law has changed in my favor." Jenna shook her head and Susan waited to make sure her client was finished before speaking up.

"Usually, yes, but not in this case. Because of the resurgence of *Roe v. Wade* debates and too much to lose politically, no lawmaker in America wants to touch IVF—so they haven't—and our laws are antiquated as a result."

"And how is this good for us?" Jenna asked skeptically. She felt like she and Susan were traveling down a legal rabbit hole and she needed to find the ground floor.

"Because we will use Waller's report to our advantage," Susan said triumphantly. "When I read through the report in detail, I was ready to kiss Mr. Waller on the lips for his gift, and I seriously considered attempting to fly the man to New York to serve as a witness, but unfortunately Louis Waller died last month."

"Well, that was timely," Jenna said. She was still not sure where Susan was going with all of this. "But how can he or his report help us?" And then, like a strike of lightning, Jenna remembered where she had heard the name Waller before. She shook her head and felt the wind go out of her sails. "No," Jenna said sadly, "I remember now. The Waller Commission's report is the argument that Ed's attorney used against me in the divorce."

Susan sighed, but she did not look the least bit flustered or put off track. "Well, then he wasn't using it right. I have just reread the darn thing from start to finish. Waller set his focus not on parental rights or custodial rights of the adults involved, but rather on the *rights of the embryo itself.* The whole reason that the council was established was because there were embryos that had been left in a Melbourne clinic after both parents died in a plane crash—meaning, parental rights were not the issue in question. Instead of fighting Cassandra over whether Mia is legally more rightfully hers or yours, we are going to focus the judge's attention on Mia's rights—where or with whom does Mia have a right to reside?"

"Mia's rights?" Jenna said out loud. And then more softly, when the dots connected in her mind, "The Rioses that Dr. Daugherty knew?" The approach was an interesting concept, but it felt risky. "Why do I feel like we are tiptoeing backward into the deep waters of the abortion debate?"

"Because we are," Susan said. "Bear with me. Strangely, proponents of stem-cell research who consider themselves progressive find themselves on the same side as conservative antiabortion advocates when it comes to embryo rights. The two sides could not be more diametrically opposed, but in this *one* case they are bound to one another based on the argument of embryo rights. This is what makes bioethics so interesting and reproductive law so complicated—it is the only arena in which you will find feminists siding with the Catholic Church." Susan paused. It was a confusing concept, and she wanted to make sure Jenna was following her line of thought. "Mia belongs with her biological mother. That is our argument. Mia has rights based on legislation left over from old Australian law, and we are going to do all that we can to call those laws into action. I need you to trust me, Jenna. It is our best way forward, I promise."

Jenna considered Susan's position for several seconds. All of what Susan had said was true, and it seemed to Jenna that the only way forward was to look back at the old law. "Let's do it," she said solidly to Susan. "I trust you."

twenty-one

Lucie was still thinking about Jenna's proposal when she walked into her aunt Estephi's apartment for the weekly Hernandez family dinner. Estephi, her husband, Lucie's uncle Oscar, along with her cousins, Luis and Nery, arrived in New York almost ten years before. But unlike Lucie's parents, who began the immigration process as soon as they arrived in the US, Uncle Oscar focused on finding work for himself, Estephi, and their two teenage sons, and never got around to the long, expensive, and arduous process that it took to become a US citizen. When the three men were deported the year before, Estephi had been at work at a dry cleaner in her neighborhood and came home to find her apartment ransacked, and her husband and two adult sons gone. Though Aunt Estephi had received word that all three men had been released from the detention center and were back in her hometown of Flores, it did not make their being gone any easier to bear. The men had never been arrested, never caused trouble, and had never been as much as one minute late to work in the ten years that they lived in the United States, but that was not enough to let them stay, and now Aunt Estephi was left paying for her apartment alone.

"Mi hermosa sobrina!" Aunt Estephi called out when Lucie opened the door to her aunt's tiny apartment in Queens. It was not an easy commute to make every other Sunday, but for that reason, the sisters, Estella and Estephi, alternated each week where the weekly dinner was held. This week was Aunt Estephi's turn.

"Hello, Tia," Lucie replied, giving her aunt a kiss on the cheek.

"You grow more and more beautiful every time I see you, my niece," Estephi cooed. "One of these days soon you will finally get married, yes?" This was a recurring question and one that until three months ago, Lucie had not minded so much.

"Tsk, tsk, tsk." Lucie's mother came out of the kitchen clucking. "We thought that she would already be engaged, but—" Estella threw her hands into the air—"this girl is loco and doesn't want to get married!"

"Leave her alone, Mama," Maria chimed in, holding Carmen on one hip and a pot full of rice on the other. "Can someone come give me a hand in the kitchen, or is the lady with the baby going to have to do it all by herself?"

"I know what I want to do." Estephi reached her hands out to Carmen and tickled the girl's belly, causing her to squirm and giggle as Estephi took her from her mother and into her own arms. "I want to cuddle with Carmen!" And she made a *zoom* noise as she spun Carmen around in circles.

The four women, five counting Carmen, were equally dependent upon one another and for both Estella and Estephi, Lucie was glad that her aunt and mother had one another to lean on after so much loss. Though Estella begged Estephi to come live with her after Oscar and the boys were taken away, Estephi turned the offer down each time saying that she wanted to be in the apartment when Oscar and her sons returned, no matter how far into the future that may be. Every time the subject came up, a silence would follow wherein everyone at the table privately accepted that Oscar, Luis, and Nery would never see the New York streets again, but no one had the heart to say such words out loud. Lucie wondered if her aunt would leave the US at some point voluntarily and return to Guatemala if it was the only way to see her husband or sons. She could barely imagine what life would be like if she lost her Aunt Estephi too. Lucie feared that her mother would never survive such a loss.

After much shouting, laughing, and yet more clucking from Estella, the meal was finally prepared, and Carmen was put down for her afternoon nap so the adult women could eat their meal in peace. The smells wafting over the table were like a piece of heaven to Lucie and Maria, and like a piece of home for Estella and Estephi. Meat stew flavored with cinnamon and coriander, cumin-infused rice, and garlic roasted corn, beans, and tortillas were standard fare for the weekly meal, along with Estella's famous chancletas for dessert.

"How do they say in the US?" Estephi asked to no one. "Ah! Yes! Bon appetit!" and everyone laughed, including Estephi, at her own mix-up of the languages. The four women sat down and collectively sighed, making all of them burst into laughter for a second time. Aside from Lucie, who only worked her cleaning jobs, each of the other women had two jobs each, making the Sunday meal much anticipated and deserved at the week's end. No one spoke for the first several minutes of the meal, as each was all too happy to be enjoying the labor of the kitchen. Estella and Estephi, the two eldest, sat at the ends of the table, and Lucie and Maria took side chairs opposite one another. There was room for more chairs beside Lucie and Maria, but someone had removed the empty chairs after Lucie's father, Alejandro, passed away, and Uncle Oscar and the boys were gone. It was too painful for both Lucie's mother and aunt to see such a physical reminder of their absence during every dinner.

Estella cleared her throat. "I saw Mrs. Martinez at the market yesterday." She took a sip of her ice water and put it down carefully before wiping her mouth with her napkin.

"Oh?" Lucie asked. "And how is she doing?"

"Mom—" Maria cut in, making a sideways glance at Lucie, but Estella put her hand up to silence her oldest daughter.

"Maria, I am only making conversation, that's all. I thought Lucie might like to hear what Mrs. Martinez said to me." Estella raised her eyebrows and took another sip of her water.

"It's okay," Lucie said to Maria, who rolled her eyes at her mother. "What did Mrs. Martinez say, Mom?" she asked.

"Just that Freddie is depressed, that's all."

"Mom!" Maria nearly shouted. "It's not fair for you to keep bringing Freddie's name up all the time!" Lucie was thankful for her sister. Only Maria knew why Lucie had broken things off abruptly with Freddie several months before.

"I just thought she should know!" Estella shouted back. "The poor boy wanted to marry your sister, and she can't even speak to him? She can't even give him a reason for why she will not see him? It is . . . it is . . . what is that damn American word—ah—*rude*."

A sharp pain ran from Lucie's chest down to the pit of her stomach whenever Freddie's name was mentioned. She would never be able to tell her mother why she had to break things off with her boyfriend of almost three years. Her mother would never understand, just as Freddie would never understand. She was broken now, tainted, and a guy as good as Freddie no longer deserved to be with someone who could do something as horrible as what Lucie had done. Freddie could never find out Lucie's secret, and Lucie knew that it would be impossible to hide from him, so the only way forward was to break things off with Freddie.

Aside from having Maria as her confidante, Lucie felt like she was completely alone in her pain after separating from Freddie. She had loved him, but when she broke things off she had said terrible things to Freddie to make it easier for her to walk away and for him to let her. And that's exactly what he had done—he let her walk away that day on the sidewalk outside his parents' apartment when she told him that it was over.

"I need to get some air," Lucie said quietly, and Maria looked apologetically in her direction, mouthing a silent "I'm sorry" before Lucie pushed her chair back from the table and she opened the sliding door that led out to the tiny balcony overlooking St. Michael's Cemetery. The burning in her stomach that began when her mother mentioned Freddie's name grew worse with each passing minute. She began by rubbing on her stomach to try to ease the pain, but by the time Maria pushed open the sliding door to join Lucie on the balcony, Lucie was crying and clawing at her stomach with both hands.

"Hey," Maria said soothingly. "Hey, it's okay. It's okay. You are going to be okay." And she held her younger sister in her arms tightly until she could feel Lucie relax. Maria glanced inside to see her mother and aunt talking animatedly about something, making both women laugh, and then she pulled Lucie back from her and looked her right in the eyes.

"You did the right thing, do you hear me?" she said sternly.

"You did the right thing." And she pulled Lucie back to her as she cried. "There will be other guys, Lu, there are always other guys. You'll be okay, don't worry."

With the afternoon soured, the two younger Hernandez women helped their mother and aunt clean up in the kitchen and then said their goodbyes. Carmen woke up cranky from her nap, so Maria and Lucie left their mother to visit with her sister while they took the bus back to Bedford Park.

Later that night, when Lucie was already in bed, Estella came to sit on the end of her bed and gently nudged her daughter awake. "Hey," she said softly. "Hey, are you awake?"

"No," Lucie said sluggishly.

"Look, mija." Estella looked to the ceiling to try to find the right words. She felt badly for upsetting Lucie earlier, but she was also worried that her daughter was making poor decisions that she would grow to regret later. "I did not mean to upset you, my pobrecita. I just worry for you, that's all."

"You shouldn't," Lucie said sleepily.

"I *should* and I *do*," Estella said sternly, throwing her hands in the air. "Look at me. Look at your sister. Look at your aunt Estephi—all of us women alone, without a man in our lives—and you, you have the chance to have a *good* man in your life, and you will not accept him? I cannot make sense of it. You do not have to suffer just because the rest of us do. I hope that is not your reason for leaving Freddie, because you think that you will be leaving your family behind?"

"That's not the reason," Lucie said into her pillow. She felt like she was twelve and her mom was trying to have *the talk* with her for the first time. This was the problem with Latino women; they were extremely nosey and lived with you forever. Estella patted Lucie's foot on top of the comforter and sighed a heavy, audible sigh.

"Okay, if you say so," she said. "Get some rest. I'll see you in the morning."

Lucie did not reply and pulled the covers up over her head. She did not want her mother seeing the single tear that slid down her cheek.

***

The next day, Lucie opened the door to her building, stepped out onto to the brick stairway, and blew out a big sigh while she wiped her face with her dry hands. What was she going to do? It was a lot of money that Ms. Mountain was offering, but could she really do it? Could she bear someone else's child? Although she knew that it was a widely used method of conception and birth, particularly in a place like New York where people often had more money than they had sense, the act of having another person's DNA put inside of her body seemed like something out of a movie and not real life.

And how did she feel about what would happen after the baby was born? Was Jenna Ellis, a sixty-something-year-old, capable of caring for a newborn and raising a child at her age? Or was that none of Lucie's business? "Ugh," she breathed out, and she sat down on the edge of the step at the top of the stairway lost in her own thoughts and unaware of old Ms. Chu sitting at the bottom on the stairs.

Ms. Chu lived alone in one of the lower-level units of Lucie's apartment building, and for as long as Lucie could remember, Ms. Chu sat on the front steps of the building bidding each tenant a pleasant goodbye in the mornings and good evening when they returned home. A terrible kitchen fire accident in the restaurant where she worked years before caused Evelyn Chu to become legally blind, and because of this, Lucie often helped Ms. Chu with her grocery shopping and other errands. It was a task that Lucie had once dreaded (because it was at her mother's insistence that she help the old woman) but had grown to enjoy, and she discovered that helping Ms. Chu do things that normal people could do made her more thankful that she had her own vision. Lucie also found that Ms. Chu was very funny, and they often sat together on the front steps and talked about a wide array of subjects. Though legally blind, she could make out some basic shapes and colors, so she and Lucie would play guessing games to name certain objects or people walking by, and the game inevitably ended in laughter. It was an unlikely friendship that Lucie treasured, and she marveled at the woman's ability to recognize people's voices, even from half a block away.

Today, however, Ms. Chu sat silent, which was how Lucie did not at first notice that she sat on the lowest step closest to the sidewalk. She sat stooped, her dark oversized glasses covering her eyes, and because of the draped kimono that she wore, the only visible skin was that of her right hand, which clutched a cane. The cane had an ivory handle, and as a child, Lucie had thought that the cane was perhaps the most beautiful and most valuable item that she had ever seen. The handle was carved into the shape of a dragon's head and was crafted with such detail that the eyes of the dragon seemed to follow its viewer. Maria had always been afraid of Ms. Chu and was sent to her room once when she was eight because she called Ms. Chu a witch and Mrs. Hernandez had heard her, telling her to never speak ill of a person that she did not know. Maria did not call her a witch after that, but she did avoid walking past Ms. Chu whenever possible and ran past Ms. Chu's interior door when she and Lucie would carry groceries up the stairs for their mother as children.

Lucie looked down at the brick and traced her finger along the step's edge. Tiny black ants scurried across the top, in and out of the holes in the brick, and she watched one in particular as it carried a piece of cracker larger than its own body across the step and down a storm drain.

"Do not enter the circle, my dear," a raspy voice said, and Lucie looked up to notice Ms. Chu for the first time sitting at the bottom of the stairs. At first, Lucie thought that old Ms. Chu might simply be talking to herself—she was old, after all, and potentially senile—but then she spoke again, repeating herself slowly. "Do not enter the circle, I tell you," she said in a tone that sounded like a kind warning from an old soothsayer.

"What?" Lucie asked. Ms. Chu was still making no sense to her, so she stood and walked down the steps to where Ms. Chu sat. Her dark-purple kimono must be hot on a day like today, Lucie thought, but the old woman seemed not to be affected by the early summer heat. Instead, Lucie watched as the old woman grasped the ivory handle to her cane more fervently, and once she had a good grasp of it, she drew a medium-sized circle, about twelve inches in diameter, in the cement dust at the bottom of the stairs. After making the circular motion with her cane, Ms. Chu tapped the end of her cane in the center of the circle and looked up at Lucie to see if she was watching.

"Here," Ms. Chu said, "is the center of the circle—do not go in."

"I'm sorry, Ms. Chu," Lucie said respectfully, "but I—"

"The white woman," said Ms. Chu, "the one from the TV. I recognized her voice. She was here today."

"Ms. Ellis, you mean?' Lucie asked and wondered how Ms. Chu would have recognized her by voice alone and was also surprised that Ms. Chu followed local news. The story had been everywhere for weeks. Baby Mia was a New York sensation that had spread to news outlets across the country. Cassandra, Ed Mountain's widow, was the most vocal and seemed to love the media attention that she received, but Jenna had been interviewed as well, and her tearful interview with Barbara Walters (pulled out of semi-retirement just to do the interview that everyone else wanted) had been picked up by every morning talk show on the East Coast.

"This is her battle, not yours," Ms. Chu continued. "Don't enter the circle."

"What does that mean, 'don't enter the circle'?" Lucie asked, bewildered.

"There is an old Chinese story that you need to hear, my dear. It comes from a long time ago," Ms. Chu wagged her finger in Lucie's direction, "back to the fourteenth century." Ms. Chu coughed, and once her throat cleared sufficiently, she continued, "The ancient story goes that there once were two women that both lay claim to an infant. The backstory leading up to the arrival of the baby is rich with color, but that is a story that I will save for another day. The point is the two women both wanted the child desperately and claimed her as their own. Eventually, unable to resolve the dispute in their village, the powerful village minister sends the women and the baby to stand before the emperor. The wise old emperor considers the position of each woman and, at last, draws a circle of chalk around the child. Both women are instructed to pull, from arms and legs, until the baby is either pulled apart or pulled out of the circle by one of the two women—"

"That is terrible," Lucie said. "It's just like the judgment of Solomon from the biblical story, yes?" Ms. Chu did not reply, but rather held up her hand to gently silence Lucie. "The emperor drew the circle and put the child inside, but he knew that the child would be unharmed."

"How?" asked Lucie

"Because he had faith that the real mother of the child would not want her baby harmed by the pulling, so as soon as the pretender mother pulled, the real mother let go." Ms. Chu made a dramatic marking through the center of the circle that she had drawn in the dust. "By this action, the emperor knew the identity of the real mother and thus awarded the baby to her." Ms. Chu turned to face Lucie, and although Lucie could not see her eyes through the dark sunglasses, she knew that she was staring straight into her soul.

"What do I do?" she asked quietly, and felt herself come to the verge of tears.

"That," Ms. Chu paused, "is up to you. For me," she tapped the circle again, "it is not your circle, it is not your fight, and I do not want to see a nice young girl like you pulled apart by the savages just to help a rich white woman. Just as the baby was in grave danger by being placed in the circle, anyone who enters the circle must be prepared to be torn to pieces to save himself. It is valiant to think of others, but we must always think of ourselves as well. It may not be nice, but one would be remiss not to consider self-preservation and survival."

Lucie knew Ms. Chu was right. It was what she had felt all along, but between the money and watching Ms. Ellis cry, she had convinced herself that it wouldn't be so bad to help Jenna out. It was just a year of her life, less than that, and then she would be done and her mother could stop working.

And there was also the *other* reason. The secret that ate away at Lucie when she lay in bed each night. It was a weight and a chain that she carried with her every day of her life, and the thing that made her fear that God would not allow her to bear children, not after what she did.

The problem, which could not be ignored, was that Jenna's request touched upon Lucie's deepest, darkest fear—that because she had killed one baby, God would never again allow her body to conceive another—or at least not safely. She couldn't take that chance, and it looked like Jenna and Mia only had one chance. As tempting as the money was, Lucie knew that she could never go through with the surrogacy.

twenty-two

The next morning, Lucie woke early. She knew that she needed to tell Jenna the bad news, that she wouldn't be able to be Mia's carrier, but the closer the bus came to Jenna's stop, the worse Lucie felt, and the words that she had so carefully crafted earlier that morning suddenly vanished from her brain. She had practiced a million times in her bedroom mirror, but as she poured over the words again on the bus, the less sure Lucie felt about herself, and her reasoning for rejecting Jenna's offer.

With only one more stop to go, Lucie recited her reply in her mind one more time. "I can't do it because . . . You see, last year when I was with my boyfriend, Freddie . . . I really wish that I could, honestly; if I could, I would . . ." And then the worst of all, but the most honest reason that Lucie could come up with: "I had an abortion and God will strike down your baby if you put her inside of me." There it was, the cold truth. Lucie was not worthy of carrying Mia, and worse, she may actually harm the unborn child unwittingly. Lucie couldn't do that to Jenna, not after she had seen Ms. Ellis talk about her unborn daughter and the many years she had waited for her to be available for adoption. There was no other option, Lucie realized, than telling Jenna the truth.

twenty-three

Meanwhile, Jenna tried her best not to pace the apartment more than she already had in recent days. She couldn't exactly tell what she was feeling—guilt, sadness, confusion, worry—or a toxic mixture of all of them combined. When Jenna heard the phone ring at six p.m., she had a bad feeling. She answered the phone tentatively and heard Susan, her attorney, on the other end of the line.

"Jenna?" she said. "Jenna are you there?"

"Yes," Jenna replied; she had a sinking feeling in the pit of her stomach. "I'm here. What's going on? I have a feeling you are not calling to tell me that Cassandra and the other couple both dropped out of the application process." Jenna tried to laugh at her own failed joke, but she and Susan both sighed instead.

"No," said Susan tenderly. "No, honey, I wish I was. Judge

Candler called my office just now and wants to meet with us. He said 'immediately,' but I told him that I would have to get in touch with you and see if that works for your schedule."

There was silence on the other end of the line. Like Jenna, Susan had a bad feeling about the proposed after-hours meeting, but legally she was bound to pass along the judge's request to her client. Though the case did not seem to be leaning in her client's favor, she had developed a good rapport with Judge Robert Candler over the previous months, and worried that he wanted to deliver devastating news to Jenna in private instead of in the courtroom the following day where journalists, photographers, and the rest of the circus (including people that traveled from all over just to sit in on big decisive court cases—these people were weird to Susan, but what could she do, it was their legal right to observe the legal system at work) would all be present and save Jenna some embarrassment.

"Can I say no?" Jenna asked Susan slowly, as if she was still considering the question herself. It had been many years since Jenna practiced law, and this case had been a stark reminder to her that she had forgotten many basics of procedural law.

"Technically," Susan said slowly, "yes. But I am not sure that is my recommendation. His office would not tell me why the judge wanted to meet, only that he wanted to meet, so it could be a whole host of possibilities."

"But most of those possibilities are bad, correct?" Jenna asked.

"In my opinion," said Susan, "yes."

"But," Susan continued, "we just don't know until we go. I have only been summoned by a judge on the night before a verdict once before, so I am hardly an expert in that regard."

"And what was that meeting for?" Jenna asked. She and Susan both knew that she was stalling, but she stalled anyway. It didn't matter what the other case was about or why that other judge called Susan in, but Jenna needed another minute to process the request and decide what she was going to do.

Susan read Jenna's stall and began a lengthy diatribe about the other attorney in the case in question, and how the judge had called Susan in over something completely inconsequential, only to discover in that meeting, and completely by chance, that the other attorney had committed terrible acts of perjury by comparing conflicting stories that both the judge and Susan had both heard in the courtroom. She finished her story, and when Jenna did not jump in, she began another, this one about a nasty divorce case that she took on several years ago. "And I said right then and there that would be the last case I try in family court *ever*." She paused again at the end of that story and Jenna sighed.

"We should go, right?" Jenna asked timidly.

"I think we should," Susan replied.

"I can meet you downstairs in a half hour," Jenna said, and Susan could hear resolve in Jenna's voice. Susan would never tell her client that their chances of winning were slim, but their chances of winning were slim, and she hoped that whatever the judge had to say in the evening before a decision was at least worth hearing.

A half hour later, Susan picked Jenna up at the front door to her building. The two women sat quiet in the back of a taxi as the car zigzagged across the city to the judge's office.

It was now seven p.m., and Susan was surprised but not shocked that the judge's clerical assistant was still poised at her desk when she and Jenna arrived. Susan announced who they were and why they were there at such a late hour.

"Yes, of course," the middle-aged assistant said. She pushed a button on her telephone and spoke into the receiver. "Ms. Ellis and Ms. Solano are here. Yes, yes, okay." And she hung up the phone.

"You can go right in. He is expecting you." She stood up from behind the desk and led the two women through the large mahogany double doors that led to the judge's private office.

Judge Candler sat behind a large desk, which suited him, as he was a large man. Broad shouldered and square jawed, Judge Candler looked like he was a judge. He sat with his hands clasped together on top of his desk and moved his thumbs back and forth, crossing them and uncrossing them several times. Jenna filed this observation away mentally as she sat down in one of the two large, rounded leather club chairs that sat facing Judge Candler's desk.

"Ms. Solano," he said, addressing Susan. "Thank you for acting expeditiously on my request to meet." Susan nodded and said of course, and though nothing in what the judge had said signaled the need for a legal pad and pen, she instinctively rifled through her briefcase and pulled out a yellow legal pad and paper, looked up at the judge, and sat poised to write. What she anticipated writing, Jenna had no idea, but she hoped that Judge Candler got to the point soon, for better or worse.

Judge Candler looked at Jenna. They were probably roughly the same age, Jenna thought to herself, and then also thought inwardly that he must think she was either insane or reckless, or both, to be considering becoming a mother at her age. "What am I doing?" Jenna meant to say only to herself but accidentally said out loud.

"What was that, Ms. Ellis?" the judge asked, not fully hearing what Jenna had said.

"Nothing, Your Honor," Jenna replied, feeling embarrassed and tired. "I just . . ." She paused. The attorney in her told her not to speak first. *Don't ever let your client speak over a judge*, she could hear herself whispering to a client long in the past. *You never know what he is going to say, so stay quiet until you hear what the judge has to say.* Susan put a light hand on Jenna's thigh. This was the silent signal to STOP TALKING.

Thankfully, Judge Candler stepped in and saved Jenna. He was a judge through and through, and as fair minded as they came in circuit court, but nonetheless, he could not help feeling a small amount of pity for Jenna.

"Ms. Ellis, I hope that you know the weight with which I bear your input in this case." Jenna nodded and took in a deep breath. Judge Candler continued, "You are the biological mother in this case, after all, and I believe that a biological parent's input is and should carry more weight than other parties in custodial cases such as this. However, you must also know that this is not a typical custody case." Jenna nodded again and wondered where the judge was going with his comments. Did he have a question for her that had not already been covered in court?

"I must ask you a difficult question, Ms. Ellis," he said after a short pause. "Given the parties involved, which do you feel would give Mia the life that you imagined for her twenty-nine years ago?" Susan shifted uneasily in her seat and was shocked that the judge would ask such an inflammatory question—on the night before a decision, of all times. "If the answer is yourself," the judge continued, "then that is all that you need to say. But I would like to hear from you that you feel that you are the most fit to raise this potential child."

"Jenna." Susan put her hand this time on Jenna's forearm. "You do not have to answer right now. Go home. Think about it overnight. We can meet with Judge Candler in the morning, surely." Susan looked to the judge, and he nodded in agreement.

"Of course," he said, "I was not expecting you to make any rash decisions tonight, and certainly my intent was not to sway you in any way. For my own peace of mind and for the fairness of the case, I needed to hear from you as to your thoughts regarding the best possible outcome for Mia, that's all."

Susan was incensed and stood up angrily to leave. What was Judge Candler doing? She picked up her briefcase jerkily from the floor and held out her hand to shake with Judge Candler coldly. "Thank you, Judge, we will see you in the morning. My client declines to comment at this time." Jenna looked at both Susan and Judge Candler and smiled.

"Susan," she said calmly, "it's okay." Jenna turned to Judge Candler. "I knew what you would ask me from the moment Susan called this afternoon and asked to set up this meeting. The reason I knew what you would ask is because it is the same question that I have been asking myself for the last several months, or years, for that matter. I have had a long time to think, too much. My mind knows what the right thing to do is, and my heart pulls for another, but the cold reality is that I am sixty-two years old. That is the hand that I have been dealt. It was not my choice, but it is the reality of the situation." All three people in the room sat in silence for several seconds.

"I want Mia, I mean—" Jenna paused and looked down at her hands folded over one another. "What I meant to say is, the embryo, to go to the adoptive couple. That is my wish. She deserves the life of a normal little girl, a normal person, not someone who will turn thirteen years old the same year that her mother turns seventy-five. That's not what I want for her." Judge Candler nodded and Susan sucked in a deep breath and looked to the floor.

"I only have one request." Jenna suddenly felt the weight of twenty-nine years lift from her shoulders. Sitting in the chair, she felt weightless, like she was flying—or drowning. "Would it be possible to forward my contact information to the couple through their attorney? I do not need direct contact, and may prefer not to for my own well-being, but I think that Mia's parents should have access to me and my medical history. I am happy to sign over the rights to my medical files to Susan. They may also have questions about ancestry, however, and I want them to have anything that they might need or want to know for Mia's, for the child's, sake. More than anything, I want her to live a long and healthy life; that's all that I want."

Judge Candler nodded. "I think that is not only a reasonable request, but a prudent one, for the health and benefit of the child-to-be. I will make sure that Ms. Solaro and the counsel for the couple are in touch regarding that subject. Thank you both for coming in for this unconventional meeting. We are living in unprecedented times, Ms. Ellis, and I appreciate your willingness to discuss this matter openly. It is probably no solace to you, but in my personal opinion, you should be commended for truly putting the best interest of this embryo ahead of your own desires. Thank you."

"Thank you," Jenna said, and for a moment, she felt dizzy and eerily similar to how she felt when Carson and David were destroyed. But then a second feeling came over her, and she was surprised at how much peace she felt. In the cab on the way over to Judge Candler's office, she had played the scenario out in her mind several times, and although she desperately wanted to find a reason to come to a different conclusion, she knew what the right answer was. It was always the same. Let Mia live. Let Mia grow. Let Mia live a good and normal life with parents that loved her and that could continue to love her for a longer time than she could. Mia deserved it. She smoothed the crease in her skirt and stood up to leave. She shook Judge Candler's hand and he said that he would see them in the morning. He also mentioned that of course the conversation had that evening was off the record, so to speak, so if Jenna had any second thoughts about her decision, to let his office know first thing in the morning.

Susan and Jenna walked in silence out of the judge's office, down the elevator, out on to the street, and Susan waved a cab to the curb. Susan gave the driver the address for Jenna's building and within minutes, the car came to a stop and Jenna's doorman opened the passenger door cheerfully. "Good evening, Ms. Ellis!" he said in more of an announcement than greeting. George was one of those people that appeared eternally optimistic. Jenna guessed this was mostly due to his young age—the inevitable heartbreak of life had not yet struck him—but she found the quality endearing, nonetheless.

"Hello, George." She turned and looked back into the cab. "I'm okay, Susan. I really am. I will see you in the morning."

"Okay, hon," Susan replied, though that bad feeling in the pit of her stomach reemerged. There were dark circles under Jenna's eyes, and she suddenly looked ten years older and one hundred percent defeated. Something told Susan not to let Jenna go up to her apartment by herself. She couldn't pinpoint the exact feeling, but something was definitely off. The car was starting to pull away when Susan stopped the driver and rolled down the back window. "Jenna!"

"Yes?" Jenna said, turning around in the doorway. The light from the lobby cast a strange glow around her body, making her look angelic, or ghostly.

"Are you sure you are okay? Maybe I should come up for a little while, and you know, just sit with you? It's been a hard day."

Jenna shook her head. "Really, I promise I'm fine. I'll see you in the morning. Eight a.m.?"

"Eight a.m.," Susan replied, and she rolled the window up and the taxi sped away from the curb. Jenna watched the taillights of the car until it took a left on Seventy-Fifth Street then turned to go inside.

"Hello again, George," she said, trying to match his cheerfulness. "A good night for you, I hope?"

"Yes, ma'am," the Southern transplant replied. "Nothing beats living in New York City. I hope all is well for you?"

Jenna nodded. "All is good, George, all is good."

Something tickled at George's brain. He couldn't say what or why, but Ms. Ellis seemed *off*. Then again, George reminded himself, Ms. Ellis was not normal by any stretch, and she was probably the most eccentric woman that he had met in his two short years in the city, but he couldn't shake the feeling that something was wrong.

"I hope that you have a good rest of your evening and a wonderful, fulfilling life," she said as he held the elevator door open for her and she stepped inside. Now he knew something was wrong, but he was also told specifically by his boss on the first day on the job to *stay out of tenants' affairs*—at *ALL* times—no matter what.

"Good night, Ms. Ellis, I will see you tomorrow," George said as the elevator doors closed. He had a bad feeling about the night ahead but couldn't determine what to do about it, so he went back to his front desk and opened a new game of solitaire on the computer.

***

213

Jenna stepped off the elevator on the fifth floor as she had done for the past fifteen years, but this time she walked slowly, taking notice of as many details as possible. The small black scuff marks just beside 5B's door, the way that the carpet was pulled up slightly and had buckled near 5E, and how her own front door, 5F, was the most unadorned, uninviting door of all on the fifth floor. *I wonder why they have never said anything to me about it*, she thought to herself. Not that there was anything unappealing about her front door; it was just plain and completely impersonal, as if the apartment was vacant.

She opened her door, put her purse down, and watched Jack, the oldest of her cats, jump up onto the counter in the kitchen to greet her. "Hello, kitten," she said soothingly to the almost all-white Persian. She pet his head and moved past him to the coat closet, where she found a long scarf looped around the neck of one of her winter coats. She tugged on it to test its strength and thought that it would probably work. She set the scarf on the table and looked around to see if any of the other cats had wandered into the living room expecting their dinner, now that she was home. Several gray-and-black tabbies came out from under the sofa and one orange cat, Tom, slipped out from the bathroom. He liked to nap in the sink and had more than likely been there all evening since Jenna went out to meet Susan and Judge Candler. The cats all began to meow in unison, signaling that they were in fact ready for dinner, and with each passing second, they grew louder and more anxious. "Hold on, hold on," Jenna said, laughing. "No need for a mutiny. There is plenty for everyone. Just be patient."

She poured food into each of the cats' personalized feeding bowls on the kitchen floor and then took out one large mixing bowl and filled it with the remaining food left in the bag. The food filled the bowl and was slightly falling out over the edges. *Good, this will be enough*, she thought to herself. Then she took out a second mixing bowl and filled it up with water. She put both bowls up on the counter of the elevated bar that separated the kitchen from the living room. She didn't want the extra food and water to be too easily accessible down on the floor, because then, some of the cats, Cashiers, namely, would eat half the food in one sitting. They needed to have to root around for it a bit, when they really got hungry. She didn't know how long it would take for someone, most likely George, or Ellie, to use the spare key and come in to find her.

She debated pouring herself a glass of wine, but after some thought, she decided against it. She wasn't exactly sure what happened to a body after one hanged oneself, and the last thing she wanted as Ellie or George's lasting memory was the smell of stale wine that somehow made its way out of her body after death. She wished she had done more research, now that she thought of it, but now there was no time. For the first time in her life, she would have to "wing it," and though morbid, the idea of not researching, but rather throwing caution to the wind, gave her an eerie jolt of excitement. Her law school friends would be so proud of her for it. She smiled, thinking about what they would say— not about her killing herself; surely, they would be upset in that regard—but about the fact that she finally did something without researching it to death, literally.

She picked up the scarf again and decided to tie it to the bedroom door handle. No reason to hide herself away in her en suite bathroom or back in the guest room where no one would find her. It was better for whoever came in the apartment first that she be right out in front. She tied one end of the scarf tightly around the handle and began to make a loop on the other end when the phone rang. She didn't plan to answer, and finally the answering machine picked up the call.

"Mom? Mom, it's me, Ellie. If you are there, pick up."

Jenna paused with her hand still on the scarf. Ellie said *Mom* once more, and she let the scarf hang from the handle and went to the phone.

"Hey, sweetheart," she said, a little breathlessly, "what's going on?"

"I'm just checking on you." Ellie sounded nervous and fidgety to Jenna, but she decided she was probably just paranoid. "I mean, are you okay?" Ellie asked. "Tomorrow is a big day."

"It is, and I am," Jenna said, "but I am ready. At this point, no matter what happens, I've decided that I will be okay, and more importantly, Mia will be okay."

"Really?" Ellie asked. "You know, it is okay to say that you are scared, Mom, or nervous, or however you might be feeling. There is literally no one else in the world that knows how you feel right now."

"Gee, thanks. You make me out to be a real winner," said Jenna, though she was smiling. "The judge will make the right decision, I feel sure of it."

"I love you, Mom."

Jenna tapped the phone on her forehead and tried not to cry.

"I just want you to know how much I love you," said Ellie, and Jenna thought that she could hear her crying on the other end. "No matter what," Ellie continued, "you still have me. And I need you."

"I love you too, sweetheart," Jenna said. "I'll see you in the morning. I'll be the one dressed in black in the front. Can't miss me." This made Ellie laugh, and Jenna felt relief.

"Okay, see you there. Kevin and I will sit as close to the front as we can," Ellie said and hung up the phone.

Jenna looked at the scarf hanging from the doorknob. "I can always do it tomorrow," she told herself and she went to bed.

twenty-four

S usan arrived in the lobby of Jenna's building at 7:30 a.m. She thought about Jenna for the entirety of the night and could never quite get the bad feeling that had come on so suddenly in the cab to go away. When Jenna stepped off the elevator at 7:40, the agreed-upon meeting time, Susan had never been more relieved or happy to see her client.

"All right, Superwoman," Susan said jokingly to Jenna, "you ready for this?"

"Ready as I'll ever be," replied Jenna, and she followed Susan to the car waiting for them outside. The courthouse was filled with camera crews, news anchors, and people of all shapes and sizes, all trying to get a glimpse of any one of the players entering the courtroom. The car that Susan had arranged for that morning purposefully had tinted-out windows, and as they pulled closer to the courthouse and saw the media circus that had assembled on the front steps, she was glad that she had also made arrangements with one of the courthouse guards to allow she and Jenna to arrive and enter on the backside of the building, away from the cameras and shouting reporters. As their car made the turn and moved slowly through throngs of people standing in the street in front of the courthouse, Jenna and Susan both spotted Cassandra at the same time.

She was wearing a hot-pink women's suit, not unlike the ones favored by Hillary Rodham Clinton, and her hair was pulled back into a sophisticated bun. She was smiling and taking questions from reporters, stopping every few words to hold her face in position for the still shots that she knew the newspapers and magazines needed.

"I'm so sorry that you had to see that," Susan said to Jenna. "Please take a right here, sir, we need to get out of this zoo and around to the back of the building as soon as possible."

"You got it," the driver mumbled, and honked his horn a few times to get bodies to move out of his way so he could make forward progress. The honking caused some, reporters included, to turn around, and the savvy ones knew that someone that hires a car with blacked-out windows doesn't want to be seen, therefore they are *exactly* who needs to be photographed.

A woman with an ET press badge rushed toward the car and began banging loudly on Jenna's window. "Ms. Ellis?" And then, "Ms. Ellis! A comment? A word? What do you think about letting your unborn child possibly go to a complete stranger?"

"Don't move," Susan warned, even though she knew that Jenna knew better than to roll down her window and give any legitimacy to the woman's questions. "They can't see in. It is just a good guess. She is counting on you to roll down the window and prove that her hunch is right."

By this time, several other reporters were banging on all the car windows and the driver was getting angry. His Jamaican accent tore through the tiny slit in his driver's side window to say, "Back off, mon! Back off or I get out and I make you back off!"

He kept his foot on the brake, but revved the gas, and the sound was enough to make the mob back away from the car just enough for it to drive forward and out of the crowd. He turned right to go around the building, and then took an immediate left and went around the block before circling back from the other direction to get to the back door.

"These people, they are crazy, yes?" he said as he pulled to a stop at a door a guard held open for Susan and Jenna. There was no one else in sight.

"Thank you," Susan said as she quickly exited the car with her briefcase and star client to go in for the final day of the biggest case of her life. Though she already had a feeling about how it was going to end, the meeting in the judge's office last night confirming that suspicion, she was proud of the case that she had presented on Jenna's behalf. Her client had every right to fight for this embryo, this child-to-be, that contained her own DNA. Susan only felt sorry for Jenna that the outcome was most likely one that would leave her empty yet again.

The two women snaked up several sets of stairwells and slipped into the courtroom just as reporters were filing in the front door of the courthouse. Several caught sight of Jenna and yelled out to her from the other side of the metal detectors. They shouted to Susan, too, but Susan pressed Jenna forward through the door of the courtroom without a word. They took their seats at the desks in front of the gallery, and Susan nervously began pulling paperwork out of her briefcase, even though there was no reason to do so. And then they sat.

When the judge finally arrived and took his seat, he let out a loud sigh as he put his reading glasses on to his nose. The verdict was what Susan feared, and what Jenna had already known; Mia would not go to either herself or to Cassandra. Mia would be handed over to the anonymous couple that Jenna prayed would give Mia the life that she deserved.

Jenna and Susan exited the courthouse by the same door that they entered. Another, different hired driver was waiting there on the curb. Jenna had wanted to speak to Ellie after the verdict, but the inside of the courtroom was such a zoo that she had only briefly made eye contact with her daughter before crowds blocked her from Jenna's view.

When the car arrived at Jenna's building, members of the press were waiting. George did his best to keep members of the press out of the lobby and as far away from the entrance as he could, but he was only one man against at least thirty hungry journalists.

"Get out as quickly as you can, and go straight inside," Susan said sternly to Jenna as the car pulled to the curb. "I'll take their questions. There is no reason or need for you to stand out here and take this." With that, the car stopped, and Jenna took a deep breath before opening her door. When she did, the sound was deafening, every one of the reporters hurling different questions at her.

"Ms. Ellis! Ms. Ellis!" they yelled. "How do you feel about losing your own DNA in court?" And another, "Ms. Ellis! Does this mean you will appeal the court's decision?" "Ms. Ellis! Where is Mia going and when will the new parents implant?"

Jenna stammered. It was more than she could bear. "I—I don't know," she answered the young, slick-looking reporter that had asked about Mia's parents. He shoved a microphone in Jenna's face as she stared blankly at him, not knowing what to say.

"Ms. Ellis is not answering any questions at this time!" Susan yelled, though it didn't for a second deter any member of the mob. If anything, they crowded in more closely than before, and Susan and George pushing and shoving together were barely able to get Jenna safely inside the building's double front door.

"Go!" Susan yelled from the other side of the glass door. George had closed it as soon as he deposited Jenna inside and blocked the entrance with his body. "Call me later!" Susan pushed her way back through the throngs of bodies and squeezed herself into the car. *The press will stay out here all night,* she thought to herself, *but at least Jenna is safely back in her apartment by now.*

***

Jenna had considered suicide before—many times before—but only now did she realize that all of those times had been different, overcharged with emotion stemming from one inciting event, like finding out about yet another of Ed's affairs or Ellie telling her that she would rather her mother *not* attend the mother-daughter weekend for her sorority for fear that Jenna would do or say something embarrassing. It was in these moments that suicide seemed the most plausible option for ending the pain brought about by intense anger, anxiety, or sadness.

But that was all wrong. In a moment of absolute clarity, Jenna felt a stillness that she had never felt before. It made perfect sense; ending one's own life was not about ending the pain, it was about giving up the pain, handing the anger and the anxiety and the sadness back to the world saying, "Here, take this, I don't need it anymore." The screaming or crying was replaced in totality with acceptance and peace.

As such peaceful acceptance settled her thoughts, Jenna knew that this time she was sure, this time she was ready to depart from this world. She felt . . . free. A supreme calmness washed over her as she envisioned leaving this life and accepting whatever it was that existed on the *other side*. Ellie would be fine. Mia would be, well, she would be what she would be, and in that thought a second reason for ending her life presented itself. She couldn't live to see what became of Mia. Simple as that, Jenna knew deep down that it would kill her to know that Mia was born a healthy, happy little girl who lived with another family, strangers to her and Mia both, and it would also kill her to know that Mia did not survive the thaw. It was the end of a story that Jenna could not live to see the end of for herself. Of that much she was sure.

With her newly found peace, however, Jenna did have second thoughts about her method. Using her scarf to hang herself on her own doorknob now seemed to be dramatic, and drama was something that Jenna was trying to avoid. And then she remembered the sleeping pills that her doctor had prescribed to her years ago when she was in the worst part of her Mia obsession. She could take them, she thought, all of them at once, and drift peacefully to the afterlife, positioning herself tastefully on the sofa or in her bed. She wondered if it would be assumed that, if found this way, she simply died in her sleep? It was possible—by way of an aneurysm or stroke. *I'm not that lucky*, she thought to herself, *but at least it is better than George or Ellie walking in to find me dangling at the end of a scarf.*

Plan in hand, Jenna began to prepare the apartment for her departure. She again put food in the cat bowls and left water in the sink. She folded all of the clothes that lay scattered across her bedroom floor, so the apartment would look neat and tidy, and she took a piece of paper out of her writing desk and wrote the only thing she knew to say to Ellie—"I'm so sorry." She wrote nothing else, because nothing else needed to be said. She was so sorry for so many things and she hoped that Ellie would employ the sentiment whenever she needed. Her daughter was due at least that, an apology for years of being thought of second, second fiddle to Mia.

She left the note on the kitchen table and put a coffee cup on top of the upper left-hand corner to make sure one of the cats did not accidentally push the note to the floor once she was asleep.

twenty-five

S everal weeks later, when Ellie and Kevin were finally allowed into Jenna's apartment to clean it out, they took large, black contractor garbage bags and only one small, plastic container in which to put some of Jenna's personal items. When the superintendent opened Jenna's apartment door, Ellie put her hands to her nose and mouth and gagged at the noxious smell.

"It's all yours," the super said, leaving Ellie and Kevin standing in the doorway, as neither one really wanted to go inside. Ellie took the first steps in and surveyed the damage. At first glance she was not sure that anything at all would be going home with her in the plastic bin. Everything from the drapes to the furniture to the countertops was covered in black from the soot and smoke. The smell, a mixture of cat feces and wet dog, was strong, and in place of her hands, Ellie pulled her turtleneck sweater up over her face to cover her nose and mouth.

"It's disgusting in here," she said, turning to Kevin, who had followed her into the apartment and was opening a few kitchen cabinets to survey the contents inside. Ellie took another step and then made a sour face as she lifted her foot and recognized cat poo on the bottom of her boot. "The damn cats!" she said as she rubbed her heel against the carpet trying to rid herself of the terrible smell now attached to her foot. "I hate them, they are like big rodents with no redeeming qualities." Ellie continued into what had once been her mother's bedroom and saw more of the same—every surface covered in thick black. It was going to take more than black contractor bags to clean out the apartment, she realized.

"I wouldn't say that about the cats," Kevin called out. He was back in the kitchen, opening and closing drawers, this time not inspecting, but rather sweeping the entire contents of each drawer into a large, black trash bag. "It was the damn cats that saved your mother's life. You should thank them, really."

"I'll give you that," Ellie called back, "but that is the last compliment they will ever get from me. Thank God that George took care of taking them all to a shelter." She picked up a sweater from Jenna's dresser; it was one Ellie remembered her mother wearing many times at Christmas, long ago, when she was just a kid. She lifted the sweater closer to her face to see if by chance it retained any trace of the perfume that Jenna wore before the divorce. The perfume was the smell of Ellie's childhood, when her mother was happy, and Ellie believed that their merry trio, including her father, would last forever. For years afterward, and especially in the big department stores at Christmas, whenever Ellie walked past a perfume counter and caught a brief hint of the smell, she was immediately transported back to those idyllic days.

"Anything worth saving in here?" Kevin asked, peeking his head around the bedroom door opening. Ellie put the sweater that she held back in the drawer. It only smelled of cats and smoke, and not the slightest trace of jasmine, tuberose, or lavender that she sought.

"No," Ellie said sadly. "It's all going to have to go, Kevin—this is going to take us forever to clean this mess out."

"Not necessarily. If there is truly nothing to keep, I can call one of those disposal crews to come in and take everything out for us. I just wanted you to be sure there was nothing here worth saving. Nothing you were sentimental about?" Kevin stepped over the clutter on the floor and made his way over to where Ellie stood, putting his arms around her. "I'm just glad that George thought to come look for her. We are very lucky, El. It's all going to be okay, I promise."

At this, Ellie turned into her husband's chest and cried. She thought about the note that George had given her at the hospital on the night of the fire, the night that the firemen broke down Jenna's door to find her unconscious on the sofa, thinking that she suffered from smoke inhalation until they saw the note and the empty bottle on the coffee table, that simply said, "I'm so sorry," as the words burned violently behind her eyes no matter how tightly she closed them.

Jenna survived because of George—and the cats, according to Kevin. George had seen Jenna go up to her apartment after the trial and he did not remember seeing her come back down when the building was evacuated later that night as an electrical fire broke out in between floors four and five. George knew that Jenna had more cats than she told the super about, and he worried that she would try to stay in her apartment to save them, instead of bringing them all, however many there were, down to the lobby.

When he didn't see Jenna standing curbside with the other tenants, he urged the firemen to check on her apartment.

No one answered the door, so the firemen broke the door down, finding Jenna slouched on the sofa and twelve mewing cats surrounding her body. Jenna was taken to the nearest hospital. Several other tenants were transported via ambulance for smoke inhalation and other minor fire-related injuries. Thankfully, because Jenna was taken in a separate emergency vehicle, none of her neighbors were aware of the real reason for her hospitalization following the fire.

The firefighters were able to contain the fire to only the fourth and fifth floors, but there was major interior structural damage, so it took a full two weeks for Ellie and Kevin to be allowed back in the building and access the smoke damage in Jenna's unit.

Jenna was released from the hospital, and to Ellie's relief and surprise, checked herself into Anderson Valley Recovery Center—a mental health and wellness facility set on a sprawling forty-four acres in New Canaan, Connecticut. The adult inpatient wing was the largest of the buildings and looked more like the main house of the Kennedy Compound than a mental health facility. The plan was for Jenna to stay for at least one month, but Ellie suspected that she may need more time than that, as she was already three weeks into her stay. Thankfully, when Ellie spoke with Jenna after her first week at Anderson Valley, her mother sounded stronger—almost, dare she say, happier—than any time in the past twenty years. Jenna raved about the beautiful grounds, the gourmet organic meals, and her roommate, Esther, a painter from Manhattan that had "also suffered the death of a child" and never recovered from it despite it happening decades before, and that she and Esther had "bonded deeply" within days of meeting.

Ellie was tempted to mention that Jenna had not suffered the death of a child, but decided to keep her comment to herself. She did not tell her mother that she and Kevin would clean out her apartment while she was distracted at Anderson Valley; she also had not found the nerve to tell her that it was her and Kevin that now had custody of Mia, and not an anonymous couple, or rather that they were the anonymous couple—Ellie couldn't quite work out in her head how to say it, much less explain it to her mother, which was part of the reason that she had not told her at all.

Surprisingly, Jenna had not mentioned Mia once since the trial's conclusion. With the fire and then moving her to Anderson Valley, it all happened so fast that Ellie wondered if Jenna had tabled her thoughts of Mia for the moment in order to focus on her mental well-being, but she knew better. She wondered what her mother had said to Esther about Mia, and also wondered what Jenna may have said about her.

All the while, Kevin was eager to begin the IVF process for Mia's transfer to Ellie, which put her on edge and, for the first time in her marriage, at odds with her nearly perfect husband.

"I'm not ready," she said to him a few weeks after the trial, once they received word that Mia had safely been moved from BabyGenix to another facility in the Midwest, its name and location known only to Ellie, Kevin, and their attorney. Kevin was visibly disappointed by Ellie's strong reaction and it had caused a silent wedge between them for days afterward.

"I'm sorry," he had said after days of chilly silence between them. "I just always wanted a big family, you know, the typical 'house full of laughter and joy' dream, and when I found you, I knew that you were the person that I wanted to build that dream with. You are going to be an incredible mother one day, Ellie, and I think that together we will be incredible parents—but, I realize that I need to give you the time that you need to come to the idea in your own time. I love you."

Ellie remembered Kevin's words as he continued to hold tightly to Ellie in what remained of Jenna's old bedroom. All the emotional highs and lows from the last month broke Ellie's heart and flooded out of her body through her tears. She had no idea what the next few months or years would look like, but she was glad that she had Kevin by her side.

One Year Later . . .

When doctors released Jenna from treatment at Anderson Valley, they cautioned Kevin and Ellie about her *stable but fragile* mental emotional state. With knowledge from Jenna's records mentioning the fire in her apartment building on the night of Jenna's overdose, Dr. Derek Anderson urged Ellie to consider having Jenna live with her and Kevin instead of immediately transitioning to living independently. Kevin was happy to bring Jenna back to Asheville, and offered to fix up the extra bedroom in the house that was meant to serve as a nursery in the future.

"We can put a crib in our bedroom," he suggested to Ellie as they made the long drive from North Carolina to Connecticut to retrieve Jenna from Anderson Valley. "The room is more than big enough, and don't babies sleep in those small beds anyway for the first few months?"

"You mean a *bassinet*?" Ellie asked. She smiled at her husband's lack of familiarity with baby equipment, especially for someone who was chomping at the bit to have a child.

"Yes!" he exclaimed. "Thank you, a bassinet. Anyhow, I think that would work out just fine. It wouldn't have to be forever, but you heard what Dr. Anderson said on the phone—he said that your mom is still very fragile."

"You are sweet, but I don't know that having Mom live with us is what I want," Ellie said, sighing. "I know that sounds terrible, and I am a terrible person, but I just don't—"

Kevin took his right hand off the steering wheel and reached across for Ellie's. "Sweetheart, you are not a terrible person. You don't have to explain a thing. I cannot imagine being in your position. It's your call, that's all I am saying. I am happy to have your mother live with us, but if you prefer that she not, we can find her a nice apartment in one of the new buildings in downtown Asheville. A new one is going up every day, so finding something quickly would not be hard to do."

Ellie nodded. "I think I would like that. An apartment for Mom would give her some privacy, but she would still only be minutes away in case she needed me." Ellie's voice trailed off and Kevin knew that her mind was wandering through the past into the present and beyond to the future. He did not envy her for such a complicated relationship with her mother. His own family was your run-of-the-mill Midwestern model of stability—a father that worked as an accountant, a consummate mother whose only job was to raise her children, and siblings that he shared deep bonds and happy memories with. He felt badly that he could not say the same for Ellie, and he looked forward to the day when he and Ellie could start their own family, and he could share all his favorite traditions with her. Christmas morning in a small suburban one-story house, hot cocoa on cold mornings before school, and snowball fights in the front yard, all experiences that Ellie had missed out on in her own childhood. Ellie once confided in Kevin that for all the expensive trips that her mother and father took her on before the divorce, the Eiffel Tower on New Year's Eve,

Christmas in Rome, and Fourth of Julys spent in the Bahamas, Ellie could not remember a single Christmas morning when she didn't feel the anxious tension between her parents and the realization that the three of them were only so far from home so they could leave the troubles in the city behind for a couple of days, and pretend for just a weekend that they were a normal, happy family.

When they arrived at Anderson Valley, Jenna was waiting, sitting patiently on a bench inside the large front lobby. Plush sofas and tufted chairs were scattered about, in soothing colors of pale green and turquoise. Jenna looked as calm and peaceful as a child waiting for her parents to retrieve her from school. Jenna's face lit up when she saw Ellie and Kevin walk through the front door, and she ran to hug them both, wrapping Ellie in a tight embrace.

The drive back to Asheville was uneventful. Jenna had gone into Anderson Valley with only the clothes that she was wearing, and so she left just the same. Kevin carefully and dutifully explained about the fire in her apartment building, and that none of her old furniture or clothing had been salvageable. He had expected the worst, but instead of being hysterical, Jenna smiled.

"Even better," she said. "I didn't need any of that stuff anyway. It reminds me of too much. Thank you both." She reached from the backseat over the center console to squeeze Ellie's shoulder in the front passenger seat. "Thank you both for cleaning the apartment out—or trying to. I would have never been able to step back in there, I don't think."

"No problem," said Kevin, "and we are going to find you a brand-new apartment in Asheville. You would not believe all the construction downtown. It's turning into its own little metropolis down there. If you have any complaints at all, it will be for all of the tourists."

"But I am a tourist," Jenna laughed, "or at least I feel like one. It has been over forty years since I left Asheville for college."

"Well, then you will fit right in downtown—and I bet that in no time, you will feel like a local again. Just don't go joining a drum circle in the square without letting me vet them first." Kevin and Jenna both laughed while Ellie stayed quiet. She was glad that Kevin had taken the lead in explaining to Jenna how the next few days and months would go. But Ellie wasn't in a laughing mood. There was still one more important piece to reveal. She was pregnant.

twenty-six

It took Ellie another month to muster up the courage to tell her mom about the pregnancy. Jenna had settled easily into a *hip modern loft* (as described by the real estate agent) in downtown Asheville and seemed to be inching closer to healthy every day. She spent her days reading in her sunlit apartment unit, taking walks to the local public library, and spending her afternoons in Ezekiel's Coffee House, chatting with locals that she had met and become friendly with.

"You need to tell her," Kevin said several weeks after they moved Jenna into her new apartment. "You will be showing soon, right? I mean, I don't know how all of this goes, but I am pretty sure that you will not be able to successfully hide something like pregnancy from your own mother, who also happens to live three minutes away from here."

"I know," Ellie groaned. It was a lazy Sunday morning, and she and Kevin were still lying in bed. She put a hand to her lower abdomen, and still couldn't believe that it was real—*she* was real.

"I'll tell her tomorrow," Ellie said solidly. "We are having lunch at Vic's, and I'll go back to her place afterward and give her the news."

Kevin watched the wrinkles on Ellie's brow and how they had not relaxed since they had begun the conversation. "You realize that your *news* is good news, right?" he said, rubbing her arm gently. "You shouldn't have to feel guilty about it. In fact, I bet that she will be thrilled. What she wanted was for you to be happy, and for Mia to be happy. That is the important part to remember."

"I know," Ellie said again. "You are right. It will be fine. I'll tell her tomorrow and finally everything will be out in the open and we can all move on with our lives."

***

In the end, Ellie chickened out on half of what she intended to relay to Jenna. She told her that she was pregnant, which made Jenna cry tears of joy, but she did not have the fortitude to tell her mother the rest of the story—the more important part of the story of Ellie's pregnancy.

The not-telling would be the final blow. Years later, as happy as Ellie was in her life with her family, and her children, she would be forever haunted by that day in Jenna's apartment after their lunch at Vic's. The day that she didn't tell her mother the whole story, and the last day that she saw her mother alive.

***

After Ellie revealed to Jenna about the pregnancy and that it was in fact a girl, Ellie did not hear from her mother for a couple of days. The day after, Kevin suggested that Ellie call or go over to Jenna's apartment, but Ellie resisted. "I'm sure she's fine," Ellie said. "She is probably just processing everything. I want to give her some space to come to terms with having a grandchild." Kevin backed off and figured that Ellie knew best at how to handle her own mother.

On the fifth day, unbeknownst to Ellie, Kevin stopped by Jenna's apartment on his way into the office. Her car, the light-blue Mini Cooper that she purchased after moving to Asheville, was parked in her space underneath the apartment building, but after knocking for several minutes, no one came to the door, and Kevin had a bad feeling. He knocked one more time, loudly, and when there was still no response, he pulled out his cell phone and dialed Jenna's number. It rang then went to voicemail. He called again with the same result. Next, he dialed the apartment manager's number. When he got David Smith on the phone, he asked if he could come let him into Jenna's apartment with the master key, and that he worried that something could be wrong, as she was not answering phone calls or the door.

Inside the apartment, there was a note on the counter. Kevin's heart sank, and his palms went clammy when he saw the note scrawled in Jenna's messy writing. He didn't need to go into her bedroom to know what he would find there. He read the note in its entirety, and then called out to David, who had hung back to finish a cigarette in the outer corridor, to call 911.

> *Dear Ellie and Kevin,*
>
>   *I want you both to know how much I love you. Because I love you so much, I want to no longer be a burden in your lives. Please do not be upset with me—it is for the best, I promise.*

Christina McClelland

You will be wonderful *parents, I just know it. Give that little one a hug and a kiss for me next year. I am so sorry that I am not strong enough to stay. It will be much better this way— for all of us.*

All my love,
Jenna

PART VI

Snowflakes

twenty-seven

North Carolina

The doorbell rang loudly, and Kevin and Mia raced each other to answer it, Mia giggling happily as she ran for the door.

"Daddy!" Mia squealed. "I want to open the door for Lala and Doc!" Kevin smiled and picked his daughter up, holding her high above his head and spinning her around like an airplane before setting her back down in front of the door. "Not if I get there first!" he laughed.

"No, Daddy, No!" Mia laughed in reply. "It's *my* birthday!" And she put her hands firmly on her tiny hips.

"Okay, I give up," he said to Mia and she beamed back at him. "Go ahead, Your Majesty, it is your day, after all," he said. "Let in your royal guests." Kevin made a dramatic bow toward the front door.

"What's all of the banging around out there?" Ellie called out from the kitchen. "Kevin—please don't encourage Mia to run in the house. I don't need a trip to the emergency room today," she added, though Kevin could tell by the tone in her voice that she was smiling, even from in the other room. He looked at Mia when they reached the door at the same time and made a quiet gesture with his index finger. Mia giggled even louder.

Mia struggled with the heavy door handle but insisted on opening the door on her own and waved off her father's offer for help. She was exceptionally strong-willed despite her tiny stature, and Kevin's parents often jokingly remarked that they hoped to never be on the opposite side of an argument with her. She was not one to back down; that was clear even at her young age. But for all her fiery tendencies, Mia was also remarkably kind-natured. There was not a stray cat in the neighborhood that went unfed or a dog that went unnoticed by Mia. She doted on her baby brother, adopted just two years after she was born, and held her guinea pig, Dolly, like a baby doll, even dressing Dolly in tiny doll clothes when Dolly would allow it. Loving to find symbolism in anything and everything, Ellie thought that it was appropriate that Mia's pet was named Dolly—not after the cloned sheep of the '90s that caused all the media frenzy, of course—but nonetheless, Ellie found the coincidence amusing after all that she and Kevin went through to keep Mia out of Cassandra's hands.

After several seconds of struggling, the door finally opened, and Mia ran into her grandparents' outstretched arms. Kevin's parents had driven all the way from Cincinnati for her fifth birthday party, which had the theme of "Royal Princesses," since, according to Mia, she loved all the Disney princesses equally and could not decide on one princess to base the party on. She had nearly spun herself into a tizzy in the weeks leading up to the party over it, until Ellie gave her the idea of incorporating all the Disney princesses into her theme, which satisfied Mia.

At five years old, Mia was precocious, lovable, bright, and exceedingly funny. She had her maternal grandmother's soft auburn hair that was wavy when it air-dried, and the same hazel eyes as Ellie. Aside from an irregular heartbeat that kept her in the ICU for several days after her birth, Mia was the picture of health, and by all accounts a happy, thriving, normal five-year-old, completely and blissfully unaware of the firestorm that erupted simply by bringing her into the world. Ellie and Kevin had endured several agonizing days of waiting to see if she would survive the thawing process in the lab, and then the greater challenge existed to see if she would remain viable once placed into Ellie's uterus.

After the trial, and Jenna's subsequent mental health treatment, Ellie could not bring herself to talk about, much less consider, pregnancy with Mia, even though the plan had been all along to thaw and implant HN3-8B as soon as the trial was over — mostly to dissuade Cassandra from filing years of appeals. And though Ellie felt in her heart that she and Kevin absolutely and one hundred percent did the right thing by fighting for Mia, her mother's health was a hard burden to carry, and on bad days made Ellie wonder if she had done the right thing at all by jumping into the custody battle without telling her mother.

Ellie had watched Cassandra carefully on the last day of the trial. The long trial period had been a roller coaster of emotion, testimony, and mudslinging, reminiscent of Jenna and Ed's divorce twenty years before, and watching it all made Ellie glad that she had been shuttled away to Asheville. When the verdict was finally read, Ellie was watching Cassandra carefully and thought that the best way to describe Cassandra's reaction to the verdict was relief.

For a mere second, Cassandra's facial muscles relaxed along with her shoulders and she smiled. Only a millisecond later, however, she stiffened her smile, conjured up tears, and put her hands to her face, waiting for her face to be amply tearstained before she took them away again. Ellie remembered looking at her mother's face next. Jenna turned around to look for Ellie, and when their eyes met, Jenna mouthed, "I'm so sorry," and Ellie could see that her mother's eyes were full of tears.

Ellie started to mouth "I love you" back when she was pulled in for a hug by Kevin.

"I love you," he breathed quietly into her hair. "I love you so much. We are going to be great parents." Ellie wanted to believe him. She also wanted to share in his joy, in his excitement of the moment, but she found that she could not be happy when her mother was so unhappy and visibly deflated.

"I haven't seen her like this—" Ellie started to say to Kevin, until a reporter tapped Kevin on the shoulder and asked if he could get his thoughts (knowing only that Kevin was the son-in-law to Jenna Ellis and nothing more). She finished the sentence out loud, but to herself: "I haven't seen her like this since the divorce." And Ellie's heart broke for her mother all over again. *I hope that she can somehow forgive me*, Ellie thought to herself, before following the crowds of people out of the courtroom and into the July heat.

Cassandra landed on her feet, as everyone surely guessed that she would. She gave numerous interviews on daytime TV talk shows, making the morning talk show circuit as well, and in the end got a book deal and the subsequent windfall of money that she had been after when the trial began. *My Life Alone* by Cassandra Mountain hit the *New York Times* bestseller list immediately after publication and received decent reviews, all while Cassandra quietly underwent several plastic surgery procedures in Florida before going on the book tour set up by her agent.

To celebrate the book's success, Cassandra and her mother moved back to Florida and spent $10 million building a mansion on Miami's Star Island, where they spent days soaking up the Florida sunshine and eating crab claws from Joe's (hand-delivered to her home whenever they were in season). They shopped and lounged and did whatever they wanted for the most part. Cassandra's mother, Doris, had become something of an internet sensation herself, in her own way, posting daily (and sometimes hourly) pictures of her lavish lifestyle on her "internet blog" (her words) entitled *The Bitch Is R$ch*, which chronicled her rise from a single mom living in a Central Florida trailer park to a woman who lounged lazily on tacky, red-silk, damask-covered furniture. The most revolting, and tantalizing, post came just weeks after Jenna's move to Anderson Valley—leaked to the press undoubtedly by an unnamed employee. Doris posted a photo of herself and Cassandra at a five-star New York restaurant clinking their champagne glasses together, with a caption of *Finally, we got what we always wanted. One less B*@# to worry about. Enjoy the looney bin, JE!*

But all the attention that Cassandra got post-trial was not even close to the media attention directed at Ellie and Kevin. Hordes of reporters tracked Ellie down everywhere she went for months. It had been the trial of the century, according to major news outlets, and some even said that it bumped the OJ Simpson trial from its throne as far as the sheer number of Americans who tuned in online or on TV to follow the trial and see who would be awarded with baby Mia. No one could get enough. When Jenna disappeared quietly after the trial, suicide rumors swirled and the press thought they had died and gone to heaven, because what could be more salacious, or juicy, than a suicide to cap off a tragic set of circumstances to begin with? Fly-by-night "investigative reporters" and photographers circled Ellie like sharks in bloody water asking her where her mother was and how come no one had seen Jenna Ellis in weeks. What all the reporters wanted to know, they hoped in vain Ellie would tell them—what were the names of HN3-8B's adoptive parents? And who would raise Ellie's biological sister?

After pressing Cassandra for weeks and with Jenna out of the picture, Ellie and Kevin were the only people left to hound—no matter how many times Ellie insisted that she had no idea who now had custody of HN3-8B.

Ellie and Kevin never did a single interview. They were offered over a million dollars by one outlet for a "fifteen-minute interview and your mother will not even be mentioned." But they turned it down. They turned them all down, because for one, they didn't need the money. When Ed died, although Ellie and her father had been estranged for many years, she was still well cared for in his will. She was a Mountain, after all, and his only living child. This drove Cassandra crazy, and at one point, shortly after Ed's death, she considered suing to take part of Ellie's inheritance, in the name of Charlotte, of course, but no attorney would take the case.

Most frozen embryos are transported from one cryobank to another via FedEx, but with all the media attention, Ellie and Kevin did not trust putting Mia into a box of liquid nitrogen and having it packed in the back of a truck with everyone's online purchases. In what felt like something out of a Hollywood movie, just one day after the trial ended, HN3-8B was taken out of the BabyGenix lab in the dead of night by four privately hired drivers, in a highly specialized transport vehicle made especially for cryopreserved specimens. Mia left New York after twenty-nine years at BabyGenix and was safely deposited in an undisclosed location in the Midwest. Only Ellie, Kevin, and their attorney knew the name and exact location of the new storage facility. Even the hired drivers had been tricked, being told by BabyGenix staff that the delivery that they carried were frozen organs of a celebrity who had recently passed and wished for them to be donated to science. Of everyone involved, BabyGenix may have been the most fatigued by overflow of media at this point. Dr. Daugherty retired instead of returning to work after the trial, and Gunnar Sharp resigned from BabyGenix. He gave a single interview wherein he calmly recounted the day twenty years before when he first met Jenna Ellis Mountain and watched two of her three embryos be destroyed. He admitted that he felt pity for Jenna on that day in 2000 and had made a life goal to watch over Mia during the long storage period. He said at the conclusion of the interview that Mia had moved on, and it was time for him to move on as well.

"It has been a long twenty years," Gunnar said tearfully. "I got married, had children, got a divorce, and still Mia was there. She was always there, and now she will finally live the life that Ms. Ellis wanted." Unfortunately, most of the press treated Gunnar, an immigrant from New Zealand, like he was soft in the head, and after that interview, no one seemed interested in hearing from him again, which suited him fine. He quietly sold his apartment in Queens, moved to New Jersey, and found work at a local fish hatchery.

Ellie and Kevin, too, had no more use for Ellie's native New York. Despite growing up in the city, Ellie never felt at home in New York, and as soon as she cleaned out her mother's apartment, she and Kevin settled back into their quiet life in North Carolina. She waited a year before moving forward with the thawing and implantation. As far as her neighbors knew, Ellie and Kevin were like any other happy expectant parents. Even Kevin's parents had no idea that the identity of Mia's biological parents was someone other than Ellie and Kevin. They simply assumed that Ellie had chosen Mia's name out of honor and memory for Jenna.

But Ellie had nightmares about the question that she knew would be asked of her at some point. She tried to guess when it would happen in order to help herself prepare for how to answer. Would it be at a cocktail party? Soccer game? Mia's school? She wondered who would be the first to be brave enough to say what they wondered—does Mia know who her biological parents are?

In her imagined scenarios, Ellie decided that it would be best to give an honest answer, should anyone ever ask. She would say, "She knows who her parents are—and that's Kevin and me. Beyond that, we will have a conversation with her about her DNA at a later date when she is old enough to understand genetics." And then, because Ellie was sarcastic by nature, she typically added, "We know that Mia is bright, but I think that five is a little early for a lesson in embryonic biology and reprogenetics. Don't you agree?" Maybe that was too harsh. Ellie knew that it was inevitable that one day she would in fact have to tell Mia where her genetic makeup came from, and Ellie cringed at having to watch Mia read through old news stories about herself, about Jenna, about Ed, and about the fact that she could have potentially been only a few years younger than the woman that she called *Mom*.

And yet, as hard as that conversation would be, she was also certain that she did not want to wait until it was too late. Kids could find anything these days on the internet, and all Mia would have to do would be to type in her first name, Mia, and a flood of articles would cover the screen. Ellie did not want her to find out that way. She would tell her, when it was right.

For now, she, along with Kevin and Mia, was focused on her swollen belly that held Mia's twin brothers. As it turned out, Ellie's uterus, after years of "hostility" toward an embryo, was completely hospitable to Mia, so much so that her OB-GYN gave her the green light to adopt two more embryos, or technically one embryo, which was then split to create identical twins, that were implanted six months before Mia's fifth birthday. Their names would be Connor and Joseph, and though they were only inches in size, hidden, tiny, and abstract to most of the world, to Ellie they were fully grown boys, her sons, with blonde hair and green eyes (according to genetic testing), and most likely short in stature but full of "thrill-seeking traits." The boys would not be genetically related to Mia, or to either Ellie or Kevin, but they would be her brothers all the same, just as was her adopted brother, Evan.

Ellie and Kevin never corresponded with BabyGenix after they left New York. When Mia was two, they decided to try for traditional adoption and turned to a well-known Christian adoption agency, Celia Bird-Wynn, to assist them with the matching process that led to six-month-old Evan becoming a part of their lives. Evan was a joy from the start, and though his dark features differed from Mia's, the brother-sister duo bonded immediately and had retained a high degree of loyalty and love for one another from the day Evan came home. So much so that as a toddler, Mia would swat away strangers' hands that attempted to tickle Evan in his stroller, saying possessively, "That's *my* brother."

In contrast to Jenna's experience with BabyGenix, Celia Bird-Wynn Adoption Agency (CBWAA) treated Ellie and Kevin as cherished partners from the start of the adoption process. They provided innumerous resources for a healthy and happy adoption transition and even required counseling with a CBWAA psychologist prior to completing the adoption. The counselor coached Ellie and Kevin on all sorts of issues from when and how to tell Evan about his biological parents, and healthy ways to make Evan feel secure in his place with his adoptive family, while knowing that more information about his biological parents was always available. Evan's adoption, as were all Celia Bird-Wynn adoptions, had been "open," meaning that the biological parents and the adoptive parents were given contact information and encouraged to update one another on a yearly basis. On Evan's first birthday, Ellie sent a card to Evan's bio mom with a picture of a smiling Evan, his face covered in birthday cake and icing. His mother replied a few days later with an email telling Ellie how much it meant to her to know that Evan had such a wonderful and loving family.

It had felt strange at first, to have so much intimate contact with the bio parents, but as the counselor explained, the truth about Evan's adoption would be brought out in the open at some point in his life; commercially available DNA kits had made discovery of genetic heritage easy and accessible. In addition, she explained that research showed strong evidence that being transparent about the adoption process and a child's bio heritage at an early age while the psychological pillars of trust were still being formed was truly beneficial for everyone involved—especially the child. "The last thing you want is for Evan's parentage to be revealed at a time when you were not expecting to have that conversation—like in an emergency room, when medical aid necessitates the information that had been previously hidden from the child." After weighing both possibilities, it made perfect sense to Ellie and Kevin to proceed with CBWAA's protocol for an open adoption.

Ellie was so happy with how CBWAA treated all members of the process respectfully that she and Kevin decided to use the Embryo Adoption arm of the agency when they were ready to adopt again. Matching the process of traditional adoption at CBWAA, the process of embryo adoption was also open. Unlike BabyGenix, all CBWAA testing of embryos centered on the health and well-being of the pre-implanted embryo. Ellie and Kevin received no information about their chosen embryos eye color, hair color, or body type. What they were given was detailed health history information on the genetic parents and assurance that the embryo showed no signs of genetic disease.

There were no forms to fill out suggesting specific genetic traits or mysterious fees. Instead CBWAA employed a fairly simple match process of prospective parents with embryos put into an adoptive pool by other parents who wanted their embryos to live on instead of being destroyed. It made Ellie happy to know that she could provide a life for these unborn children—a life that her mother had wanted for all three of her frozen embryos.

In Ellie's closet, high up on the top shelf, she kept a few of her mother's personal items. She didn't take much from Jenna's apartment in the end, because truthfully there was not much that Jenna had accumulated in recent years that reminded Ellie of the Jenna that existed before her obsession with Mia. There was one small frame, however, that Ellie took from Jenna's bedroom. The frame held a simple ecru piece of paper. On the paper was a quote:

Any change in custom or practice in this emotionally charged area [of assisted reproduction] has always elicited a response from established custom and law of horrified negation at first; then negation without horror; then slow and gradual curiosity, study, evaluation, and finally a very slow but steady acceptance.

—Dr. Sophia Kleegman, Pioneer in Human Fertility
New York 1966

twenty-eight

California

L isa Correa was flipping through racks of brightly colored silk dresses when the hairs on her forearm stood on end. She could sense, no, she could *feel* someone watching her. Glancing to each side, down long racks of expensive clothing, Lisa told herself to relax, she was the only customer in the boutique. She tucked an errant piece of highlighted bang behind her ear.

It was no surprise that she was jumpy. Her nerves had been on edge all morning, made worse by a text from her ex-husband alerting her to the fact that he would be bringing his new wife to their daughter, Alecia's, high school graduation the following afternoon. "It will be fun," he had texted. "The whole family together."

Because of all the walking and standing around during the event, Lisa had planned to wear a simple teal-blue shift dress with flats to the graduation ceremony and party afterward, but now, with the news that her daughter's new stepmother would be in attendance, Lisa felt the sudden urge to buy something new for the occasion—as well as make an appointment to have her hair blown out at the salon.

She looked at the fitted pink dress that she held in her left hand and lifted it toward the natural light coming in through the front glass walls of the store. The fabric had a slight shimmer to it. Lisa took care of herself, working out several times per week, and because of her efforts, her figure had remained relatively attractive for her age.

"That would look fantastic on you," an accented voice said from behind her.

When Lisa turned to see the shop girl perched on a high stool behind the cash register, not only did the hairs on her arm stand up straight, every hair on her body felt like it had been hit with an electrical current. For a moment, all the air in the shop felt like it had been sucked out with a giant vacuum. She couldn't take her eyes off the pretty, young, and very familiar looking salesgirl.

The girl, who looked to be only slightly older than a teenager, stared back at Lisa and appeared to be struck with the same electric shock that Lisa was experiencing, but not to the same degree. Where Lisa was in utter shock, the girl simply looked curious.

Because of the text from David at seven, a hectic morning, and a hormonal meltdown from her younger daughter, Anastasia, Lisa had been somewhat frazzled when she walked into the boutique. Normally, she enjoyed chatting amiably with the girls in the boutiques, remembering how she once felt when she was the girl behind the counter, and not the well-heeled wife of a doctor. Ex-wife. But today, with so much on her mind, Lisa had not even looked up to see the shop girl who welcomed her when she entered the shop.

Now, Lisa couldn't *not* notice her. Now, she could have picked the girl out from a crowded plaza in her native Argentina—at night. The resemblance was unbelievable.

"What event are you shopping for?" the girl finally asked. She looked down at some mailers and business cards on the shop counter. She began to stack and straighten the cards while waiting for Lisa to respond. It took several seconds for Lisa's voice to find itself again.

"Graduation," Lisa said, clearing her throat. "My oldest daughter graduates from high school tomorrow, and I wanted to find something, something new for the occasion." Lisa held the dress up again to the light. "Is the shimmer too young for me?" she asked. "I can't tell."

"I think that cut would look great on you—and I think the shimmer is fun. You are celebrating, after all, right? Graduation only happens once, you know. Here." The girl came out from around the counter with a set of small keys on her wrist. "Try it on, and then you can decide for yourself. If you need another size or color, just let me know."

Lisa nodded and followed the girl to the back of the shop where three small dressing rooms were divided on the interior by heavy white curtains. She placed the hanger on a wall hook and turned to close the dressing room door. The girl smiled, and the jolt that made Lisa's hair stand on end rocked her body once again. She looked just like her. *Just like me*, Lisa thought to herself.

After shimmying herself into the tight-fitting dress, Lisa stepped out of the dressing room to look at herself in the large floor-to-ceiling mirror mounted on the back wall of the shop.

"Oh, I love it!" the girl exclaimed from the front. She came out from behind the counter and walked toward the back of the shop, where Lisa stood critiquing herself, gently pulling the fabric that stopped at her upper thigh to see if she could get one more half-inch out of the dress.

"Where are you from?" Lisa asked. She tried to sound casual, but she knew that the pitch of her voice exposed her nerves. She had found the courage to ask the one question that burned in her brain from the moment that Lisa turned around and saw the girl for the first time.

"Melbourne," the girl said, smiling. "I came to the US two years ago and fell in love with it." She picked up a shirt that had fallen off its hanger, and carefully slid the silky fabric back into place. "But I only started working here last week. Today is only my second day."

"What is your name?" Lisa tried to keep her eyes focused on her own image in the mirror, despite fighting every urge to look the girl over with a fine-toothed comb, comparing her every curve, freckle, and dimple to the ones on her own body.

"Alexandra," the girl said, "but most people call me Alex." Once Alex put the hanger back on the rack, she walked closer to Lisa. "Well," she said, holding her hands out, "what do you think?"

Lisa tugged at the hemline once more. She thought about David and blew out a big sigh, which Alex took to be a sigh of relief. Lisa knew that she looked great, and that was the point, wasn't it? It was all so silly, the need to compete with her ex-husband's new wife, but that was exactly what she was doing. "I'll take it," she said, and Alex clapped with delight.

"You look ah-mazing in it," Alex said, smiling. "Definitely wear it more than just the once—promise me?"

Lisa laughed. How much this young girl reminded her of her own two girls. "I promise," she said as she went back into the dressing room to put her own clothes back on.

Out at the register, Lisa couldn't shake the feeling that she needed to ask one more question of her new friend Alex.

"Alex?" she asked. "Can I ask you a question?"

"Sure thing. I am pretty much an open-book type of person," Alex said, smiling. She was neatly folding Lisa's new dress and wrapping it up in pale pink tissue paper.

"Why Los Angeles?" Lisa felt herself fidgeting. "You said you fell in love with the US, but was there a reason that you chose LA specifically?"

Alex glanced up at Lisa, and she felt the jolt of lightning for a third time that day. It was the girl's eyes. They looked just like—

"Personal reasons, I guess you could say," Alex replied. She paused. "I've always wanted to come to LA. I guess you could say I have a kind of connection to it that I can't explain."

In that moment, Lisa wanted to jump across the counter, take the girl in her arms, and bear-hug her until the poor girl couldn't breathe. *My niece. She couldn't be,* Lisa told herself. *You are acting crazy. Of all the boutiques in Santa Monica. There is no way . . .*

Alex tore the receipt from the register and slid the paper across the glass counter. "If you could just sign here," she said, pointing to the line at the bottom and handing Lisa a pen. Once Lisa hastily scribbled her name, Alex put a copy of the receipt in the shopping bag filled with pink tissue paper. "You're all set," she said cheerily as she handed the bag across the counter and into Lisa's hands. "No kidding, you rock that dress. Enjoy your event."

"Thank you," Lisa said, "and enjoy LA. I'll see you soon, Alex."

Lisa's stomach lurched as she left the shop, and it took a full five minutes to regain her normal breath as she walked to her car parked on the curb a block away.

When Lisa was young, everyone told her that she looked just like her aunt Elsa. Elsa was her mother's youngest sister, and she often joked that Elsa and Lisa took all the "skinny genes" and left the large-boned genetics to her and Lisa's younger sister, Genie. They all lived on the same street back then, and Lisa remembered going to Aunt Elsa's house often, and she also remembered her cousin Claudia. After Claudia died, Aunt Elsa and Uncle Mario moved to another part of the city and Lisa did not see her favorite aunt as often. And then, one day, when Lisa was in middle school, both Elsa and Mario were gone.

Lisa's mother and grandmother were so distraught in the aftermath of Elsa's death that for many years, Lisa had been too afraid to ask her mother any questions about her beloved aunt's death. *Where was she when she died? And why were they there? Why had Elsa and Mario gone to Australia a few years before? And why was Aunt Elsa so sad when they returned?*

By the time Lisa was old enough to feel comfortable asking the questions, both her mother and sister were gone too. Old age, a hip fracture, and pneumonia took Lisa's mother, and breast cancer took her sister.

The next day, Lisa watched her oldest daughter walk across the graduation stage in a beautiful white robe and tasseled cap. When Alecia smiled for the photographer on the end of the stage, Lisa felt the jolt again. Her daughter's smile *so* closely resembled the dimpled smile of the shop girl on Montana Avenue that Lisa met the day before. She looked down at her pink dress. She felt silly for buying it in such a rush. David had complimented her on it, which he almost never did, and certainly never had while they were married. Lisa put David out of her mind and smiled. Her daughter Alecia was happy, and that was all that mattered. She took a deep breath in and assured herself that any family resemblance between Alex and her aunt Elsa was merely a coincidence.

PART VII

Remorse

twenty-nine

Birmingham, Alabama

Nearly fifteen years after Ed Mountain's death, a notarized letter arrived in Regina Mountain's mailbox. In her early nineties, Regina was frail and suffering from mild dementia, but, as she insisted on never leaving her Mountain Brook home in any way other than a casket, she had remained in her massive white-brick castle surrounded by twenty-four-hour caregivers.

Althea came in the mornings around seven to prepare Regina's hot peppermint tea and breakfast, usually cold oatmeal with cranberries, and Melissa, the overnight nurse, would leave once Mrs. Regina was out of bed and dressed out of her nightgown and into clothing for the day. At three in the afternoon, Patrick the physical therapist would come to the Mountain home to assist Regina in her daily exercises, and then Althea would begin dinner prep at five, just in time for Melissa to come back on her shift at

261

seven p.m. Regina's shiny, thick blonde hair lost its luster many years before, and had turned white and thin, showing patches of bald scalp in some places.

The letter that arrived was thick and looked official, so, instead of opening it (as she did for most of Mrs. Mountain's other mail), Althea left the letter on Regina's bedside table, in hopes that her boss would open it before her afternoon nap. Since Mr. Mountain's death some years ago, the Mountain residence did not receive much correspondence other than junk mail and constant requests for political donations, so Althea's interest was piqued as to what this important-looking letter could be about.

Regina in fact saw the letter and opened it on a Tuesday afternoon, after her lunch of minced turkey and lady peas, and opened the cream-colored envelope with care before carefully sliding the folded letter out. When she did, something smaller fell out, and when she looked down to her lap, she saw that it was two things — a note enclosed in an envelope and a man's platinum silver wedding band. Regina turned the ring around in her fingers and did not need to put on her reading glasses to know what the engraved inscription on the inside of the ring said. *Together in Love, ECM and JEE.* Regina had told Jenna that it was in bad taste to engrave a man's wedding band, something reserved for women's jewelry, but her new daughter-in-law had not listened. *That girl never heeded any of my good given advice,* Regina thought to herself with a huff. The two women did not hit it off when they met, and Regina had never forgiven Jenna for it.

The other item, the smallish notecard, had unkempt handwriting scrawled across the front. It read: To Jenna. Regina first put the note aside and turned her attention to the larger, business-sized letter addressed to her. It read:

Dear Mrs. Mountain,

As no person has made a claim to the contents of the safety deposit box owned by Edward C. Mountain III located in Ameris Bank, Freeport, Bahamas, the contents have been dispersed to the decedent's next of kin—which, according to the bank files signed by Mr. Mountain—is you. Please find the contents of the deposit box enclosed here in this envelope. With the entire contents of Mr. Mountain's box dispersed, the account is now closed. Many thanks for your longtime business with Ameris Bank, and best of luck.

Sincerely, John P. Mayfair
Bank Manager, Ameris Bank, Freeport

Regina turned the smaller envelope with Jenna's name on it over in her hand. Her fingers traced over the engraved initials of ECM on the back flap and felt an unusually deep sting of loss for her son. She was the only Mountain left, well, besides Ellie, but she had not heard from her granddaughter in years. The Andersons, close family friends of the Mountains, kept in touch with Ellie through their granddaughter, who attended the same upper-crust-girls-only summer camp in North Carolina with Ellie, and the two women had remained friends into adulthood. Mrs. Anderson told Regina several years before that Ellie had three children, and that one of them was named Mia. Like everyone else, Regina assumed that this was out of reverence for her mother.

She carefully loosened the back flap and opened the note. Inside was a note, also handwritten, presumably by Ed. It was short.

Dear Jenna,

Please know that I am sorry—for everything. Also, please tell Mia that I am sorry.

I hope that one day, you both can find it in your hearts to forgive me.

Best, ECM III

Holding the notecard like a delicate flower, Regina put the stationery card and the ring back in the envelope. She ran her fingers over Ed's monogram once more, and then dropped the card in the wastebasket beside her bed.

"Althea!" she called out in a raspy croak.

"Yes, ma'am," Althea called back, hobbling into the bedroom. The day nurse was only twenty years younger than her employer and had two bad knees in desperate need of replacement, but not the time, or the money, to do so.

"Althea, take my trash bin out if you would—it's practically billowing over." Regina motioned loosely with one skinny outstretched arm in the general direction of the trash can, her knuckles sticking out like rocks underneath her thin skin. It was a wonder that she could still get any of her jewelry on.

Althea looked down at the nearly empty silver-plated waste basket. A large engraved M was intricately etched into the center of a ring of roses on the front, and when Althea looked inside the waste bin, all she saw there was a single envelope in the bottom. She had worked for Mrs. Mountain long enough to know not to argue with the woman, though, so she picked up the small wastebasket and emptied it into the larger black trash bag that she held in her hand.

"I'll go ahead and take the trash out to the curb now," Althea said through labored breath, "so Miss Melissa won't have to worry over it in the morning." She gently shook the contents into the larger bag. Then, once tied up, she took the bag outside to the large green trash bin on the street and tossed it in, where the bag would sit, overnight, until the City of Birmingham took it away the next day.

That night, Regina enjoyed her usual dinner of mashed potatoes and small, cut-up bits of beef pot roast, while sitting in front of the TV watching *Wheel of Fortune*. After dinner, Melissa served her dessert—one cup of strawberry ice cream—and helped a crankier-than-usual Regina Mountain dress for bed.

the end

Author's Note Continued

In 2010, the California Institute for Regenerative Medicine (CIRM) estimated that there were well over one million cryo-preserved embryos in facilities all over the United States.* Due to lack of information, political infighting, and strong pushback from various lobbying groups, the number of frozen embryos continues to grow with each passing day, and by the year 2020, the number of stored embryos could top three million by conservative estimates. Even with the advent of the embryo adoption industry, which alleviates a small percentage of the excess embryo population, there is no time limit for storage of cryopreserved human specimens in the US, and experts worry that without public awareness and regulation, the issue of "abandoned embryos"—those left over from IVF treatments that are never intended to be used—will never be solved, and a crisis will eventually ensue.

My goal was to accurately portray the monumental success as well as emotional hardship that can be found in studying the scientific progression of in vitro fertilization over the last forty years. However, because the fertility industry is largely unregulated in areas such as embryo disposition post-IVF and IVF treatment itself, practices often vary widely from clinic to clinic.

This book is a work of fiction based on the true story of Mario and Elsa Rios, a couple that simply wanted to fulfill a desire to become parents once again after suffering a devastating loss, and the immeasurable impact that their tragic story had on assisted reproductive technology (ART).

The fate of the Rioses' "orphaned embryos" remained shrouded in mystery long after a Los Angeles court ruled that the embryos had no legal rights to the Rioses' estate. It was unknown to the general public (as well as members of the media at large) whether the two unused Rios embryos were discarded, implanted in an adoptive womb, or remained frozen in time. Many wondered if descendants of Elsa Rios could be living among the seven billion humans on earth. In the course of my research for this book, a credible source close to the Australian team caring for Elsa Rios at the time of her care in the Test Tube Baby Program confirmed what some speculated—the Rios embryos were placed in an anonymous donor pool in Australia's embryo adoption program for infertile couples, and both were implanted unsuccessfully, putting to rest any rumors that purported otherwise.

*Lomax, Geoffrey P. and Trounson, Alan O. "Correcting misperceptions about cryopreserved embryos and stem cell research." *Nature Biotechnology.* April 2013. Number 4, vol. 31, p. 288–290.

Acknowledgments

Many people supported me in every step of the creative process that led to the publication of *A Circle of Chalk*. Thank you first and foremost to my husband, Walter, and two girls, Mabry and Emily, for allowing me to follow my crazy dream, and for sharing me with my beloved characters for over a year while this book was written and edited.

Thank you also to Kathy McClelland for being the earliest reader of the completed manuscript and for supplying me with valuable feedback and support to keep moving forward. My fabulous book club also read early versions of the book and provided enormous support and helpful critique. These wonderful ladies include Stephanie Stephens, Erica Cummings, Melanie Paidipalli, Ann Reid Young, Bradley Sosebee, Emily Graney, Morgan King, Suzanne Loyd, Erin Harris, Amy Douglass, Lauren Ralls, and Mary Lorraine McDonald. My sisters, Celia Johnson and Caroline Barnes, along with Katie Oblinger, were early readers as well, in addition to serving as my wall to bounce insane ideas off of in the early stages of the story's creation. Stephanie Walstad gave me the courage (and tips) to walk confidently into early pitch sessions—I tried my best to evoke "feelings" no matter what. To Susie Pryor, my perennial mentor and gold standard, thank you for your openness and willingness to add value to this book—and to my life in general. I am grateful to have you in my corner.

Thank you to Dr. Alan Trounson for his wisdom and insight

into the world of IVF at its inception, and for being so very gracious with his time and support of the project. Dr. Trounson is responsible for the development of cryogenic storage of embryos as we know it and was one of the first scientists around the world to successfully create life outside of the womb—he is truly amazing and is a rock star in the medical scientific community.

To so many special friends, thank you—for loving me, believing in me, and spurring me on. Special thanks to Schuyler Espy, Sarah Stewart, Melanie Adams, Adrienne Oliver, and Julie Farmer. You have stuck by me for the long haul.

To Maria Panizo, I would forget to leave the house with my own head if it wasn't attached and I didn't have you! Thank you, thank you, for all your hard work and dedication to Walter, me, and especially to the girls over these last many years. You are an amazing woman and can truly do it all!

Thank you to the team at Lanier Press for supporting *A Circle of Chalk* and guiding me through the publication process.

Last, but not least, thank you to my mother, Claire Cole, for (somehow) finding time to read to my sisters and me every single night of my childhood despite being a full-time working mom. She read everything from *Corduroy* to *Little Women* to the three of us girls, while we all snuggled up in one big wooden antique bed. Reading aloud in many different animated voices, my mom inspired not only my love of books, but of storytelling as a craft. Thank you, Mom, for your unwavering love, support, and prayers. It, along with the support of all mentioned above, and so many more, is the only reason that this book is in print.

CPSIA information can be obtained
at www.ICGtesting.com
Printed in the USA
LVHW030214120720
660355LV00005B/439